SILENCE
Your
DEMONS

First published in Great Britain in 2022 by Be World Class.
Copyright © Simon Hartley 2022

The moral right of the author has been asserted.

A CIP catalogue record of this book is available from the British Library.

ISBN 978-1-3999-2237-1

Typeset in Minion Pro by Beamreach Book Printing

Be World Class Ltd
Lister House
Lister Hill
Leeds
LS18 5DZ
https://be-world-class.com

MIX
Paper from
responsible sources
FSC® C100431

Papers used by Be World Class are from well managed forests and other responsible resources.

SILENCE
Your
DEMONS

be world class

Simon Hartley

We all have demons.

You know… that voice in your head that chips away at you… constantly pelting you with doubts, criticism, and self-judgement.

It's the voice that tells you you're not good enough…

… that you're stupid… fat… ugly… that no-one likes you… or you'll never do it.

That voice.

If any of that resonates, this book was written for you.

I really hope you like the story.

But, above all, I hope it helps you silence your demons.

Chapter One

THE END

The light shone straight into his eyes, obliterating everything else. Gradually, the murmurs died down and the room fell silent. For a moment, Seb Hall stood motionless, transfixed, dazzled, desperately trying to remember what was next, as he rolled the cold metal tube between his fingertips.

He searched the gloom just beyond the cone of the spotlight, scanning the faces on the front row. There she was… his mum. She looked like he felt – a rabbit caught in the headlights. The audience were growing restless, coughing, shifting in their chairs, muttering. She stared at the glistening flute in his hand.

"Play!" she mouthed. She did not look happy.

What was he supposed to be playing?

"Ahem. Are you ready?" asked Mr Bamfort. The small bald music teacher stood on the edge of the stage, looking even more irritated than usual.

"Uh, yeah," came Seb's feeble croak.

"Shall I play you in?" Mr Bamfort asked.

"Thanks," he replied, his mouth dry, heart pounding.

A sinister voice came from the dark shadows of Seb's mind. *This'll be interesting…*

He shuddered at the sound.

"Fine," said Mr Bamfort, pulling his stool up to a small piano. "'A Happy Dawn'. On three… One, two…"

A string of playful notes skipped from the keys of the piano. Like children set free into a playground, they danced joyously into the air. Seb raised the flute to his lips and took a breath. To his horror, a series of awkward notes stumbled out. They did not sound like gleeful children playing. More like a funeral march.

Oh God. It's even worse than I imagined, the sinister voice in his mind said.

For a while they played on. The melancholy sounds of his flute wrestling with the cheerful notes from the piano. It was awful; like the Grim Reaper dancing with Tinkerbell.

They're laughing at you, you know.

This was supposed to be a glorious moment, his one chance to make her proud, and it was falling apart. Months of practicing until the early hours, and this was all he had to show for it. He caught a glimpse of her, shielding her face… humiliated. She probably wished she'd never come, wished he was not her son.

He caught a sob in the back of his throat and his flute squealed indignantly.

What are you doing? growled the voice.

This was a nightmare. His worst fears were becoming real. He screwed his eyes up, trying to hold the tears back, but it was no good. Any moment now, he would break down on this stage.

Loser!

He took the flute from his lips, turned on the spot and ran. He hit the bar on the fire exit and burst through it. Cold air flooded his lungs. The blue green imprint of the spotlight swam before his eyes, but on he ran. There must be somewhere he could hide. Somewhere quiet, where he could disappear. Somewhere no one would find him.

Slowly the world came into focus. Ahead was the rusty corrugated iron bike shed. Maybe that would do. He tucked himself behind the wall and slumped onto the concrete floor, desperately trying to catch his breath. What had he done? Tears streamed down his face. He curled up into a ball, clutching the flute to his chest.

"Seb," called Mr Bamfort. "Where are you?"

"Sebastian!" came his mum's hysterical cry.

Maybe, if he sat here long enough, they would give up. How he'd love to just disappear. That way he wouldn't have to endure the interrogations. He already knew the questions…

What on earth happened?

Why did you just run out like that?

He hadn't even finished the piece. But what was the point? It was a horror show. Playing the flute was the only thing he'd ever been good at. It was the one thing he loved. But, clearly, he was no musician. He was a failure… a loser…

More shouts, this time much closer. Footsteps echoed off the walls. They couldn't be more than a few metres away. If he kept quiet, perhaps they would pass. He held his breath and stared at the scuff marks on his shoes. He wasn't ready to see anyone. Maybe in a few minutes. Right now, he just needed to be alone.

"What are you doing down there?" His mum's voice was so shrill it was barely audible. There she stood, hands on her hips.

He didn't reply.

"We're going home," she announced, her voice dropping an octave. "Come on."

Seb didn't need to look at her to know she was wearing *that* look… the look he'd seen so many times before. It was the look she gave him when his report came back from school or when he received exam results. It was that look of pure, unadulterated disappointment.

For a fleeting moment, she seemed so proud that he'd been invited to perform at the annual recital. Seb suspected she'd been waiting for something like that for years. But it had gone.

She marched ten metres or so before she turned around to see him still cowering in the corner of the bike shed.

"I haven't got all day," she barked. He glanced up to see whether she actually had steam coming out of her ears.

He sighed. It was no good. He couldn't stay here forever.

Slowly he pushed himself to his feet and slumped along behind her. The journey back was going to be torture. He knew exactly what she'd say. He'd heard it all so many times before.

"I feel so let down."

"I'm disappointed."

"I can't believe it."

"What will they all think?"

He opened the car door and crawled inside.

***

Seb lay on his bed, staring at the ceiling. The emotion that he'd been holding back for what seemed like an eternity was spilling out. A hot tear trickled down the side of his face. Then another. Before he knew it, the stream had become an uncontrollable torrent.

Beyond his bedroom door, the stairs creaked, and heavy footsteps crossed the landing. He couldn't let his dad see him this way. He buried his head in his pillow to muffle his sobs. For a few moments he lay there as thoughts rattled around his head.

I can't go on like this.

I'm seventeen.

I've got a whole life to live.

I've got to do something.

He sat up and wiped his eyes. Sobbing wasn't going to get him anywhere. He needed answers. For a few moments he sat, gazing blankly into space. Then, one by one, the cogs in his head began to turn. Like a rusty machine that hadn't worked in years.

An idea… then a second… and a third. One after another they emerged and were rejected. And then something clicked.

He went to his desk and opened the drawer. There, beneath the pens and sheet music was a book. This was no ordinary book. It was a brand new, leather-bound notebook – a Christmas present from his dad. He had been saving it for some special purpose. Perhaps this was it. Maybe this was the book in which he'd document his journey from nobody to somebody.

He lifted it out of the drawer, like a museum curator holding a priceless artefact, and laid it down on the desk. Now all he needed was his best pen and the perfect opening line.

He turned to the first page, searching for the right words, pen hovering over the page. But nothing came. As always, his mind seemed to have failed him.

With a sigh, he replaced the lid on the pen and slid the book back into the drawer.

Another day, maybe.

Six months later

"Seb… SEB!! Get up! You're going to be late. I'm leaving in twelve minutes," his mum yelled from the bottom of the stairs. "If you want a lift, you'll have to be ready."

He flew out of bed, flung some clothes on, raced downstairs and jumped into the passenger seat of his mum's aging red hatchback, slamming the door behind him.

"Careful!" she snapped.

With a huff, she screeched through the farmyard gates, narrowly missing the post van, sped out of the village and through the winding country lanes towards the nearby town of Yeoborough.

"First day at college and you're already late," she said as the hedgerows flashed past.

"You'll have to be more responsible now," she continued. "You're seventeen. You'll be driving soon, if we can scrape enough money together for lessons, that is. Anyway, you can't rely on me to get you out of bed every morning."

He didn't reply. His gaze followed a money spider that was climbing up the side of the rear-view mirror. Every now and again a jolt would knock it off. Seb watched it abseiling on its tiny thread and then climb back up, only to be knocked down once more.

He knew that feeling.

The car squealed in protest as she slammed on the brakes. The seat belt cut into his chest. "Mum!"

"Have you listened to a word I said?" she snapped. Her sharp features were illuminated in the morning sunlight.

"I know." He sighed. "I need to be more responsible."

"Humpf." She screeched away from the junction.

He sank into his seat.

Sandy would have been special, he thought. Sandy would have made her proud. He'd have been a "straight A" student. He would have been selected for the school sports teams or starred in the school play. He would have given her something to tell the neighbours.

Maybe she wished it was Seb who had died on that fateful day, instead of his older brother.

With the words "Don't be late" ringing in his ears, he stepped out of the car and looked up the grassy bank towards the college. The imposing grey concrete block towered above him; shabby and unloved, decorated only with patches of rust and chipped stonework.

Slowly he wandered up the path towards the entrance. Withered trees that had been baked during the scorching summer heat stood forlornly around the entrance. It reminded him of the local hospital. A small road looped around a roundabout, at the centre of which stood a dead rose bush. Next to the huge glass doors was a six-foot-high sign, adorned with the words "Welcome to Yeoborough College." Even on a bright sunny morning, with a backdrop of blue sky, it looked distinctly uninviting.

The glass doors slid open.

Hundreds of students were packed into the reception area. Through the mass of jostling bodies, Seb noticed an array of tables manned by slightly frantic looking college staff. They were all wearing shocking pink T-shirts with the words "Here to Help" plastered across the front.

He checked the time on his phone. He was already late for his first class.

Great first impression, said a sarcastic voice from the deep recesses of his mind. *Well done.*

He scanned the handwritten signs above the tables. Helpdesk… Student Registration… Lost?… Maps and Information… Welcome Packs. He snatched a map from the nearest table. His first class was psychology, on the fifth floor. He began pushing his way through the crowds towards the lifts across the hall. Then it dawned on him. The crowd *was* the queue for the lift.

Damn it.

To his left a staircase spiralling upwards.

As he passed the second floor, Seb concluded that the lift would have been a far better option. His legs were burning, and a nasty acidic taste bubbled up in his throat. To be honest, he was surprised that he made it to the fourth floor alive and was pretty convinced that he'd be dead before he reached the fifth.

Beyond his wildest expectations, Seb made it to room 534. He burst through the door, dripping with sweat and gasping for air. The room fell silent. Thirty pairs of eyes stared at him, doubled over in the doorway. The lecturer peered quizzically towards the door. He was a very well-dressed man, probably in his late thirties. His dark hair was slightly greying around the temples.

His eyes were chocolate brown, skin lightly tanned.

"Ah. Sebastian Hall, I presume?" he said in his mild Scottish brogue.

"Ye-Yes," Seb stammered. "Yes… sorry… sir," he panted. "Sorry I'm late. Stairs…" he spluttered, pointing down the corridor. The class burst into laughter. He could feel their eyes boring through him, like white-hot laser beams. Beads of sweat rolled down his face. More than anything, right now, he wanted to shrivel up and disappear.

The lecturer smiled gently and gestured towards a seat at the front of the class next to a plain looking girl wearing horn-rimmed glasses.

"I'm Mark," he said. "You don't have to call me 'sir' here. I haven't been knighted yet." More laughter from the class. "Anyway… It's nice to have you with us, Sebastian," he continued.

You are such a loser! That voice was back.

Seb sunk into his chair.

***

As he dismissed the class at the end of the lesson, Mark called Seb to one side.

"I'm sorry I was late, sir… Mark," Seb blurted out.

"Sir Mark?" he replied, raising an eyebrow. "Well, I suppose that's progress."

"Seb," said Mark. "You didn't murder anyone. You were a couple of minutes late to a lecture, and I'm sure that you'll get here in good time from now on." Mark looked him in the eye. "May I share a thought with you?" he asked.

"Uh… yeah," Seb replied.

"Experience tells me that we spend far too much time and energy worrying about what other people think of us. They will think what they want to think. They will form their opinions.

Some will even pass judgement on us. The opinions that they form and the judgements that they make always say more about them than they do about us. Anyway, I don't want to make you late for your next class. See you next lesson," he said.

He probably thinks you're mad. I didn't see him call anyone else back.

The monologue rumbled on inside his head as he made his way through the still crowded reception area towards the canteen. The echoes of Mark's words wrestled with the relentless nagging voice. He was so preoccupied he didn't notice his foot catch the trailing strap of a bag. Time slowed as he sailed through the air. Books fell from his grasp as the ground rushed to meet him. He landed sharply on his shoulder and skidded across the floor. But the searing pain was nothing compared to the humiliation. He looked up, dazed. Hundreds of eyes; all fixed on him. From a few feet away, through the deafening silence, came a silky-smooth low voice.

"That is *so* uncool."

A tall muscular figure towered over him. He looked like a comic book superhero, with broad shoulders, a chiselled jawline and stubble. Behind him stood a group of five or six athletic lads, plus a handful of very glamourous girls.

"I-I'm sorry," Seb stammered.

"Lucky for you there's nothing *too* valuable in there," said the lad, extending his hand. Seb held out his own hand and the lad grasped it with a bone-crushing grip. In one effortless motion Seb was lifted like a rag doll and set back on his feet.

"Uh… yeah… sorry," Seb mumbled.

"You might want to watch where you're going next time, hey," said the lad, running his fingers through his jet-black hair. For a moment he examined Seb closely. Then he clapped him on the back, slung his bag lazily over his shoulder and sauntered back to his friends.

Seb scrabbled around the floor collecting his things.

Idiot. They're all staring.

"There you go," came a shy voice behind him. It was the girl with the horn-rimmed glasses from his psychology class. She handed him a book.

"Thanks," Seb replied.

"I'm Alice, by the way," she said. "Nice to meet you."

She's just saying that. She's not really pleased to meet you. She thinks you're a waste of space like everyone else.

Seb screwed up his eyes, trying to ignore the voice.

"I'm Seb," he replied.

"I know." She chuckled. "Sebastian Hall, I presume."

"Oh… course," Seb muttered, examining a patch of floor.

"I'm going to get a drink. You coming?"

Seb half shrugged, half nodded and followed Alice.

They sat with their cups of coffee in the far corner of the canteen. Like the rest of the college, it was drab and uninspiring; rows of grey tables were flanked by unbearably uncomfortable orange plastic chairs. But at least they could look out over the sunlit lawns.

"What did you think of psychology?" she asked.

"After my spectacular entrance, you mean?" he replied.

"It wasn't that big a deal. Everyone will have forgotten by now," she said. "Mark seems nice."

"Yeah," replied Seb.

"Did you study it at school?" Alice asked.

"Psychology?" he replied. "Nah. Our school didn't offer anything like that."

"What made you choose it?" she enquired. He looked up from his coffee cup. Behind her glasses she had bright blue eyes; the colour of sky. Her mousy brown hair was loose and fell just past her shoulders.

"Not sure. I guess because it's new. Means I haven't failed it yet," he said, trying to sound flippant. "And I'd love to know how this thing works," he said, tapping the side of his head. For a brief moment, her expression changed. Was that concern or judgement?

Oh, well done. You've known her two minutes and now she thinks you're mental, too. No wonder you don't have any friends, the voice taunted.

She took a sip of her drink.

"By the way, his name is Michael Malone… the lad who picked you up," Alice said. "He went to my school. He was captain of the football team, the rugby team and every other sports team we had, I think."

"Which school did you go to?" Seb asked.

"St Joseph's," replied Alice.

"The posh school?" Seb blurted out, almost choking on his coffee.

"It's an independent school, yes," Alice said, looking slightly affronted.

He paused for a moment, desperate not to offend her. In many ways she was an unremarkable looking girl, but there was something about her. If friendliness and kindness had a look, she would have embodied it.

"How come you're here? Doesn't St Joseph's have a sixth form of its own?"

"The sixth form building burned down at the end of last year," Alice said. "It was pretty freaky. Some people said it was arson but apparently there's not enough evidence to prove it."

"Well… I'm pleased you're here anyway," said Seb, to his own surprise. "And your friend Michael seems nice enough, too." A look of concern crossed Alice's face.

"Just… be careful there," she said seriously. She checked the time and drained her cup. "Right, must go," she announced. "I have another class."

"Uh… me too," replied Seb. "See you in psychology."

Alice smiled, picked up her bag and gave an awkward little wave as she headed out of the canteen. Not wanting to be late for his second lesson in a row, Seb pulled his bag over his shoulder and set off for philosophy.

***

Thankfully the day drew to a close without any further catastrophes. He lay back and stared at his bedroom ceiling once more. Why did life feel so tough… like he was wading through treacle while everyone else skated gracefully across a frozen pond? He'd made a fool of himself on his first day, humiliated himself in front of the entire college. There's no way he could survive two more years of this.

Exhausted, he sunk his head into his pillow. For a few moments he stared blankly into space before closing his eyes and drifting off to sleep.

Seb was in the Bluebell Wood. It was autumn. The late-afternoon sunshine cast long shadows across the fallen leaves. He knew this place like the back of his hand. It was his own personal paradise… his playground… his sanctuary. He walked along the path he'd trodden so many times before, pine needles crackling beneath his feet. Past the dense holly bush he'd hollowed out to make a den when he was eight. Past the swing that his dad had made for him just after Sandy had died, all those years ago, and on towards the pond.

But something was different. No bird song… no animals scurrying through the undergrowth… just an eerie silence. A chill wind picked up and mist swirled around him.

You are pathetic, came a vicious growl from beyond the mist. *Why can't you just be normal, like everyone else?*

Seb spun around.

"Who's there?" he shouted, his voice trembling.

Humiliated again, came the reply.

Seb turned one way, then the next. Then he caught a glimpse. Two gigantic horns flashed past then merged back into the mist. He stepped back, panic rising.

Why can't you get through just one day? Is it so hard?

A skull and a pair of eyes – pure fire, pure hatred – appeared and then disappeared in an instant.

Panic became terror. Seb turned to run.

Demonic laughter filled the woodland.

You think you can outrun me?

You'll never outrun me.

I am fear!

How to Silence Your Demons

You can see what goes on inside Seb's head.
Do you recognise these kinds of voices?
What kinds of words and phrases do you hear in your own mind?

Towards the end of the chapter, Mark gives Seb some advice.
He says, "Experience tells me that we spend far too much time and energy worrying about what other people think of us. They will think what they want to think. They will form their own opinions. Some will even pass judgement on us. The opinions that they form and the judgements that they make always say more about them than they do about us".

What do you think of Mark's advice?
How could it help you?

Chapter Two

THE THIEF

Seb woke with a start, his heart pounding, drenched in sweat. Images from the dream flashed through his mind.

What was that thing? He rubbed his head, trying to erase the images. It was just a dream. But this was like no dream he'd ever had. It was so vivid, so real. And that voice, laced with hatred.

You'll never outrun me. I am fear.

Slowly, he pulled himself out of bed and crossed the dimly lit landing to the bathroom. How long had he been asleep? The full moon shone through the window filling the small room with a soft light. He stood at the sink, splashing cold water over his face and caught sight of himself in the mirror. His ginger hair was matted and stuck to his head, so saturated it looked almost black. His blue-green eyes stared back, terrified.

Seb wiped his forehead with a towel and took a deep breath. For several moments he stood, staring at his own reflection, making sure he was still alive. Although he had just turned seventeen, he still had that gangly teenage look. Many of the lads his age now looked like men, but whenever Seb looked in the mirror, he saw a boy.

He wandered back through to his bedroom and checked the time on his bedside clock. Large green numbers bore through the film of dust. It was 1.32 a.m. He stared around his small and very plain bedroom. The walls were bare. His small desk, littered with sheet music and books, stood out against the sea of beige.

His bed gave an indignant creak as he sat down. He could do without a sleepless night. Somehow, he needed to survive another day at college. But he didn't want to close his eyes. What if he walked straight back into the dream again? What if that thing was waiting for him?

Don't be ridiculous! he told himself. *It was just a dream…*

***

Seb headed to the canteen to meet Alice. They'd agreed to have a cuppa and discuss their psychology assignment. But, as far as he was concerned, it was just another chance to see her. It seemed a bit bizarre on the one hand. He'd only known her for a few days. But there was something about her. She was special. He'd never really had a best friend; someone he could talk to about anything. Maybe she could be the one. That would be amazing. But it might be too much to hope for.

He spotted her at a table in the far corner and headed over.

"What's up?" she asked. Seb paused for a moment.

This'll be fun. Gonna tell her about your nightmares? About dreaming of monsters? Ha ha haa!

"Oh, nothing much," replied Seb uneasily. "You?"

Alice took a mouthful of coffee. "Me neither," she said.

He took a slurp of his own coffee. The sharp bitter flavour seemed to press buttons in his brain.

"Who do you talk to about… stuff?" he asked to his own surprise.

"Stuff?" she asked.

"You know… personal stuff," he replied a little awkwardly.

"I dunno… all kinds of people, I s'pose. Friends. Gemma from my old school. Megan. My cousin Harry, sometimes. Mum and Dad, a bit. Depends what it is," she replied.

"What about the big stuff?" he asked.

"Big stuff?" she repeated. She placed her cup back on the table. "I guess… not many people. Maybe Gemma a bit." She paused for a moment.

"A few years ago, I was really sick. There was a time they didn't think I'd make it. It was my heart," she said. "They didn't tell me that… they kept saying everything would be okay, like parents do. But I knew. Anyway, there were lots of nights I felt too scared to go to sleep in case I didn't wake up. I didn't really know who to talk to, so Dad asked one of the counsellors at the hospital to chat to me. It really helped. He told me to write a diary. I called it George. George was the one I could tell anything. Sometimes I'd share stuff with Sam, the counsellor. Sometimes I'd let George share it so that I didn't have to… you know, when saying it out loud was just too hard. Even now George is probably the one I talk to about the big stuff."

"Wow," he said. "I… I… Uh… Is it alright now? Your heart?" he asked.

"Should be," she replied. "Fingers crossed."

The alarm on his phone chimed from inside his pocket.

"Ah shit, got to go," he said. "Music. Fancy walking down to the bus stop later?"

Alice smiled and nodded. "Defo," she replied. "See ya later."

He wandered down the corridor towards the music block, his head spinning. Poor Alice. He'd had no idea. And he thought he had it tough. A couple of nightmares and tripping over Michael's bag. It was nothing compared to that. What did he have to moan about?

He caught sight of the sign for the gents.

Probably best to go now, he thought to himself.

He nudged the door open, checking for occupants. It seemed

empty. Good. He stepped in and was met by the overwhelming smell of rotting cabbages and old people. He held his breath to avoid gagging, then took the closest cubicle and sat down.

Bang.

The outer door crashed open. There was a scuffling of footsteps and hushed voices.

"You'll keep your mouth shut if you know what's good for you, Jonny," said the first voice.

"Mike, I'm not going to say anything, I just don't think it's a good idea," replied the second. Seb now recognised the first voice; it was Michael Malone. Slowly he raised his feet, so they weren't visible below the cubicle door.

"It'll serve him right," Michael continued. "Imagine making Collins captain instead of me." There was a slight pause. "Anyway… He always leaves it unlocked, so it's not like I'm breaking in. You just do your job, okay? OKAY?" demanded Michael.

"Okay," replied Jonny, sounding less than comfortable. The door swung open again and then slammed closed with another crash.

Probably wise to wait a few minutes, Seb thought to himself. *There's no point looking for trouble.*

***

Seb entered the octagonal music room. Despite its lack of windows, the room was bright, illuminated by the many skylights in the ceiling. The wood-clad walls gave it the colour of soft brown sugar. Unlike most classrooms, the floor was tiered so that the back of the room was several feet higher than the front. A large screen filled the front wall, making it look like a mini cinema.

He found a seat towards the back and took his flute from his bag. Perhaps, if he stayed in the shadows, he'd avoid humiliating himself yet again.

Miss Sophie Burrell was in her mid-twenties. She was slim with long dark hair, which glistened as it moved. Her chestnut brown eyes sparkled and seemed to cast a spell over him. Whenever she spoke to him, Seb found himself completely tongue-tied. During his very first music lesson, she'd asked the class to introduce themselves. It wasn't a complicated task; just say your name, the school you came from and your favourite instrument. After several other students had spoken, the baton passed to Seb. He stood up, opened his mouth and blurted out, "Sebastian, Miss, I mean Sophie... sorry... Sophie Hall. No, uh, sorry. Not Sophie. Sorry, me... uh, Sebastian Hall, Miss Sophie... from St James' School. Um, flute... I mean, that's what I play." This was met with howls of laughter from his fellow classmates.

Now, keen to avoid further catastrophes, Seb decided to hide in the far corner.

Sophie gently tapped her conductor's baton on her desk and the class fell silent.

"Today," she said, "we're going to try something a little different. You've all got your instruments, so I thought we'd play a little piece together. You'll find the sheet music on your stands. We have enough instruments and musicians for a mini orchestra, but we'll need to do some reorganising. So, could we have strings over here, please?" she said, pointing to her left. "Percussion at the back, brass on the right there and woodwind to the left."

Seb made his way down to the middle tier of the music room. As he moved into position a thought struck him. He was the only one in the woodwind section.

"Okay," Sophie said as they found their places. "In this piece of music, there is a section for each family of the orchestra, except the percussion. Strings, you take the first. Brass, you take the second and woodwind... well, Sebastian, you take the final section. In between each one, you'll find a 'tutti' that the whole orchestra plays together, a bit like the chorus of a song."

Oh hell. A solo.

Wonderful. Another chance to make a fool of yourself.

But before he could get himself too worked up, Sophie counted them in and the first bars of Mozart's "Eine Kleine Nachtmusik" filled the room. It was a piece Seb had grown up with. He smiled as the notes danced playfully around him. As the strings faded away and the first tutti approached, Seb pursed his lips, lifted the flute and began. He loved playing in an orchestra. There was something magical about it. The sounds of his flute blending harmoniously with the other instruments. He marvelled as the strings and brass sections played their pieces almost faultlessly. As the second tutti tailed away, Seb realised that his solo was next.

His stomach lurched. Every drop of moisture in his mouth evaporated in an instant. How was he going to create a note? He licked his lips in desperation and lifted the flute. To his great surprise, he heard a note. It was a little sharper and harsher than the one he normally played, but it was a note. Then a slightly hurried second, followed by a wobbly third.

But as Seb listened to each note, he became immersed in the music. He forgot where he was, or that he was playing a solo, and lost himself in the sound. One by one, the notes became softer and more melodic. He hit the final note and held it briefly before gently tailing off. As it faded away, he took the flute from his lips and opened his eyes.

The class broke into spontaneous applause. A blond girl in front of him turned and mouthed, "Wow."

This is a joke. It's a set-up, protested the voice in his head.

He glanced sideways and saw Sophie clapping too, beaming at him. Seb was dumbfounded. What had just happened?

***

At the end of the lesson, with the sound of congratulations still ringing in his ears, he set off to find Alice. He checked the time.

Damn it. He was late.

Maybe if he took the shortcut between the sports hall and the design block, he could catch her.

The narrow lane had high concrete walls on both sides, which cast a dark shadow. The warm afternoon sunshine faded as he stepped into the shade. About halfway down, parked by the sports hall entrance, stood a tatty yellow car, patches of rust visible through its faded paintwork. Beyond it, a silhouetted figure. The muscular man seemed nervous; constantly checking to see if he was being watched. As he drew closer, Seb recognised him. It was Michael Malone.

Seb hesitated. What was he doing? Michael turned and walked towards him. Praying he hadn't been spotted, Seb dived behind the old car. The footsteps grew louder, echoing off the high walls as Michael got closer. He screwed himself into a tiny ball, trying to force himself out of sight… waiting until Michael passed. But, as he drew level with the front doors of the car, Michael stopped. Seb froze, not daring to breathe. There was a moment's silence, then…

Clunk.

The handle lifted and the car door eased open. The suspension gave a thud as Michael leaned across the car. Seb felt an unnerving twitch in his nose.

Uh… Uhhh… UUUhhhhh…

Above him, Michael rummaged around in the car. The twitch intensified. Finally, Michael emerged from the car and stood up.

AACHOO!

"What the…?"

In the blink of an eye, Michael was behind the car, picking Seb up by the throat and pinning him to the wall. For the briefest moment, there was a flash of pure rage in Michael's grey eyes.

Then his expression changed and he relaxed his grip.

"Ah… it's you," said Michael, his silky smooth voice returning. He released Seb and examined him closely. "What's your name, my clumsy little friend?"

"Uh… S-Seb," came the trembling reply.

"Seb, what?" asked Michael.

"H-Hall."

"Well, Seb Hall, you don't look like you're stupid enough to poke your nose into other people's business… or get yourself into trouble. Am I right?" asked Michael, surveying him intently.

"R-right," replied Seb, nodding furiously.

"Good," said Michael. "Then I'm sure you'll want to do the smart thing."

Seb continued to nod.

"I tell you what. How do you fancy hanging out with us, being part of my crew?" Michael asked.

Seb's eyes nearly popped out of their sockets. "Me?" he asked, failing miserably to hide his shock.

"Sure," replied Michael. "Of course, we'd need to agree on something first." He paused and his expression hardened. "This never happened. I was never here and nor were you. You didn't see anything… so there's nothing to say. Do we have an understanding?"

Seb nodded again. "Yeah," he breathed.

"Excellent. Trust me… I'm far better as a friend than an enemy," Michael said with a wink. "How about coming down to the beach with us tomorrow evening? You can hang out with the guys."

"Yeah… cool," replied Seb, his voice still shaking.

"Good. Eight o'clock," said Michael. He clapped Seb on the shoulder, turned and sauntered back down the alleyway.

Seb stood, frozen to the spot. What was that all about? What had Michael been doing in that car? Whichever way Seb looked at it, the whole thing seemed very dodgy. But, like Michael said, it was none of his business. And he'd just been invited to join his crew… to hang out with the cool kids. For a second, Seb imagined what it would feel like to be popular, surrounded by pretty girls, all giggling at his jokes.

Then he remembered… Alice. He was late. She would have left the main building by now and might even be on her bus.

He set off at breakneck speed for the bus stop. Unfortunately, Seb was no athlete. As he reached the main entrance, his chest seized up. Despite the fire tearing at his lungs, he rounded the corner and sped down the hill. As he crossed the lawns, he spotted Alice boarding her bus. He tried desperately to call her name, but all he could muster was a breathless croak. She took a seat on her own next to the window. As the bus pulled away, he caught her eye. Was she crying?

He tore up to the bus stop, doubled over, panting. He pulled his phone from his pocket and dialled her number. It rang… and rang. Maybe her phone was in her bag. Maybe she couldn't hear it. Maybe she'd set it to silent during her last lesson and forgotten to turn it back on.

She's ignoring you. She doesn't want to speak to you.

No. It couldn't be.

He typed a hurried text.

Alice, I'm sorry. I can explain.

He stared hopefully at his phone, waiting for the text alert to chime. Nothing. The seconds ticked by, which seemed like hours. Still nothing.

"Damn it!" he shouted. An old woman sitting at the bus stop tutted at him disapprovingly.

***

He stormed into the house, threw his bag on the kitchen floor, burst through the back door and out into the farmyard. The euphoria of the music lesson seemed like a distant memory. In the space of a few hours, he'd had a pretty scary encounter with Michael Malone and probably lost Alice.

He hurdled the rickety wooden gate, stormed across the paddock and down the hill. Past the pond, shrouded by his favourite willow tree. Anger was enveloping him, like a dark blanket.

What have you done?

On he marched. Over the creaking iron gate at the bottom of the field and up the craggy, potholed lane. Storm clouds gathered above him, obscuring the sun. He stepped from the lane and strode across the field to the edge of the wood. This was his sanctuary. Here everything made sense. Here he would find solace.

The musty smells of autumn filled his senses as he pushed his way past the outstretched branches, beyond the treeline and into the wood. He followed the familiar path, dry twigs and pine needles crackling beneath his feet. In just a few moments, he'd be sitting on his thinking rock in the middle of the woodland and his mind would be at peace again.

A chill wind whistled through the trees and the mist descended.

You are such an idiot. You've lost her, your only friend.

"Stop it!" he shouted. His words echoed through the empty woodland.

Believing she'd like you... that she'd want to be friends with you?

He grabbed his head and forced his hands over his ears.

"Shut up!" he yelled.

Ha ha haaa! You think you can silence me?

"Leave me alone," Seb pleaded.

A shadowy outline emerged through the mist.

That head… horns, curled around its bony skull, eyes of fire, flaming nostrils. Then an enormous smouldering body, huge shoulders, arms like tree trunks, claws like daggers. From its back rose two gigantic bat-like wings. As it opened its mouth, Seb saw only fire.

It was the demon from his nightmare.

But this was no dream.

How to Silence Your Demons

Seb received a spontaneous applause after his flute solo, but he struggled to feel proud of himself. I'll bet you've done something that you could feel proud of too. Maybe, like Seb, you thought people were just saying nice things to make you feel better.

What have you done that you could feel proud of?

How could you accept when you've done something good and start to feel proud of yourself?

Seb beat himself up when he got to the bus stop late and missed Alice.

How can you avoid beating yourself up if something like this happens?

Chapter Three

THE TRIAL

Seb spun on the spot and ran.

You cannot silence me! bellowed the creature.

Roars of laughter echoed menacingly around him.

Trees passed in a blur as he sped back along the path. Trailing brambles tore at his legs, branches whipped his face and arms… but on he ran.

More laughter.

You cannot escape from me.

His mind was a whirlwind. Ahead he saw the gap in the trees. He burst through it and out across the open field. Thunder rumbled overhead. Lightning crawled across the darkening skies, but Seb didn't care. He was focused on one thing… home.

He sped down the hill, through the paddock, across the farmyard, straight into the house and up the stairs to his bedroom.

He lay on his bed panting, a tornado tearing through his head. After that disastrous music recital, he'd made a promise to himself. He was going to put a stop to this. He was going to find some answers. His mind wandered to the leather-bound notebook. It had been sitting in his drawer for months. Now and again, he'd thought of getting started, but he never knew what to write.

Go on… What have you got to lose? said another voice. This one wasn't a vicious growl. It was calm, almost soothing – like an old friend.

He walked over to the desk, pulled out the book and gently opened it. The blank page stared back. How was he ever supposed to find that perfect opening line?

And then a rather bizarre thought struck him. What if it didn't need to be perfect? What if it just needed to… be…? Trying to find the perfect line was the one thing that had stopped him in his tracks. Maybe he just needed to get started.

He pictured Frodo and Samwise looking across to Mount Doom at the end of *The Lord of the Rings*. Crossing Mordor had seemed like an impossible challenge. What was it that Sam said?

"Let's just get to the bottom of this hill, Mr Frodo."

He picked up his pen.

Dear Jerno,

There… I did it. I wrote something.

Firstly, sorry for giving you such a cheesy name – it was the first thing that came into my head. Jerno the Journal. It'll have to do for now.

Anyway, I need answers!

I'm sick of never feeling good enough. I don't want to be a loser. I hate being a failure. I don't want to be alone… and I'm scared.

I'm scared of the Demon in the woods.

I'm scared I've lost Alice.

… and I don't know what to do.

What would you do?

He glanced down at the words on his page, half expecting that the answers would appear before his eyes like in Tom Riddle's diary. But he was no wizard, and this was no magic diary. He was the only one who could put ink on this page.

Well… I'm not going to find all the answers right now. It's going to take time.

Where are the answers to my greatest questions? How do I break free from my fears? How can I discover the secrets of self-confidence? Sitting here? Maybe. Here I find the questions. But answers? Maybe the answers are out there… in the world. But where to start? Perhaps I should start in safe, familiar places. But then I must adventure beyond! That, I think, is where the real answers lie.

He put down his pen. He hadn't found the answers, but he had just taken the first little step.

His mind turned to Alice. He never meant to upset her. And, now he thought about it, there was something he could do to put it right. He picked up his phone and began to type.

> I'm really sorry I missed you this afternoon. I ran into MM again. If you let me buy you a cuppa tomorrow morning, I'll tell you all about it.

A couple of seconds later, he heard his message alert chime.

> Ok. Canteen tomorrow at 9? X

He smiled.

> Great!

***

Alice was already sitting at their normal table when he arrived.

"Coffee?" he mouthed over to her.

"White and sweet," she mouthed back with a smile. As the lady behind the counter made their coffees, Seb wondered exactly what he should tell Alice. He'd promised Michael that he wouldn't mention their meeting in the alleyway, and yet he already had in his text to her last night. Whichever way he sliced it, he'd put himself in a sticky situation.

He slid Alice's coffee across the table and sat down.

"White and sweet," he said with a slightly uneasy smile. "Sorry about last night," he began, "I got held up."

"Yeah… So, you met Michael Malone. What happened?" she asked.

"He invited me to hang out with his crew, at the beach," he replied casually. "Although the nearest beach is miles away."

"He means the lawns next to St John's Church in town. They call it 'the beach' for some reason," Alice replied. She looked away, clearly troubled by something.

"Don't worry," he said quickly. "I'll still be your friend too."

"Don't be dense, Seb," she replied. "I know Michael Malone. I spent five years at school with him, remember." She paused for a moment. "Just be careful, that's all. I don't want you to get caught up in… well… stuff you don't want to be caught up in."

"Like what?" he asked, a note of concern creeping into his own voice.

Alice looked down at the table. "I don't know for sure," she said, almost in a whisper. "Nothing was ever proved. It's just that… I don't know… a lot of dodgy stuff seems to happen wherever he is." She looked Seb in the eye. "I just don't want you to get hurt."

Seb felt a warm glow somewhere deep inside him that had nothing to do with his coffee.

They finished their drinks in silence before Alice headed off for her art class and Seb set off for music.

***

The music room was full. Everyone seemed preoccupied setting up their instruments, so Seb slipped in quietly and headed for a seat in the back corner of the room.

"Ah, Seb," Sophie called. "Could I have a quick word?"

A few heads turned.

That doesn't sound good, Seb thought.

"I was wondering if you'd like to audition for the college orchestra. We're entering the British Colleges Orchestral Championships this year. Obviously, we're looking for the very best musicians." She paused for a moment. "And I think you've got real talent."

Seb stared open mouthed, like a lizard hoping to catch a fly.

She doesn't really mean that, came that all-too-familiar growl. *She's just being nice.*

"Are you sure?" he asked meekly.

Sophie smiled. "Yes, I'm sure. Auditions are this afternoon in the Main Hall. See you there at three o'clock?"

"Uh… okay… sure," he said.

Something glowed within him. He would love to be part of the orchestra… part of something special. And Sophie thought he was good enough. Him. He'd never been good enough for anything in his life.

It took a moment for Seb to fully comprehend what he'd just agreed to. Had she said *this* afternoon? A little tingle of panic began to surface. He needed time to get ready, time to prepare. Normally it took him *days* to get his head around these sorts of things. He checked the clock on his phone. He had less than four hours.

***

As he wandered into the canteen at lunchtime, Alice came to greet him. She was not alone. In fact, she was with a lad. He had boy-band looks; tall and slim, with blond wavy hair that he kept flicking off his face. With a wink and a smile, the lad said, "See ya, Howsa," and sauntered off.

"What's wrong with you?" Alice asked, before even saying hello.

"Who was that?" asked Seb, trying to sound as casual as possible.

"Oh, just Tim. He went to St Joe's too. He's a year above us," she replied. Seb didn't answer.

"We were seeing each other for a while last year," she continued. "He spotted me in the corridor and came to say 'Hi.'"

Seb frowned. "Why did he call you Howsa?" he asked, failing miserably to hide his disapproval.

She smiled. "It was a nickname. My form tutor at school gave it to me. You know, it kinda stuck." Seb looked blank. "My surname is Commons, so, Howsa Commons… You know, House of Commons," she replied, shrugging.

He tried to force a smile but ended up grunting instead.

"Yeah… I get it," he replied.

"We're just friends, you know," she said.

"It not that," Seb blurted out.

"Well, what's up, then? Is it Michael Malone?" she asked.

"No, not this time," he replied with a sigh. "Sophie, my music teacher, just asked me to audition for the college orchestra."

Alice's face lit up. "That's wonderful. Well done!"

His expression didn't change. "I know… b-but…" he stammered. "You don't understand. The audition is *this* afternoon."

"Yeah, so what?" She chuckled. "My friend Gemma is in your music class. She said your solo the other day was amazing."

Seb frowned. He hadn't realised that Alice knew anyone in his music class. Gemma, a very accomplished violinist, normally sat at the far side of the music room with a couple of other girls. They were the kind that whispered and giggled.

"Why did she say that?" he asked.

"I've known her for years. Our parents are friends. We went to the same schools, the same summer camp, the same theatre group. She saw us in here the other day, so I guess she thought I'd be interested."

They watch you, they see your failings, they talk… What else do they say?

Seb began imagining the audition and his stomach churned. How many people would be there? Who would be listening? What were they going to ask him to play? What if he didn't know the tune? What if he messed up? What would Sophie think of him?

He desperately didn't want to let her down. And the more he thought about it, the more nervous he became.

"I'm going to get some lunch," Alice said. "Are you coming?"

"I'm not hungry," he replied as his stomach flipped again. Whichever way he looked at it, this audition was a disaster waiting to happen.

At two o'clock Alice said goodbye, wished him luck and headed off to biology, leaving Seb stewing in his own thoughts. He didn't know how long he'd been staring into his cold cup of coffee when he heard his name.

"Seb… Seb… You comin'?" asked a cheery voice from the other side of the table.

"Huh?"

He looked up to see Alice's friend Gemma with her violin case tucked by her side, looking curiously at him. She was quite short and very slim. She had ginger hair that fell to the middle of her back, and a pretty face scattered with freckles. Although she must have been at least sixteen, Gemma looked a lot younger.

"Audition?" she said, motioning with her violin case.

"Oh… Uhhh… Yeah… Sure. What's the time?"

"Ten to three," she replied. "I'm off. You comin'?"

Reluctantly, Seb picked up his flute and his bag, and trudged towards the main hall.

"It's super-cool, ya know, bein' asked to audition… Don' ya think?" Gemma asked.

"Yeah, I s'pose," Seb replied dully.

"Wonder what we'll play," she continued excitedly, talking more to herself than Seb. "Handel, maybe. Or Bach. Or Mendelssohn. Oh!" she said, stopping suddenly in the middle of the corridor. "I hope it's *A Midsummer Night's Dream*. That's an epic piece for the violin."

Seb let her talk. In truth, he wasn't really listening. He just wanted to keep the contents of his stomach where they were. And, if he opened his mouth, he feared they may end up sprayed across the chequered floor.

As they arrived at the main hall, Gemma wished him luck and rushed over to join her friends. The hall was a cavernous space; comfortably big enough to seat three or four hundred people. At the far end there was an old wooden stage, with a set of rickety steps on either side. Down one side of the hall were blackout blinds, which partly covered the floor-to-ceiling windows. Shafts of light illuminated the columns of dust swirling in the air. In front of the stage were two rows of grey plastic seats. On the front row, there sat a couple of dozen students. Behind them, members of the music department.

Sophie perched on the front of the stage. "Good afternoon, and thank you for coming," she announced . "In just a moment we'll begin by giving each of you a piece of music. It isn't a particularly difficult piece, and this isn't a test, so please enjoy it. We just want to hear you play and see how you could fit into the orchestra. Okay, any questions?"

There were no questions, so Sophie handed out sheets of music to each student.

Seb looked down at his piece, "The William Tell Overture", by

Rossini. He'd heard it enough times and liked the tune, but he hadn't performed it in ages. He closed his eyes and replayed the tune in his head. It was a dramatic piece, but the flute section was calm, melodic and playful in parts. As he played to the tune in his head, his mind began to race.

Are there any sharp or flat notes? How loud is the start of the second section? How long should the pauses be? What's the tempo again?

Before he knew it, the tune in his head was crumbling. The rhythm was ebbing away. The melody was fading, and he was left staring at a page full of dots and lines. Although he'd been reading sheet music most of his life, it was like his memory had been wiped.

At the tap of Sophie's conductor's baton, the room fell quiet.

"Okay," she said. "First up, Seb Hall."

Oh no. Not me. I'm not ready, he thought.

You don't know it, do you? said the sinister voice in his mind. *Here we go again. Just like the music recital.*

Seb picked up his flute and crept towards the stage. The old wooden steps creaked beneath his feet. His stomach felt like a washing machine on spin. His palms were greasy. The narrow metal tube slipped in his fingers. He looked out across the hall and saw faces staring at him.

The dust swirled like mist, thicker and thinker, solidifying. The Demon's horned skull appeared, then the eyes.

They're waiting, it taunted.

Just play it, he told himself.

He took a hasty breath and pulled his flute to his lips. A strangled squeal echoed through the hall.

Idiot!

The Demon's hot breath was on his neck. His mind was racing, his heart thumping. He looked again at the music and tried to follow the notes, but he was running out of air.

Clawed fingers wrapped themselves around his neck, their grip tightening, choking him. Desperation set in. He gasped and lost his rhythm entirely. The flute slipped in his fingers, he missed a few notes and his mind went into meltdown.

Pathetic! the Demon spat. *They're all laughing at you.*

Seb faltered his way to the end of the piece, lowered his flute and stared at the floor, devastated.

He could sense everyone's eyes, fixed on him. He dared not look at Sophie. He couldn't bear to see the disappointment. She'd recommended him, and he'd let her down. This was his chance to be part of the orchestra, part of something special – to impress Sophie, make up for the recital, maybe even make his mum proud… and he'd blown it.

How to Silence Your Demons

You can see what makes Seb nervous.
What makes you nervous?
What gives you confidence?

What makes you nervous?

What gives you confidence?

After Alice mentions keeping a journal, Seb thinks it could
help him too.
Alice's journal is called George. Seb has called his Jerno.
Do you think that keeping a journal would help you?
If so, what would you call it, and what would you write in it?

Chapter Four

FIRESTARTER

"I'm really sorry," Seb muttered, almost in a whimper.

"Would I be right in thinking you're a bit nervous?" asked Sophie.

"You could say that," he replied, inspecting a splinter of wood protruding from the dusty stage.

After a second or two of torturous silence, Sophie asked, "What's your favourite piece at the moment? When you're playing on your own, with no one else listening, what do you choose to play?"

Seb looked up and caught her eye. To his surprise, she didn't look disappointed at all. Her expression was thoughtful and concerned. He didn't need long to think about the question.

"There's this piece from a film called *The Last Samurai*. I watch it with my dad. It's his favourite. It's called 'A Hard Teacher.'"

"What does it mean to you?" she asked.

Seb drew a breath. "There's this American army captain, Nathan Algren, who is brought in by the Japanese emperor to help their army defeat the Samurai. This is in, like, 1870 or something," he began. "In the first battle he gets taken hostage by the Samurai and they bring him back to their village in the mountains. He spends a few months with them, watching them.

He learns they're not barbarians at all. They are courageous, spiritual, honourable people – probably like the Native Indians he'd massacred on the plains of North America. He develops this great love and respect for the Samurai, but he doesn't belong. He is an outsider. He's alone. Most of the tribe hate him. He's drowning in his own guilt and self-hatred, but, at the same time, he desperately wants to belong. This music sort of sums up his struggle to find himself, to belong, to win their respect."

The words tumbled effortlessly out of his mouth. It didn't occur to him that there were other people in the room. He didn't even realise that he'd completed a full conversation with Sophie without stumbling over his words. As he told the story, he saw the scenes from the movie playing in his mind. He remembered the advice that one of the Samurai, Nobutada, had given Algren before he fought.

"Too many mind.... Mind the sword... Mind the people watch... Mind the enemy. Too many mind... No mind!"

Nobutada was telling Algren to forget about the people watching, forget about what they thought; to stop thinking and just fight.

"Could you play that for us now?" asked Sophie. Seb nodded. He closed his eyes.

No mind, he thought. *Just play.*

Slowly, he raised his flute, filled his lungs and began.

The notes floated from his flute and a beautiful, sombre, haunting melody filled the room. Seb pictured Algren standing in the Samurai village. He was the only white man. He stood facing his opponent, sword in hand. Before him stood a Samurai warrior, his eyes filled with hatred. Seb felt Algren's guilt, his loneliness and his deep desire to belong, all battling within him. He felt the emotions flow and, as he breathed into the flute, the feelings became sound.

As he released the final note, a tear rolled down his cheek. He opened his eyes, half expecting to be surrounded by the fields and mountains of Japan.

Sophie stood in front of him, wiping a tear from the corner of her own eye, beaming at him. "That was absolutely beautiful," she said gently.

Others looked emotional too. An older woman next to Sophie had her hand clasped to her mouth. Someone whispered, "Stunning." Others muttered "Amazing", "that was incredible" and "I can't believe that's the same boy".

Sophie took a breath and turned to the other musicians. "Okay, second up today, please could we have Melissa White."

Seb climbed down from the stage and sunk into his chair. What had just happened? He hardly had time to process it when he saw Melissa ascend the steps onto the stage. She was jaw-droppingly beautiful, with brown eyes and soft olive skin. Her long dark brown hair was slightly curled at the ends and shimmered as it caught the light. She glanced over at him, held his gaze for a moment and smiled. A bizarre cocktail of terror, excitement and awe surged through him – like plummeting through the most incredible paradise, on his way to certain death. He could feel the ground rushing towards him. Any second now he'd be dead. But, for this one exquisite moment, he was in heaven.

Melissa stood, calm and serene, placing her sheet music on the stand. Time slowed as she raised her clarinet to her lips and began to play. The notes sounded distant and faint… as if they were part of some other dimension. Seb was transfixed.

The rest of the audition passed by in a blur. Gemma and the others took their turns to play but, in truth, he wasn't really in the room. His mind bounced back and forth between his own horrendous performance and daydreaming about Melissa. Had she really smiled at him?

As Seb filed out of the hall following the final audition, a deep gravelly voice called his name. He turned and saw a portly middle-aged gentleman beckoning him over. The man had thick grey hair, a walrus-like grey moustache and bushy eyebrows that were so huge, they looked just like a second upside-down moustache stuck to his forehead. He wore a faded pair of tweed trousers and matching jacket. They must have been old favourites because the gentleman seemed not to notice, or care, that they no longer fitted him around the middle. The brass buttons were so strained, they looked like they might ping across the room at any moment.

"Sebastian, I'm Colonel Walmsley, head of music here at the college," he said gruffly.

Seb muttered a small "hello" in return.

"You know that we're entering this year's British Colleges Orchestral Championships, don't you?" he continued, moustache rippling. "Well, there is no doubt that you've got real talent, but, in a competition, you have to be able to perform under pressure. You..." He looked at Seb and paused, as if to emphasise the word "You". "... need to be able to control your nerves. If you can play the way you did for that second piece, you'll be a great asset to the orchestra. But we can't have the boy that played the first piece, now can we?" Colonel Walmsley attempted to straighten his jacket, made a small grunting noise and nodded, as if to say, "Right, that's that, then." Then he turned on his heel and marched out of the hall, leaving Seb dumbfounded.

Dejected, he made his way through the labyrinth of corridors back towards the main entrance. Maybe he'd spot Alice on the way down to the bus stop. He could do with someone to talk to. He stepped out of the huge glass doors and heard a familiar voice.

"Well... if it isn't our friend, Mr Hall."

Seb spun round. It was Michael Malone and his gang.

"I believe I invited you to join us at the beach. Are we not worthy of your presence, Mr Hall?" Michael enquired as he strode towards him.

Seb froze, not knowing what to say. After his encounter with the Demon, he'd completely forgotten about meeting them.

"Uhhh... I'm really sorry... Orchestra," he said, gesturing towards his flute case. The assembled crowd began laughing, but Michael raised his hand and they fell silent. He moved closer, surveying Seb suspiciously.

"Well, do you want to join the crew?" Michael asked, pointing at the group standing behind him. "Or have you got better offers?"

All eyes were now trained on Seb.

"No... no better offers," replied Seb hastily.

"Mmmmm," said Michael, considering him carefully. He placed a hand on Seb's shoulder and looked him directly in the eye. "Obviously, there's no such thing as a free lunch. I'm sure you know that. So, if you want in, you'll have to earn it." At these words, Melissa appeared behind Michael's shoulder and winked at Seb. "Fancy earning your way in, Mr Hall?" Michael asked.

"Uh... Yeah, sure," Seb replied, failing to hide his trepidation.

"Good. I have a little assignment for you. Think of it like a test, to see if you have what it takes," Michael continued.

"W-What is it?" Seb stammered.

"All in good time, my clumsy little friend," Michael replied. "All in good time." And, with that, Michael casually turned and re-joined his crew.

Seb stood for a moment, not quite sure whether he'd been dismissed or not. Then he slipped around the corner and sped down the hill towards the bus stop.

He spent the whole of the bus journey home staring mindlessly out of the window. He wasn't sure how to feel. What was that all about? Was that good? Was he in trouble? As the bus weaved its way through the country lanes towards the village, he replayed the conversation with Michael, then the one with Colonel Walmsley. What did Michael mean by "You'll have to earn your way in"?

Was there some kind of bizarre initiation? And what did Colonel Walmsley mean by "We can't have the boy who played that first piece now can we…"?

Each time he replayed those words, he became more convinced that he'd blown his chance. He began to wonder if Melissa had smiled at him at all, or whether he'd imagined the whole thing. She was bound to be in the orchestra. For a few moments he indulged his imagination.

They'd both be in the woodwind section. Maybe they'd have to sit next to each other. They'd get chatting. She'd see beyond the clumsy idiot. Maybe he'd do something heroic, and she'd fall instantly in love with him…

The bus driver slammed on the brakes and Seb was jolted back to reality. If he'd screwed up this audition, he'd probably screwed up his only chance of getting to know her. Or maybe not. She was in Michael's crew. If he passed this test thing and got in… But he'd never pass. Whatever Michael had in store for him was surely another opportunity to make a fool of himself. He'd failed the audition. He was about to fail this test. His only chance of being popular, of being someone, gone. The more he thought, the angrier he got.

He was on autopilot as he stepped off the bus next to Cokendale Parish Church and made his way across the village green to his house. He burst through the front door, stomped up the stairs and slammed his bedroom door behind him. Tears welled up in his eyes and a cold, hard lump formed in his throat.

"Are you okay in there?" his dad called gently from the other side of his bedroom door.

"Fine," snapped Seb.

"Okay," came the unconvinced reply. "By the way, your mum's just found some discounted tickets for the London Symphony Orchestra in a few weeks' time. Wanna come?"

"No!" The word burst from his mouth before he could stop it.

A moment of silence followed.

"Are you sure?" his dad asked. Seb detected his dad's confusion but couldn't stop himself.

"Sure!" came the defiant response.

"Okay… if you're sure. Dinner's in an hour." His dad's words echoed across the landing as his footsteps descended the stairs.

What did he say that for? The London Symphony Orchestra! It would be amazing. He should tell him he'd changed his mind. He should say sorry.

He buried his head in his pillow. Why did he feel like he'd won a fiver and lost a tenner? Why was his mind rebelling against him? He felt like he was about to explode. He needed an escape. He needed to be alone.

Completely dejected, he headed across the farmyard, through the paddock and out towards his favourite thinking spot deep in the woods. It was a boulder that the wind and rain had cunningly shaped into a comfortable seat. It was a quiet, undisturbed spot, overlooking a small pond. He'd spent many hours staring into its depths when Granddad Bill had died three years ago. It was a tough time for everyone but especially hard for Seb. Granddad Bill was his hero. During his younger years, he had been a sailor. Seb loved the summer holiday visits to his cottage on the coast. Together they would sail across the bay in his dinghy, *Jack Tar*, chasing pirates and hunting sea monsters. They fished from the jetty, catching mackerel and cooking them on the barbeque. To Seb, Granddad Bill was immortal. He had never even considered the possibility that he might one day die.

The sky darkened as he left the lane and crossed the field towards the wood. He barely noticed the first cold drops of rain hitting his face as he passed through the treeline and stepped onto the leaf litter that now carpeted the woodland floor. It was like a noisy street market inside his head, with more voices than he could count, all competing for his attention.

He heard Colonel Walmsley say, "We can't have the boy that played the first piece."

And Sophie's voice saying, "That was beautiful."

Then Michael: "There's no such thing as a free lunch."

In amongst these was another, more sinister voice.

You've blown it… lost your nerve.

He reached his thinking spot. There was the boulder. He rested his hand on its smooth surface and a mist began to descend. Thicker and thicker it swirled around him, eclipsing the autumn colours behind an impenetrable wall of white.

That Colonel was right. You'll just let everyone down. Melissa would never be interested you. You're a nobody. A loser… Weak… Pathetic…

"Stop," he yelled, putting his hands over his ears.

Laughter reverberated around his head. The Demon appeared through the fog… its fiery eyes, full of hatred… its flaming nostrils…

You will buurrn! it hissed.

Seb stood open-mouthed as it reared up in front of him, its wings flexed, its mighty claws bared. An orange glow issued from its smoky chest as it coiled back like a cobra, ready to strike. Instinctively, Seb dived behind the boulder. A split second later it unleashed a torrent of white-hot flames that engulfed the woodland around him. Seb curled into a tiny ball behind the rock, eyes tightly closed. The noise was deafening, like he'd been suddenly dropped into the eye of a hurricane. He could feel the searing heat surrounding him… and then it stopped.

For a moment, Seb thought he must be dead. Then he heard the boulder crack in half. He sprang to his feet and ran.

Laughter echoed through the trees behind him. The mist was so thick Seb could hardly see. Which way was he going? He clattered through the branches, stumbled over fallen logs. This was not the path. He glanced behind and saw the Demon crashing through the trees. The cold air tore at his lungs but fear drove him on. Ahead he saw a dark mass… a deep ditch.

You'll never jump that, came a triumphant roar. *I've got you now.*

If he missed his jump and ended up in the ditch, he was mincemeat. But what choice did he have? If he stayed where he was, it was only a matter of seconds.

He jumped. Time slowed as he launched into the air. The opposite edge of the ditch inched closer, but would it come close enough? The ditch passed beneath him. More in hope than expectation, he threw his arms and legs forwards, desperately reaching for the bank. With a crash he landed, right on the edge of the ditch, and rolled across the woodland floor. Somehow, he'd made it. A searing pain tore through his right thigh.

You will not escape me! the Demon bellowed. It had crossed the ditch.

Seb scrambled to his feet and ran for the field. The pain in his leg intensified with every stride but adrenaline drove him on. The Demon crashed through the woodland behind him. He glanced over his shoulder. It was gaining on him.

With an enormous THUD, Seb was knocked off his feet. It felt like his shoulder had been smashed with a baseball bat. He lay on his back, staring upwards, stars spinning in his eyes. A torn piece of his jacket hung from the branch of a tree. Had he run into it?

A hollow laugh filled the woodland. It was upon him. A mighty claw scythed through the air, smashing the branches above his head. Seb was showered with splinters. It recoiled again, ready to strike. Without thinking, he bounced to his feet and ran towards the Demon. A look of startled surprise flashed through its fiery eyes. Seb dived underneath its immense body, rolled out beneath its arrow-head tail, regained his feet and sprinted for the treeline. The huge monster turned like an ocean liner, crashing into tree trunks.

Through the trees he saw the field. On he ran, propelled by fear. The pain was unbearable. With one last effort, he stumbled through the treeline and collapsed into a heap at the edge of the field, gasping for air. He lay on his back, covered in blood. The cold rain lashed his face, but he didn't have the strength to stand up. At any moment, the Demon would appear and finish him off.

This, he was pretty sure, was the end.

How to Silence Your Demons

Seb's demon becomes really scary during the audition.
What do you find scary?

[ ]

When he was feeling nervous, Seb found that immersing himself in the music helped him.
What have you done to help you feel less nervous?

[ ]

Chapter Five

DIAMONDS AND DEMONS

Seb closed his eyes, fully expecting to hear that sinister voice announce his death. The seconds ticked by.

Any moment now and it'll all be over. This is it, he thought.

Nothing.

Seb opened his eyes. Still nothing. Slowly he rolled over and pushed himself onto his feet. Blood poured down his sodden face. His whole body ached. Was the Demon playing games with him? He neither knew nor cared.

The rain was beating down harder than ever now, and rumbles of thunder echoed through the clouds in the distance. He turned his back on the woodland and started hobbling across the muddy field towards home. If the Demon struck him from behind, it would all be over. If it didn't… he would keep taking one painful step at a time. Down the potholed lane… up the steep hill of the paddock…

Lightning crawled across the dark sky as he crossed the farmyard. Slowly, he eased the back door open, hoping not to alert his parents. They seemed to be having a rather heated conversation in the living room. Maybe he was in luck. If he kept quiet, he might just make it to his bedroom unnoticed. The last thing he needed was a barrage of questions.

Carefully, he tried to slip his boots off. Normally this was a pretty straightforward task. He'd had them so long they were loose enough to kick off. However, the warmth of the kitchen seemed to have awoken his body and pain seeped back in. Wincing with every movement, Seb removed his boots and dragged himself to bottom of the stairs. He placed his foot onto the bottom stair.

Creak!

"Is that you, Seb?" called his mum.

"Just gonna take a shower," he called back, trying to disguise the pain. But his voice betrayed him. The living room door swung open and he heard his mum's footsteps approaching.

"Where have you b— Oh my God!" she exclaimed as she caught sight of him. "What the hell happened? Are you alright? What have you done? Oh, Seb." Was she angry or concerned?

"I'm okay, Mum, I just fell in the wood. There was this ditch. I didn't see the edge and slipped," he replied. It was almost the truth.

"It looks like you've been mauled by a bear," she cried. Hearing the commotion, his dad appeared behind her at the doorway.

"Let's get you to the hospital," he said calmly. "They can clean you up."

The last thing Seb wanted right now was a four-hour long visit to hospital, with the accompanying interrogation from his parents.

"I'll be fine, honestly. I just tripped. I'll take a shower and get cleaned up… I'll be fine!" He could see his mum shaping up to argue. "Seriously," he insisted, before she had a chance to speak. "I'll come down and you can check the cuts to see if they need a stitch. If they do, I'll go to the hospital. Okay?" Reluctantly they agreed. Seb headed upstairs.

He stood in the shower. The warmth seemed to wash away the numbness and pain swept back in. He looked down. The water was a reddish-brown mixture of dirt and blood. Bits of leaves and small twigs littered the bottom of the shower tray. As the pain built to a crescendo, Seb turned off the water and stepped out of the shower. Now, for the first time, he caught his reflection in the mirror. No wonder his mum had looked so anxious. His face was torn to shreds. He had a deep gash on his right ear and his shoulder was a mess. There was an inch-long wound that looked pretty deep. His thigh was weeping too and, even with handfuls of tissue, he couldn't seem to stop the flow of blood. Slowly, Seb dressed and hobbled downstairs, clinging tightly to the bannister. His dad stood at the bottom of the staircase, wearing a look that said, "We're going to the hospital so don't even think about arguing."

"I'll put some shoes on," Seb muttered.

To his surprise, the journey to the hospital was quiet. There was no interrogation, for which Seb was eternally grateful. The current affairs programme on the radio filled the awkward silence. But Seb's mind was whirring. He kept replaying the scene from the woodland, half thinking he'd imagined it. Then his dad drove over a pothole in the road. The sudden jolt sent a new wave of pain through his leg, which snapped Seb back to his senses. This was not imaginary.

They pulled up to the front of the accident and emergency department.

"I'll drop you here and find a parking space. It might take me a few minutes. You okay to check yourself in?" his dad asked.

"Fine. Thanks, Dad," replied Seb. Delicately, he extracted himself from the car and limped through the automatic doors into the reception area. It was packed.

Just my luck, we're going to be here hours, he thought.

The nurse at the desk asked him to take a seat in the waiting area. He found a pair of chairs, right on the end of a row, next to the vending machine. Seb gently lowered himself into one and closed his eyes.

This was getting out of hand. He'd landed up in hospital but, to be honest, he was lucky to be alive. And, it was getting worse. This thing was gaining strength. It wasn't just invading his nightmares anymore. It was there in the audition… and now in the woods. What next?

He desperately needed to do something. But what? What could he do? This was a demon. How the hell was he supposed to kill a demon?

"Sebastian Hall," the nurse called from the desk.

This would have to wait.

***

Seb awoke from a fitful sleep. He was still in the clothes he'd worn to the hospital. Through his curtains he could see the faint light of dawn. It was 6.27 a.m. For a fleeting moment Seb thought about going back to sleep. He could take a sick day from college. Surely the fact that he had been to hospital would be a good enough reason… and what difference would one day make?

The email alert chimed on his phone. He reached into his pocket to check the message. It was Sophie.

Hi Seb,
I've got some feedback from your audition.
Could you pop in at morning break to the music block?
Thanks.
Sophie

Maybe I should go in, he thought.

There was also a text from Alice.

How did your audition go? I'm dying to hear all about it.
Meet me for a cuppa tomorrow before psych? A xx

Seb re-read it a couple of times, particularly the last couple of characters. Two kisses at the end of a text. Did that mean anything? Seb's heart suddenly felt lighter and a smile crossed his face. Although every part of him seemed to ache, he forced himself up. Wincing with pain, he pulled on some fresh clothes, hobbled downstairs and made his way to the bus stop.

***

Seb walked into the canteen and scanned the room for Alice.

"Hey," she called cheerfully from over his shoulder. Seb turned to greet her and watched as her expression changed. Her eyes searched the cuts on his face and the gash in his ear.

"Seb!" she gasped. "What happened?"

He paused for a minute before answering. Should he tell her the truth? There was a part of him that desperately wanted a friend to confide in… someone to share all this with. His grandma had always said, "A problem shared is a problem halved." But what would she think of him? Surely, she'd think he was some kind of deranged nutter, or worse still that he was lying to her. And he didn't want her to start worrying either. He saw how she'd reacted when he told her about Michael Malone.

"It's nothing," he replied. "I was walking in the woods at the back of my house and fell into this ditch… stupid, really." He sounded far from convincing, and Alice didn't look like she was buying any of it. "I… I lost my footing," Seb continued in a bid to make it all sound more plausible. "I slipped on the edge. I guess I hit some branches and stuff as I fell."

Alice frowned.

"Are you sure?" she asked.

"I'm okay," replied Seb, "Honest… Now, shall we get that cuppa?"

Alice nodded and found a seat while Seb bought their coffees.

"So… how did the big audition go?" she asked a little flatly.

"My first piece was a horror show," he replied. "But Sophie gave me a second chance. I think she felt sorry for me. It seemed to go okay. She wants to see me at break time… probably to let me down gently."

Alice sipped her coffee. "Maybe not," she replied. "Gemma got an email too. How did she do?"

Seb thought for a moment. He was so busy worrying about his own performance and daydreaming about Melissa, he'd hardly noticed Gemma's. His mind drifted back to Melissa.

"Seb!" Alice asked for the third time, her voice rising slightly.

"What?" he replied, suddenly coming to his senses.

"Oh… Forget it!" she snapped. She snatched up her bag in frustration and marched off. Seb followed in her wake, trying to figure out what had just happened.

They entered the psychology classroom in silence, sat down and pulled their books out of their bags. Mark was perched on the edge of his desk, surveying the class with interest as they arrived.

"Morning, everyone," he said in his gentle Scottish accent. Today we're going to have a slightly different lesson. Some of your tutors think that their job is to get you through your exams. They will teach you what's in the curriculum and give you a great chance of achieving good grades. Some of us feel that our job is to give you more than that. We believe in providing a more rounded education. We believe in developing you as people, not just students. We want to help you to truly understand the subject. We want all of this to help you, not just at college but in life. So, today we're going 'off-piste', beyond the boundaries of the curriculum, to explore how our mental game really works and how to manage our own headspace. We'll start with a very simple challenge. All you have to do is recite the chorus of your favourite song."

He looked around the class, observing the response. "Hands up if that's too tough for you."

Seb looked around the room. There were no hands.

"Okay, great," Mark continued. "Then let us begin. First, take a moment. Think of your favourite song. Then find the lyrics of the chorus. You could find them on your phone or write them at the top of your page if you need to."

There was a murmur from around the room as everyone got started with the task. Seb thought about his favourite song. He sang the chorus in his mind and wrote the lyrics on his page.

"Okay," said Mark as everyone finished. "Has everyone got their lyrics? Does anyone need more time?

"No? Good," he said, sporting a mischievous smile. "Then let's move on. Next, turn to the person next to you and tell them the lyrics of the chorus, as you've written them on the page."

The class seemed rather puzzled but followed Mark's instructions nonetheless. Seb turned to Alice, who was looking intently at her page.

"After you?" asked Seb, hopefully.

"Fine," she muttered without looking up at him.

"At first sight I felt the energy of sun rays

I saw the life inside your eyes

So shine bright... tonight... you & I

We're beautiful, like diamonds in the sky

Eye to eye... so alive

We're beautiful, like diamonds in the sky"

Seb listened intently. "Wow," he said, "That's beautiful." The faintest trace of a smile crossed her face then faded, but she said nothing.

"Okay, now swap over. It's the same task," Mark instructed.

Seb looked at his sheet and read.

"When you feel my heat

Look into my eyes

It's where my demons hide
It's where my demons hide
Don't get too close
It's dark inside
It's where my demons hide
It's where my demons hide."

As he heard the words tumble out of his mouth, Seb began to feel uneasy. A frown took hold of Alice's brow and she looked away. What had he just said? He hadn't thought about the words or what they meant; he just liked the song. He didn't know he'd be saying them to Alice. Part of him wanted to tell her, "They're just words from a song, I don't feel that way." The problem was, he did feel like that. A frosty silence fell between them.

Now look what you've done, came the all-too-familiar growl.

"Right," said Mark, once they'd all finished. "How did that go? How did it feel? Easy? Tough? Did you feel any different than normal?" There was another outbreak of muttering. "Barney, what do you think?" Mark asked.

Seb looked around to see Barney Jones, a "straight A" student from his old school. Seb had always had a bizarre dislike for Barney. It was bizarre because he was basically a nice lad. Unlike many of the kids at his old school, Barney had never caused him grief. But he was the one person his mum always seemed to compare him to. And, of course, Seb had always come off second best.

"Um, it felt okay," Barney replied. "A bit weird... but okay."

"Alight," Mark said. "Anyone else? Jonny Martyn, how about you? Did you notice anything?"

Michael Malone's friend, Jonny, cleared his throat. "It was a bit strange. It felt a bit personal, actually... like they were *my* lyrics," he replied.

Mark nodded knowingly. "Anyone find anything different?" asked Mark, surveying the class, but no one answered.

"Interesting," he remarked. "Has anyone found it too difficult so far?"

Seb scanned the room. There were no hands.

"Right… then we'll move on," Mark said. As he spoke, his eyes lit up and a cheeky smile appeared in the corner of his mouth. "The next part of the challenge is, very simply, to sing the chorus to your partner. Exactly the same words, just add in the tune."

There was an outbreak of nervous chatter. Angela Thomas was so consumed by a fit of giggles, she could hardly speak. Maybe it shouldn't have been a surprise. She was always giggling. But how on earth could she find this funny? It wasn't funny. It was torture.

Seb felt a knot starting to tighten in his stomach.

Sing? You? Ah ha hhhaaa… laughed the Demon.

It was right. He had a terrible voice. It was barely fit for singing in the shower, never mind in a classroom full of people. He hadn't sung in front of anyone else since primary school. Apart from not wishing to publicly humiliate himself, he also felt it was unfair to inflict his singing on another human being. And, after seeing her reaction, he certainly didn't want to sing those lyrics to Alice. He turned to face her.

"I went first last time," she said calmly. Seb swallowed hard. How could he possibly get out of doing it? Maybe if he delayed long enough, Mark would stop the class and move onto the next task.

"Ladies first?" Seb offered.

"No, I insist," came Alice's reply.

Seb looked down at his sheet and took a breath.

"When you feel my heat," he squeaked. He'd started too high. He could see Alice trying really hard to stifle a giggle. Laughter was breaking out all around him. Who else had heard? Had the entire class heard?

He paused briefly and stared down at the second line. He knew it was going to sound awful before he'd even begun. He'd started too high and was getting higher. A thin wailing noise issued from his mouth as he continued to blunder his way through the chorus. It was even worse than he'd imagined. Alice's shoulders were bouncing up and down as she tried, in vain, to supress her laughter. Almost everyone in the class had lost control. Mark stood at the front of the room, smiling benignly.

"Okay, calm down, calm down," he insisted. "Take a few breaths." Gradually, the laughter subsided. "Right. Swap over now."

If she didn't think you were a loser before, she will now...

How could Mark do this to him?

Alice straightened up in her chair and began. Her voice was beautiful. It wasn't quite note perfect, but it was soft and mellow. Her words seemed to float into Seb's ears and nestle comfortably in his mind.

As she finished her chorus, he said, "You never told me you could sing."

For the first time in the lesson, Alice turned and looked Seb in the eye.

"You never asked," she replied.

Mark waited until the laughter and chatter subsided before he addressed the class.

"So, how was that? Did you feel any different from the first task? What were you thinking and feeling this time? How was it different?" he asked. Several hands shot up around the classroom. Mark worked his way around the room, encouraging everyone to share their experience. To Seb's surprise most people said that they felt embarrassed too. He had always assumed everyone else was confident and self-assured. They certainly looked more confident than he felt.

"In that case," Mark continued, "we'll move onto the third and final task this morning. I know that last one was a little more challenging, but is there anyone that *could not* do it for any reason."

Everyone seemed to be looking around, eager to see if there were hands in the air. As before, there were no hands.

"Great," announced Mark, with an even bigger smile. "The third task, very simply, is to sing your chorus again… in front of the class."

Mark's gentle Scottish accent echoed through the stunned silence for what seemed like an eternity. There was a collective intake of breath. Gradually, Seb heard frightened voices around him.

"What? He can't be serious."

"OMG!"

"I'll literally die."

Mark waved his hand to quieten the class and eventually the ruckus died down.

"The only question is… Who is first?" Mark asked. This time there was no muttering. The whole class seemed determined not to make eye contact with him. Mark reached behind him and picked up a bowl from his desk.

"I've got everyone's name on a little scrap of paper in this bowl," he announced. "We'll pick a name. That person, and their partner, can go first." Mark held the bowl in front of Seb. He reached in and picked the first piece of paper that his fingers touched.

Please, not my name, not my name, Seb begged.

Seb took the paper and opened it. Relief. It wasn't his name. It was Alice's! His heart sank.

"It says, um… Alice Commons," he muttered. There was an enormous sigh from the class.

"Ah, excellent," said Mark cheerfully. "Up you come then."

For the second time in just a few minutes, Seb felt his stomach turn to lead.

This can't be happening, Seb thought as he and Alice approached the front of the room. He stared out at the twenty or so faces, whose eyes were all fixed on him.

"Alice, your name was picked, so you can go first," Mark announced.

"Okay," she said brightly.

Alice's voice gently filled the room as she sang. Judging from the expressions on his classmates faces, they were clearly impressed too.

As Alice finished there was a polite ripple of applause around the room.

"Very good, Alice, thank you," said Mark once the applause died down. "Right, Seb, off you go."

He stood motionless, feeling like he'd just had the breath knocked out of him. His mind had been erased. Beads of sweat formed on his brow and his throat tightened up. He couldn't remember the first word of the chorus. Seb looked across at Mark, panic etched into his face.

"Do you need your sheet of paper?" asked Mark. Seb nodded and reached across the table to pick up his sheet. Desperate not to squeak his way through this, he decided to start a lot lower. He took a breath and began.

"When you feel my heat," he croaked. It was monotone, devoid of any tune. He looked up and saw a sea of smirking faces looking back. There was an undertone of giggling from around the room. Seb knew it was only Mark's presence that stopped everyone from roaring with laughter.

What have you done? The whole class is laughing again! spat the Demon.

Clumsily, Seb stumbled through the second line. He could hear his voice faltering.

"It's where my D-D-D…" He couldn't say it. How could he share his darkest, most shameful secret?

Look at you. Pathetic. I hate you! it cursed.

68

The Demon's clawed fingers tightened around his throat. It's breath, like a dry desert wind, extinguished the air from his lungs. He was suffocating. Panic rose like a serpent from within.

Breathe! Breathe! he told himself.

He gasped and felt cool air rushing into his chest. But the relief was short-lived. He gasped again and again. Faster and faster. He heard his breath, short and shallow. The room swam in front of his eyes. In and out of focus. He slipped back through his own eyes and out of the room.

How to Silence Your Demons

Seb gets worked up about the thought of singing in public.
How would you have felt if you were in that psychology class?
What other things tend to make you feel the way Seb did?

How would you have felt in the psychology class?

What other things tend to make you feel the way Seb did?

Some of the things we get ourselves worked up about seem
pretty scary in that moment. But, when we step back, they
don't look as bad.
Think about those things that get you worked up.
How do you think you'll feel about them in a week, or even the
next day?
Will you even care?

Chapter Six

THE AWAKENING

"There you go. Easy now," came Mark's calming voice. Seb felt a hand on his shoulder and the hard plastic of a chair against his back. After a moment he realised that the pattern of squares dancing before his eyes was the ceiling tiles. He sat up and the room gradually came back into focus. What just happened?

"You're okay. Just stay there and get your breath," Mark said. "We'll see how you're feeling in a few minutes. If you need to go down to the medical room, I'll get someone to escort you. For now, just relax while we finish off the lesson. Okay, let's see… Who's up next?"

One by one, the students came to the front and sang their chorus to the class. Some were visibly shaking. Others melted into a fit of giggles. It took Angela Thomas a full three minutes to complete her four-line chorus.

As the last pair returned to their seats, Mark asked the class how their thoughts and feelings had changed during the exercise. Most people admitted to feeling nervous. Some said they felt sick. Others had heart palpitations. One girl said she felt almost paralysed with fear. But no one else had reacted like Seb. No one else had a full-on meltdown.

"Interesting," said Mark. "Because it's basically the same task that you found very easy at the beginning of the lesson. All we've added is the tune and the audience. Why did that make such a difference?" Mark surveyed the class. Again, there was much muttering, but no one ventured an answer.

"The truth is, it isn't different. We make it different. But why?" he asked.

His question was met with stony silence.

"Okay… that's your homework! Thank you very much, I'll see you next lesson," he said brightly.

Seb rose from his chair, picked up his bag and started walking towards the door.

"Hang on, Seb," Mark called over the scraping of chairs. He waited for the room to empty. "Firstly, are you feeling okay now?"

Seb stared at the floor. He couldn't make eye contact but managed a feeble nod.

"Okay, good," Mark said. "I had a chat with Sophie Burrell. She mentioned that you could use a little help with your nerves. Based on what just happened, I think she might be right."

She thinks you're weak too, came the sinister growl.

Mark looked directly at Seb.

"You're not the only one who has struggled with nerves, you know. You can see that from today's lesson. You're not alone," he said. Mark gave Seb a knowing look. "Here's a little tip that helped me," Mark continued. "When my head was full of negative thoughts, I used to tell myself to stop thinking about the negatives. It didn't work." Mark reached into his pocket, drew out a blue marker pen and held it in front of him.

"Here's a little challenge to illustrate my point. Don't think about the pen. Don't think about what's written down the side of the pen, or how big it is, or the stripes on the lid. Whatever you do, don't think about the pen. What are you thinking about?" Mark asked.

"I'm thinking about the pen," Seb sighed.

"Right," replied Mark, "and it's almost impossible not to. Now, focus for a moment on the bookshelf over there. How many books can you see? What sizes are they? What colours? Are they tall, short, thick, thin, old, new?"

Seb examined the collection of books on the shelf. There was a vast array of different colours and sizes. He could make out the title on a few of them, but the spine on others was too thin. There was a particularly old book with a tatty cover that seemed to be holding all the others up.

"Are you still thinking about the pen?" Mark asked.

"What?" replied Seb, slightly surprised. "Uh, no."

Mark smiled.

"If you want to stop thinking about X, start focusing on Y," he said. "Now, don't get me wrong – this little technique is not a magic wand. It's not the ultimate solution. But it is certainly something that I've found useful. I hope it helps you too."

Seb nodded. It all sounded reasonable enough, but he wasn't sure how it would help.

"I suspect you've done something similar before," Mark went on. "We often have some really useful strategies, but we're not really aware that they *are* strategies. We don't think of them that way. So, we only use them occasionally. When we do use them, they really work, but we don't always use them when we need them."

Seb pondered for a moment.

"During my audition," he muttered, almost to himself, "when I played that second piece, I just... I just listened to the notes, felt the music and everything else seemed to melt away. All the worry, all the fear... gone. You're right – it was the same. I did change my focus."

A smile slowly crossed Mark's face.

"Remember: focus follows interest, and interest follows what you care about. Curiosity is a powerful force, if you harness it!"

...hed behind him. He picked up what looked like ...ur sheets of A4, folded in half. "Your assignment from ...A solid start. I hope the feedback is helpful," Mark said, ...g it to Seb. He paused for a moment and looked pointedly at the gash in Seb's ear.

"If you ever need to chat about anything, my door is open," he said. "Now, don't be late. Sophie will be waiting."

***

Seb arrived in the music block. Sophie was sitting at the front of the room with a mug full of steaming hot tea.

"Ah, there you are," she said. She scanned the cuts on his face. "Everything alright, Seb?" she asked.

"Yeah, fine. I just fell in the woods. It's nothing, really," he replied, not wanting to go into any detail. Sophie surveyed him for a moment but, thankfully, didn't pursue the conversation any further.

"I was beginning to think you weren't coming," she said.

"Sorry," Seb began. "Mark was helping me with my nerves."

"I hope you didn't mind me mentioning it to him. When I saw that you were studying psychology, I thought he might be able to help." Seb nodded, not really knowing what to say. He hated the thought that people were talking about him… sharing all his flaws. But maybe she was just trying to help.

"Anyway, that's not why I asked you to pop in," she continued. "Congratulations… Your audition yesterday was impressive. We would be happy to offer you a place in the orchestra."

"What?" That was the last thing he was expecting her to say. "Really? But… the first tune… I… well… It was rubbish," he said. "And Colonel Walmsley said—"

"I've spoken to Colonel Walmsley," she said. She looked into his eyes. "Seb, I believe in you."

Her words hit him like a bolt of lightning. No one had ever said they believed in him. A wave of emotion crashed over him and a tear welled up in the corner of his eye.

"That first tune… Well, let's just say it wasn't your best. But your second showed just how good you can be, when you control your nerves. That's why I thought Mark could help."

Seb took a deep breath. "Thanks," he said.

He was in the orchestra. Maybe he hadn't screwed up after all. Or maybe Sophie just felt sorry for him. He thought of Melissa. She was sure to be in the orchestra too… and in the woodwind section. Maybe they would sit next to each other, get to know each other.

But what if he couldn't control his nerves? What if he screwed up again? What if he had another meltdown? What if he let everyone down? It sounded like Sophie had put her neck on the line for him too.

"Our first practice is here, tomorrow afternoon at five o'clock. See you then?" she asked.

He nodded a little hesitantly. "Yeah… See you then."

Seb left the music block with an unusual blend of nerves and excitement. Where might Alice be? He wanted to tell her everything. Although morning break was over, they both had a free period, so he headed for the canteen.

He walked in and looked over to the table where they normally sat, hoping to see her waiting. It was empty. He scanned the room. There was a handful of people but, to his dismay, no sign of Alice. Seb took out his phone and called her. No answer. He tried again. Still nothing. Then, it began to dawn on him. Alice had been upset ever since their conversation that morning. She hadn't really talked to him during psychology either. Perhaps she was ignoring him.

Maybe she'll answer a text, he thought.

Hey. Just been to meet Sophie about the orchestra. Tell you all about it at lunch? S

He waited. Nothing. He wandered over to their usual table and sat, waiting for a response. The minutes ticked by, but Seb's phone remained resolutely silent. He tried to start the homework assignment for Mark but didn't get very far. Every few minutes he'd check that his phone battery hadn't run out or if he had accidentally switched the text alert off.

As lunchtime arrived, the canteen began to fill. People filed in and out, but there was no sign of Alice. Finally, he spotted her with Gemma. He waved. He was pretty sure that she'd seen him, but she turned away and resumed chatting to Gemma. Seb's heart sank.

You've done it now. You've lost her, the Demon sneered.

It'll be okay, his mind protested. *I'm joining Michael's crew. I can have friends. I can be popular. You'll see.*

But it didn't matter how hard he tried to convince himself. He didn't feel it. Despite being told he'd made the orchestra and being invited into Michael's crew, he'd hit rock bottom. Alice was everything. How could he be so stupid? He felt that all-too-familiar lump forming in his throat. He screwed up his eyes, determined not to shed a tear.

He wasn't sure how long he sat there, staring forlornly into space, or what had woken him from his daze. The canteen was almost empty. He checked the time. Perhaps he should make a start on his homework.

He reached into his bag for his notebook and also caught hold of the assignment Mark had just given him. As he pulled them from his bag a scrap of paper fluttered to the floor. He bent down and picked it up.

There were four words:

"Find the Demon Charmers"

He stared at scrap of paper. How did it get in his bag? Find

76

the Demon Charmers? Hang on… Who else knew about the Demon?

He screwed up the paper and threw it into his bag.

He got up, almost knocking the table over. All he wanted to do was get home and slump into bed. He didn't want to see anyone or talk to anyone. His world was in utter chaos. As Seb wandered forlornly down to the bus stop a girl called his name. Without really caring who it was or what they wanted, he slowly lifted his head. Melissa stood a few yards away, leaning casually against a lamp post.

"See you at orchestra practice tomorrow?" she asked with a smile.

Seb stumbled, his heart pounding. "Uh… Hi," he replied weakly. "Yeah, um, see you… uh… tomorrow."

She simply giggled, waved and headed up the hill towards college.

Seb stayed rooted to the spot.

Well done. Messed up yet another conversation with a nice girl. Loser!

***

The following afternoon, Seb arrived right on time for orchestra practice. As always, he settled into his seat in an empty corner of the room. Melissa glided through the door. She seemed to be heading in his direction. Where was she going? None of her friends were sitting near him. Then, she pulled up the seat next to him and sat down.

"Hey," she said, flicking her hair off her face. "By the way, I like your new rugged look."

Her eyes drifted to the scratches, still visible on the side of his face. He didn't know what to say. His heart was racing, his mind spinning.

Don't screw this up!

He knew that, "I fell over when I was walking in the woods," sounded pretty pathetic. He also knew that, "I was attacked by a demon," wasn't a great answer either. In fact, no answer sounded good.

"Ah, it's nothing." He shrugged.

"Mmmm… The strong, silent type," whispered Melissa with a grin.

Seb knew it wouldn't take long for her to realise that he wasn't the strong, silent type at all. He was just rubbish at talking to girls. Within seconds, he would be making a complete fool of himself and she'd never speak to him again.

"Good afternoon everyone," came Sophie's voice over the muttering of the crowd. "Settle down."

Phew. Saved! he thought.

"First of all, well done everyone. You all made it through the auditions and it's great to have you in the orchestra. As you know, this year we're entering the British Colleges Orchestral Championships. There is a regional heat this term. The winner of that will compete at the national final at the Royal Albert Hall in London next term. The winner of the British championships then represents all of the British colleges at the world championships next summer."

Did she just say "The Royal Albert Hall"? It was his all-time favourite concert hall. He'd dreamed of playing there ever since he was a kid.

"Now, the regional heat is just before Christmas, so we only have a few weeks to practice. Fortunately, for the regional competition, we can choose what we play. So, the piece we have picked is called 'A Hard Teacher'. It features in the soundtrack from a movie called *The Last Samurai*." Sophie glanced over at Seb.

He smiled. It was the piece he played for the audition, one of his favourites, one that he knew, one with a flute solo… His smile faded.

A solo!

No!!

How could she do this? I can't play a solo in front of all those people, he thought.

They had to win the regional heat to get to the national final and play in the concert hall of his dreams. But to do that, he had to play a solo in a competition, in front of an audience. To be honest, he didn't know what was worse, playing the solo or facing the Demon. His heart sank.

Sophie continued. "We'll build the piece during the next few weeks. Today we'll start with a few tutti pieces, which we'll play all together. She passed around the sheet music and looked up. "Everyone ready? Then we'll begin."

As they struck up, Seb remembered why he loved playing music. The notes from his flute blended seamlessly with the rest of the orchestra. The sounds danced around the room, like young children laughing and playing together. And, while the music played, Seb joined them. For those few brief moments, despite the chaos of his life, he felt free. Free from the throbbing pain, the gnawing anxiety, the Demon's voice in his head… just free.

The practice finished and everyone began filing out. Melissa leaned over to pick up her bag and her hair brushed his cheek, setting fireworks off inside him.

"See you next week," she whispered. Before he had time to answer, she'd spun around and was gliding gracefully towards the door.

What the hell just happened? Did Melissa like him? No way. She couldn't. Girls didn't like him… especially nice ones. But her hair brushed his cheek. It must have been an accident. But she said he was "rugged looking". It must have been a joke, right? Right!

For a split second he began to imagine himself and the orchestra, playing at the Royal Albert Hall... with Melissa. What was he thinking? The orchestra were not going to the Royal Albert Hall, because he was sure to mess up his solo. He was going to let everyone down. It would be like the recital but a hundred times worse.

The last couple of people left the music room and the door swung closed. He was alone. Seb sat motionless in his seat, unwilling to move or think. All he wanted was a few precious moments of peace. He took a deep breath. All he craved was silence. Another long deep breath.

He felt air filling his lungs and solid ground beneath his feet. One breath after another... like the sea gently lapping on the beach. He closed his eyes and allowed himself to slip into the stillness. At last, his mind was clear. The constant jabbering died down and he relaxed into the chair. Silence. Peace. He didn't know how long he'd been sitting there when a thought finally emerged; quiet but profound.

He needed to tell Alice everything. She was his friend. He knew that. She'd been upset with him because she knew he was holding something back... keeping something from her. The most important thing in the world right now was her friendship and he didn't want to lose it. Telling her about the Demon could be a risk. Not telling her was a much bigger risk. And, if she laughed in his face, maybe she wasn't the friend he thought she was.

Seb opened his eyes. The room was growing dark. The last dim rays of sunlight crept in through the skylights.

He took out his phone and texted Alice.

I'm sorry. I wasn't completely honest with you. I didn't just trip in the woods. I can't explain on a text but, if you'll forgive me, I'll buy you a cuppa tomorrow and explain everything.

He sat for a few more moments before pressing "send". He wasn't really sure how to finish the message. He took another deep breath, cleared his mind, added an "x" and hit send.

Seb picked up his bag, smiled and headed for the door. As he stepped into cool evening, his phone vibrated in his pocket.

See you tomorrow at morning break ☺ x.

For the first time in a very long time, Seb felt a sense of calm. He set off towards the bus stop, feeling lighter… clearer. He rounded the corner by the main reception and heard that silky smooth voice.

"Ah, Mr Hall… The very man I wanted to see," said Michael Malone, leaning casually against a wall. "What on earth happened to you?" His eyes searched the scratches on Seb's face. Fortunately, Michael didn't seem interested in the answer. "Still want to earn your way into my crew?"

This was it, his chance to be someone… be popular… be cool.

"Yeah, sure," replied Seb.

"Good… Then I have a little assignment for you. Meet me tomorrow, 1 p.m., sports hall entrance. Don't be late, there's a good chap."

***

Seb dropped his bag onto his bedroom floor, pulled open his desk drawer and took out his journal.

Dear Jerno,

Firstly… Sorry, I still can't think of a better name for you, so I guess you're stuck with this one.

Also… Why is life so bloody tough? As soon as I answer one question, another three come hurtling at me.

Why did I have a panic attack in psychology? We only had to sing a song. Why was it so terrifying?

Mark said it's not different, but we make it different. When I think about it, he's right. I didn't have a panic attack when I said the words to Alice. Singing to her was a bit harder. But singing it in front of the class…

It was like the recital, like my first audition – but on steroids!!

All I could think about was looking stupid, everyone laughing, everyone hating me. I guess I felt trapped. All I could see was disaster… my worst nightmare coming true. And there was no escape, no way to stop it.

But Mark was right.

It wasn't different. I made it different.

Why?

He stopped for a moment as his mind chewed on the question.

Maybe that's it?

I made it different.

Maybe I changed the job, in my head. I changed it from a simple task into some monstrous, impossible, life or death thing.

Instead of just singing, maybe I thought the job was to impress them all, or avoid looking stupid, or make them like me.

I was so bothered about what everyone else thought, I lost focus on what I was doing.

What did Mark say? "Focus follows interest and interest follows what you care about."?

So, I guess… If I care too much about what everyone else thinks, that's what I'll focus on.

Maybe that's enough to turn a simple task into a terrifying ordeal.

I'll keep thinking on that one!

He was about to close the journal when another thought struck him.

And then there's the problem of this demon.
It's not going away. To be honest, it's getting worse.
I don't even know where to start.
I'm scared!

How to Silence Your Demons

After the singing task, Mark sets some homework.
He says, "The truth is, it's not different. We make it different.
But why?"
Why do you think we do this?

Mark shares a little exercise, where he asks Seb to focus on a
pen, and then a bookshelf.
How could this help Seb?
How could it help you?

Chapter Seven

THE ASSIGNMENT

Bleary-eyed, Seb slumped into his usual chair in a deserted corner of the canteen and waited for Alice. He hadn't slept well. When he did manage to grab a few minutes here and there, his dreams were invaded by images of Michael Malone, the Demon and disastrous flute solos. He sat wallowing in his thoughts for a few minutes.

"Hiya," Alice said cheerfully as she sat down. "Mine's a coffee... white and sweet."

"What?" replied Seb, a little taken aback.

"You said you'd buy me a cuppa," she said with a cheeky grin.

"You're right, I did," he replied. "Back in a second." It was amazing how a few words and a friendly smile seemed to transform his world.

"Coffee for madam, white and sweet," he said as he placed Alice's cup on the table in front of her. She smiled.

"So, what's up? You haven't been yourself recently."

Seb took a mouthful of his own strong black coffee to buy himself a couple of moments before answering. The bitter, sour taste seemed to awaken his brain.

"I know," he said. "I'm really sorry I haven't told you about it. I wanted to," he added hastily, "but…" Seb didn't quite know how to explain it.

"But what?" she asked.

"I know how this is going to sound… It's going to sound like I'm some crazy weirdo."

Alice didn't reply. She sat calmly sipping her coffee and let Seb continue.

"The other day when I came in covered in scratches, I said I'd fallen over in the woods. That's true. But I didn't tell you why I was running… what I was running away from." Alice's expression changed. Calm and cheery became concerned and anxious.

"Go on," she said.

Seb drew a breath, unsure whether to keep going or not.

Just say it. Just say it!

He looked Alice in the eye.

"I was running from a… a demon," he said.

There was a stunned silence that seemed to last for hours.

"A demon?"

"A demon," Seb confirmed. "It's huge, with horns as sharp as spears, fire for eyes, claws like daggers. Oh, and it wants to kill me."

Alice's mouth fell open.

"Oh my God, Seb. What are we going to do?"

He didn't quite know how to respond. He hadn't planned this bit of the conversation.

"Lock me up?" he said flippantly.

"Don't be stupid," she replied. "What are we going to do about the Demon?"

Seb sat back in his chair.

"You mean you believe me? You don't think I'm a nutter?" he said.

"Of course I bloody believe you. I care about you," she replied.

A tear escaped from the corner of his eye and trickled down his cheek. He made to wipe it away, but Alice's smile told him she'd seen it. She reached across the table and gently placed her hand on top of his.

"We'll find a way," she said softly.

Seb took a deep breath.

"Thank you," he replied in as steady a voice as he could muster. He took another slurp of coffee while his mind tried desperately to catch up.

"The other little problem I have right now is Michael Malone," Seb said without thinking. "I bumped into him last night after the rehearsal. He told me he has an 'assignment' for me. I need to meet him at lunchtime."

Alice looked thoughtful for a moment. "You're right. Compared to a demon, that is a little problem."

The two sat for a moment, lost in their own thoughts.

"I'm scared, Alice," Seb said finally. "What the hell am I going to do?"

"I'm not sure," she replied. She took another sip of coffee. "But... maybe," she said quietly.

"Maybe what?"

"It's something Sam – you know, my counsellor – said to me," she replied. "He said he'd started to understand fear. He'd realised his fear was imaginary."

"What?" Seb replied.

"I know, right. But I think there's something in it. He told me a story. He'd been out walking across open countryside in the middle of the night. He heard these noises around him, got scared and started running," she went on.

"I don't blame him," Seb said.

"Yeah, but then he stopped to think. What am I running from? At first he thought it was the ghosts, werewolves, zombies, monsters lurking in the shadows. But none of those things actually existed. The noises weren't made by monsters or ghosts. They were probably made by rabbits or owls or something. He was imagining all the horrors from beyond the grave. So, what he was actually scared of… was his imagination. He was running from his imagination. He reckons it's the same with all fear," she said.

"Woah. That's mad," said Seb, as he scrambled to make sense of it all. "But how did that help you when you were in hospital?" he asked.

"Sam said most of the stuff we get scared or anxious about is in the future. When I was in hospital, I used to lie there thinking about what would happen if the treatment didn't work. Sometimes I'd see myself in a wheelchair, hooked up to all these drips, for the rest of my life. Sometimes I'd wonder what would happen if I died… if there was a heaven… what would happen to Mum and Dad. That's the stuff that used to scare me. But, like Sam said, I was imagining all that stuff. How did he used to explain it? The only way we can ever experience the future is to imagine it. There is no other way. So, if we're scared of something in the future, it has to be our imagination," she said.

"Wow!" Seb replied. "I've never thought about it like that."

"I hadn't either," she said. "We would talk about how the future is unknown, like a blank canvas. Our mind can't handle the void so it starts to fill it in. It paints pictures of the future. And, normally, those pictures are pretty terrifying. But they are our pictures… our imagination."

Seb sat for a moment dumbfounded, until Alice's phone chimed.

"We'd better get a move on, or we'll be late for class," she announced. With that, they grabbed their bags and headed for the door.

***

As Mark dismissed the class, Seb's thoughts turned to his imminent encounter with Michael Malone. What was this "assignment" that Michael had in store for him? Was it some bizarre initiation test? From the little he knew of initiations, they all involved a mixture of pain and humiliation; neither of which he fancied.

He walked forlornly towards the sports hall. With every step, another doubt invaded his mind. He began picturing the things Malone might have planned for him. Melissa was sure to be there to witness his humiliation too. She would see him at his worst.

Seb's heart began pounding in his chest and fear bubbled up inside. Fear, he thought, might well be imaginary… but he could feel it.

He stood at the bottom of the shaded alleyway. To his left, the sports hall towered above him like a huge grey cliff face, casting its deep shadow. To his right, the dilapidated design block, its window frames, with their flaking paintwork, looking sad and tired. Halfway up the alleyway was the dishevelled entrance to the sports hall. Should he turn back? What awaited him behind that door?

And then it hit him. He was imagining this fear. Alice was right. He had no idea what Michael had planned.

He looked up. It was a beautiful, crisp autumn day. The sky was clear and blue, and the light breeze tossed the dry leaves playfully.

This is real, he thought.

The butterflies were still doing aerobatics in his stomach, but his heart wasn't trying to beat its way out of his chest anymore. He took a lungful of fresh air and strode towards the entrance.

Seb pushed open the door, which creaked, as if to announce his arrival. The sports hall entrance was small and dingy, illuminated by a small orange light above the door. Two narrow, dark corridors led off in opposite directions to the changing rooms.

Immediately behind the door to the left stood an old vending machine, its light flickering. Above it, a spiral staircase with a rusty handrail led up to a balcony.

"Ah, Mr Hall," said that now familiar silky voice from the corridor to Seb's right. "I have a little job for you." Michael appeared out of the darkness.

Seb said nothing. He stood, rooted to the spot, in the open doorway.

A furrow crossed Michael's brow. "Get over here," he snapped.

As if on autopilot, Seb walked towards Michael.

"This is a very simple job," Malone said slowly. "So... don't... screw... this... up..."

He stared at Seb for a moment and then pushed a small package into his chest. It was a sealed brown padded envelope. Malone drew closer.

"Go to the athletics track this evening, eight o'clock," he said in a low voice. "There is a small hexagonal building. You'll meet a woman there – short pink hair, covered in tattoos. You give her this and she'll give you a package for me. Make sure you get that package... Understand?"

Seb nodded nervously.

"Good. Because I don't tolerate failure. If you're curious, look up seppuku sometime," he said casually. "I'm sure you'll be fine, though. You're a smart lad. This is your chance to prove it and earn yourself a place in the crew. I look forward to welcoming you aboard." With that, Malone picked up his bag and pushed open the door to leave.

"Tomorrow morning, eight o'clock sharp, here, with that package," he said as he swept through the door.

Seb stood alone in the dingy entrance hall holding the brown package. What was that all about? What the hell had he got himself into? For a moment he considered running after Malone and telling him he'd changed his mind. But this was his way into the crew... to be one of the cool kids. He thought of Melissa. What would she think of him if he failed?

Seb stuffed the package in his bag. He could deal with it all later. Right now, he needed to get to his music lesson.

***

Seb packed his bags at the end of a very enjoyable music lesson and heard Sophie's voice over the murmuring and clattering of chairs.

"Seb, Gemma – could I have a quick word before you go? I have some news about the orchestra," she said. "The northern regional heat is in two weeks' time, at Rippendale Cathedral. There will be a dozen colleges competing. As you know, the winners go through to the national final... at the Royal Albert Hall!" Sophie looked so excited, Seb thought she might burst.

"Obviously we'll need to rehearse our piece, so—" she drew a breath "—I've put together this schedule." She handed each of them a piece of paper with a timetable for the next two weeks.

"Wow," exclaimed Seb as he scanned the page. It contained a grid with a mass of coloured boxes, outlining the elements they would work on, which section of the orchestra would be involved during each rehearsal and how they would bring the whole thing together.

"Now," continued Sophie, "I know it's a lot of work. There are some early-morning and late-afternoon sessions. But I know it will be worth it. We've got a really good chance of getting to the final." She looked at Gemma. "Can you make all of these sessions?" Sophie asked.

Gemma nodded.

"Yeah, no worries. I only live a few minutes away," Gemma replied.

"Wonderful." Sophie beamed. "And you, Seb?"

Seb thought for a moment. He had no idea if there was an early bus or not; he supposed there must be.

"Uh, yeah," he replied, still trying to work out how he could get there on time. To be honest, it didn't really matter how he got there; this was really important to him and he desperately didn't want to let Sophie down.

"Yes," Seb said, "I'll be there."

"Wonderful! See you both at rehearsal."

Seb and Gemma picked up their things and wandered out into the autumn sunshine. With a cheery, "See ya," Gemma bounced off in the direction of the canteen, leaving him trying to figure out what to do next. Normally, he would walk down to the bus stop and head home. Today, however, he had a job to do. He checked his bag to make sure the brown package was still there.

Should he tell Alice? She would definitely want to know. Maybe she could help? But he really didn't want to burden her with it. He pulled out his phone, found her number and tapped in a text.

> Hey. Sophie's just given us our rehearsal schedule for the regional heat. Lots of early starts and late finishes. I met Malone too. Nothing to worry about. I'll tell you about it at morning break tomorrow. Coffee before psychology?

He hit send, put the phone back in his pocket and started walking down the hill towards the town. If he was going to meet this mystery woman with pink hair at 8 p.m., he may as well find something to eat and drink. He might even get started on that philosophy homework.

Seb watched the sun setting behind the buildings as he walked down into the town. The orange glow turned crimson and lit up the few fluffy clouds that floated just above the horizon. It was truly magical, as though someone had set fire to the sky. He stopped for a moment and just drank in the scene. As he did so, his thoughts ebbed away, leaving blissful silence.

No mind, he remembered. *Is this what Nobutada meant?*

Seb took a deep breath of the fresh, cold air. *No mind.* He stood for a few minutes, entranced, watching the sun slowly slip below the horizon. Then headed down the hill to find something to eat.

***

Seb sat in the almost deserted coffee shop and opened his philosophy homework. Their task was to watch movies during the Christmas holidays and identify the philosophical themes. He read the list with interest: *Star Wars* (all of them), *Harry Potter* and *Fantastic Beasts* (all of them), *The Matrix* (the original), *The Lord of the Rings* and *The Hobbit* (all of them), *The Hunger Games* (all of them), *The Avengers* (as many as you can), *Into the Wild* and *The Last Samurai.*

Not bad homework, he thought. *Maybe Dad will fancy watching some too?*

He imagined the pair of them sprawled out on the sofa, gorging on popcorn and tortilla chips. He'd always enjoyed whiling away time with his dad, doing nothing in particular. But, during the last couple of years, they hadn't done very much of it.

The door of the coffee shop slammed and woke Seb from his daydream. The sky was dark now and rain drummed on the windows. He checked his watch – twenty to eight. It was a good ten minutes to the athletics track. He'd need to set off in a couple of minutes. To pass the time, Seb pulled out his phone to check his messages.

Seppuku… What did Malone mean?

No, not now. This is not the right time. Save it for later, he thought. But curiosity got the better of him and he typed it into the search bar. The result came back in an instant.

Seppuku (切腹, "stomach-cutting," "abdomen-cutting") is a form of Japanese ritual suicide by disembowelment.

Oh my God, thought Seb. *Alice was right. She warned me.*

Seb tried desperately to convince himself it was nothing. Maybe it was a joke or a test to see if he'd crumble – part of the initiation. But his stomach didn't seem to believe him. He packed up his bag, slung it over his shoulder and set off.

The glorious sunset seemed like a distant memory. Heavy spots of cold rain pelted him as he walked back up towards the college. He hadn't thought to bring a coat when he left home that morning and the ten-minute walk seemed to take forever. With every stride he became colder, wetter and more miserable.

Who was this woman? Was he about to walk into the middle of a criminal gang, armed with knives… or worse?

His stomach flipped.

Fear is imaginary. Alice's words echoed around his mind.

Knowing it was imaginary was one thing, but it didn't stop him feeling scared. He trudged up the road, trying in vain to shield himself from the worst of the rain.

If it's imaginary, it must be coming from me. I'm painting the pictures, he thought. *So maybe I can control it.*

By now he was soaked to the skin. His hair was plastered to his face and his patience seemed to have been washed away by the torrential rain.

Yeah, maybe, but it's easier said than done.

He shook his head in despair, spraying rain and sweat into his eyes. The sweat stung.

"Arrrggghhh," he cursed as pushed the sodden hair off his face. The heavy rain didn't make any difference now. He couldn't get any wetter or colder.

Seb rounded the corner, stepped into the athletics track and saw the bizarre hexagonal building a little way ahead of him. Malone had chosen the spot well. It was poorly lit. The lone streetlamp cast its weak orange glow across the path next to the building. Rather than illuminating the landscape, it created eerie shadows. Perfect for an ambush. Seb stood a little way from the building. The woman was nowhere to be seen. The fact that this building had six sides did not help either. Was she at the back, or obscured by one of the many walls?

I might as well have a look, he thought. *It's got to be better than standing here like an idiot in the rain.*

Seb had circumnavigated the strange little building and come back to the point he'd started, when he spotted her. The silhouette of a slim hooded figure emerged from the shadows.

"You got summat for me?" she asked cautiously.

"That depends… What are you expecting?" asked Seb.

She drew closer and the light caught her face. She wasn't the fierce, intimidating woman that he'd expected at all. She was petite. A flash of shocking pink hair peered out from under her hood. Her bright hair and colourful tattoos stood out on her pale skin.

"A package from Malone," she said.

Seb slipped his bag off his shoulder, reached in and pulled out the brown padded envelope. He held it close to him. How was this supposed to work? Were they supposed to exchange at the same time? He needed to take a package back to Malone. He didn't want to imagine what would happen if he failed.

"Have you got something for me?" Seb asked.

The woman nodded, reached into her coat and pulled out a similar looking package. He held his envelope and gradually extended it towards the woman, ensuring he kept a tight grip. The woman reciprocated.

The exchange seemed to happen in slow motion. Seb grabbed the envelope from the pink-haired woman and stowed it under his coat without looking at it. She, on the other hand, ripped open the end of the padded envelope he'd just given her. He stood and watched as she tipped the contents into the open end of the package. Seb caught a glimpse of silver in the dim orange light. It looked like a metal watch strap. As the woman turned it around in her hand, he spotted a Rolex symbol between her fingers. Then she dropped it back into the padded envelope, nodded to Seb and disappeared back into the shadows.

***

The house was dark when Seb arrived home. He supposed his parents were out, which suited him just fine. After changing into some dry, warm clothes, he slumped face down onto his bed.

What the hell had he just done?

He reached for his coat and pulled out the envelope. It was tightly sealed. For a split second, he considered opening it but then thought better of it. To be honest, it didn't take much imagination to figure out what was inside. The envelope was obviously full of cash; how much, he couldn't guess. But he knew it was more money than he'd ever held in his hands before.

Suddenly he began to feel sick.

Oh my God, he thought. *I've just traded stolen goods.*

How to Silence Your Demons

Malone gave Seb an assignment. Seb felt that something wasn't right, but he didn't feel able to stop.
Has anyone asked you to do something you knew wasn't right?
How did you respond? What did you say and do?

There were probably a few reasons that Seb didn't feel able to stop. He was scared of Malone. And, he desperately wanted to be popular and to belong.
Would you do what Malone told you or not?
What would you do if you were in Seb's shoes and why?

Alice says that fear is imaginary, because we fear things that might happen in the future. And the only way to experience the future is to imagine it.

What do you think about this?

How could it help you with your fears?

Seb feels scared about meeting the pink-haired woman. But when he gets there, it's not like he imaged.

What do you imagine about the future, that scares you?

How realistic do you think your fears are?

Chapter Eight

THE CRIMINAL

Seb sat for a few moments in shock.

There must some other explanation. Maybe the woman bought it from eBay and he was just the courier?

Yeah, that's why you had to meet at a deserted athletics track at night, the Demon retorted.

Whichever way he looked at it, there was only one logical explanation. He was a criminal. Images raced through his mind.

Police knocking at the front door… A court room… He was standing in the dock. His parents stared across the court room. Then a barred cell, the visitor's room at the prison…

"What did we ever do to deserve this?" his mum asked from across the prison table. He could feel shame rising uncontrollably.

Then his dad, looking only at the floor. "I've let you down, son," he said, his voice cracking with emotion.

Seb's guilt began to swallow him. A deep hollow laugh filled his ears. He was wrenched from the prison back into his bedroom.

Someone has been a naughty boy, said the menacing voice.

Was it coming from outside?

He raced to the window just in time to see the Demon swooping back into the darkness. Through the rain-spattered glass, he could just make out the outline of the enormous, winged beast as it flew over the field beyond the paddock.

It circled back towards the house. There was something in its claws… a person. Alice!

Naughty boys get punished, it hissed as it whistled passed his window. *Maybe you need a little demonstration.*

With that, the Demon climbed into the darkness and out of sight.

He searched the dark sky. Where had it taken her? A fiery red glow appeared in the sky over the wood.

"No!" he screamed.

He flew down the stairs, taking them two and three at a time, and sprinted out into the torrential rain. This couldn't be. Alice was innocent. She didn't deserve this. She didn't deserve to be punished for his crime.

Seb tore up the lane and across the field towards the wood, pelted by the stinging rain. He could barely see. His feet slipped beneath him, but on he ran, propelled by a potent cocktail of fear, guilt and rage.

The Demon stood on the edge of the field, backed by the trees. Alice lay beneath it, motionless on the glistening grass. Was she still alive? As he got closer, Seb noticed her stirring. *Thank God.*

Criminals cannot go unpunished, the Demon announced.

"No!" Seb shouted. "Take me. It's me you want. I'm the criminal."

You seem not to value your own worthless hide, it replied. *Perhaps this way you will learn.*

The Demon reared up. Seb saw the fiery glow emanating from its smoky chest. In a few seconds it would unleash its fury on Alice. In desperation, he picked up a rock and hurled it at the Demon. It lazily raised a bat-like wing and flicked it across the field.

Pathetic, it spat. *You cannot stop me!*

Seb snatched up another rock and aimed for the Demon's head. As before, it raised its wing and casually sent the rock flying across the field. The Demon's fiery eyes fixed on Seb and it began advancing towards him. He grabbed a third rock and threw it with all his might. He didn't expect to hit the Demon… that wasn't the point. He'd gained its attention.

The Demon kept advancing, stalking him like prey.

You, it hissed, with pure hatred.

It was getting closer.

You loathsome little…

"Alice, run!" Seb bellowed.

Out of the corner of his eye, Seb saw Alice scramble to her feet and run in the opposite direction. Her silhouette blended into the shadows and out of sight.

The Demon raised a mighty claw. Seb heard the wind whistle between its bony fingers as it swept through the air towards him.

CRASH.

With a thud, he landed on his bedroom floor, dazed and confused. His heart was hammering. Sweat poured down his face.

Alice, he thought to himself.

He picked up his phone and dialled. Nothing. Maybe a text.

U ok?

Had she escaped? Was she alright?

The room swam in front of his eyes. Lights popped. He rubbed his head. Had he hit it on the bedside table? Maybe if he closed them for a moment, all would become clear again.

***

He woke early the following morning to the shrill sound of his alarm. He was exhausted, curled up on the floor beside his bed.

What was he doing here? Never mind. Maybe he could crawl into bed and have just a few more minutes sleep.

No!

His eyes snapped open.

Alice!

Panic erupted and then subsided. It was a dream, right? He paused for a moment to make sure. It must have been. Okay, maybe he could get a little more sleep.

Malone…

His heart sank. He had an appointment to keep. And, knowing that the envelope contained a small fortune, he did not want to be late. What would Malone do if he thought Seb had run off with his cash?

Let's not go there, he thought.

He dragged himself up, pulled on some fresh clothes, stuffed the package into his jacket and headed for the bus.

Remarkably, Seb didn't feel particularly anxious as he gazed out of the mud-splattered window, watching the early morning countryside speed past. He'd completed Malone's little assignment. He had the package. Surely there was nothing Malone could get angry about.

He stepped off the bus and began walking up the hill towards the college. The dreary grey buildings seemed to merge with the dreary grey clouds.

As always, the alleyway to the sports hall seemed much darker than the world around it. The tall muscular figure of Malone stood next to the entrance. Seb's footsteps echoed off the high walls around him, betraying his presence. Malone turned to face him.

"Have you got it, Mr Hall?" he asked. His voice, smooth as silk, oozed with danger.

"I've got it," Seb replied. Interestingly, the churning sensation in his stomach, which he'd felt so acutely the day before, was not there. They stood for a moment, looking at each other in silence.

"Well?" demanded Malone.

Slowly, Seb pulled the envelope from inside his jacket and held it out in front of him. Malone whipped the package out of his hand in a flash. For a few seconds he inspected the contents through the envelope, the way people do with Christmas presents before opening them. A satisfied grin gradually spread across Malone's face.

"Good," he muttered to himself. "We're done, Mr Hall… for now." And with that, he turned and sauntered off up the alleyway.

For now? Seb thought. *I thought that was it. I completed his little assignment.*

Then it began to dawn on him. Malone was never going to leave him alone. This was never going to be a one-off. It was probably the first of many "little assignments".

How could he be so stupid? He cursed as he stormed off down the path to meet Alice. What had he got himself into?

***

When Seb reached the canteen, he found Alice at their usual table in the back corner. She smiled and waved from across the empty room.

"Hey," she called as he approached. "What's with the 2 a.m. text?"

"I'm a complete idiot, that's what," he replied flatly.

He told her about the assignment that Malone had given him, seeing the strap of the Rolex watch and the envelope full of cash that he'd just handed over. Then about the nightmare with the Demon and how he'd woken on the floor, dazed and confused. For a brief moment she seemed amused, but it soon passed, and the concerned look returned.

"I think I've just committed a criminal offense," concluded Seb in a low voice. Alice stared out of the window.

"I think you're right," she said at last. "Oh, Seb. I was afraid something like this might happen."

She closed her eyes and a moment's silence fell between them.

"I'm pretty sure this is not the first time he's done something like this. Things mysteriously went missing at school too. No one could pin anything on him, but I'm sure he was involved."

"Yeah, probably because fools like me did the dirty work for him," Seb replied bitterly. "I guess that's why he's dressed from head to toe in fancy clothes."

Alice shook her head. "He doesn't need the money. His father is loaded. He owns that Car Supermarket place near the motorway. He was always sponsoring the sports teams and presenting the trophies at school… making grand gestures… always doing things to get noticed. How did Dad describe it? 'They're new money trying to be old money.' I think that was it."

"What do you mean?" Seb asked, making no attempt to hide his confusion.

"Most of the really wealthy people around here have had money in their family for generations. They own the land… you know, the sort of people who have estates and go on pheasant shoots. Dad says that Mr Malone has been trying to get in with that crowd for years, but they don't really fit in. That's why he sent Michael to St Joes, so that he could get in with their kids, and then his father could break into their parents' social circles. It's all about appearances with him."

"Is that why Malone was always captain? Because his father sponsored all the teams?" asked Seb.

"Probably," Alice said. "He would hold these huge parties at their house. I say 'house'. It's more like a mansion, with tennis courts and pools. There was a massive graduation party when we left school, apparently."

"Apparently?" Seb asked. "Weren't you invited?"

Alice gave a hollow laugh. "You had to be the right kind of person to be invited to Malone's parties. To be honest, they're not my kind of crowd."

Realisation hit him like a freight train. *They're not my crowd.* Alice was right. They weren't Seb's kind of crowd either. What was he doing trying to hang out with Malone's crew? He wasn't one of them. He didn't need to be in the cool gang. That's not who he was.

"Anyway, the big question is: What are you going to do now?" she asked.

Seb shrugged. "I don't know," he replied. "He's just said that we're done… for now. This isn't the last assignment he's going to give me, is it? And I'm pretty sure the next one will be bigger."

Alice nodded. "We've got to stop this thing," she said earnestly.

"I know," he agreed. "But how?"

They sat looking out of the window as the first spots of rain began to run down the pane.

"Well," she said. "Let's start by getting a cuppa. I'll buy this one," she said and wandered off to the counter.

Seb's mind turned to the dream and texting Alice in the night. When he woke up in a heap on the floor, he was convinced that she was in danger. He remembered picturing her running across the fields to escape. Why couldn't he separate the dream from reality?

Alice returned with two steaming cups of coffee.

"I think I'm going mad," he said as she sat down.

"What makes you say that?" she asked.

"I sent you that text last night, didn't I," he said. "I was so convinced the Demon was outside my window. I ran out into the rain to try to stop it… or I thought I did. It knocked me off my feet. But when I fell, I…" He paused and took a breath. "I'd just fallen out of bed… I dreamed the whole thing." Seb's head fell into his hands and he let out a long, slow sigh. "What is wrong with me?"

"I don't think you're going mad," she said gently. She took a sip of her coffee. "'Is this real? Or has this been happening inside my head? Of course it's happening inside your head, Harry, but why on earth should that mean that it is not real?'" she said.

Seb looked at her, perplexed. "What?" he asked.

"It's from Harry Potter," she replied. "You've read Harry Potter, right?"

He was no less confused by her answer. "Of course I've read Harry Potter," he replied.

She shook her head. "It's the conversation Harry and Dumbledore have at Kings Cross station. You know, right at the end of the story, after Voldemort hits him with the killing curse in the forest."

He was starting to catch up with her now. "Okay, yes, I remember," he said. He thought he could see where she was going with this. "So, you're saying that Harry wasn't actually standing on Kings Cross station… so it was all in his head," Seb said.

"That's right," said Alice. "But Dumbledore said that didn't mean it wasn't real."

Seb thought for a moment. He didn't really understand, but he didn't want to look stupid either.

"Okay. But they're two wizards in a fictional story. How does that help me right now?"

Alice peered into her mug of coffee, as if looking for the answer.

"I don't know," she said finally, "but somebody will. Come on, we're going to be late for psychology." And with that, she took a final swig of coffee, picked up her bag and left.

Seb followed, shaking his head in disbelief.

***

Mark was perched on the edge of his desk, surveying the class with interest as they came in and took their seats. Once the general murmuring and clattering had died down, he spoke.

"Good morning. You may remember a little while ago, we went 'off piste', beyond the boundaries of the curriculum, and spent a session looking at your own mental game. I'd like to do that again today"

An outbreak of nervous chatter spread across the classroom. Was this going to be like the singing task he gave them? After a moment or two, Mark stood up and the class fell silent.

"Personally, I've always learned the most when I've followed my interest and my curiosity. So, this morning, we're going to follow yours. Take a few minutes to think about challenges that you're experiencing in your life. Perhaps there are anxieties, doubts or fears that are holding you back. Take a minute or two to think about it. Feel free to chat amongst yourselves," he added. "I'll come back to you in a few minutes and see what you think."

The classroom erupted into noisy conversation. A few people seemed concerned about the prospect of sharing their darkest, innermost secrets with the rest of the class. However, others were talking about challenges they'd like to raise. Seb looked at Alice, who was deep in thought and furiously scribbling notes. Not wanting to interrupt her, he began thinking of his own challenges.

He could tell them about feeling so nervous in the audition that he could hardly play a note... or never feeling good enough... or maybe the challenge of facing a fire-breathing demon that wanted to kill him... or Malone... or becoming a criminal... or going mad... or he could just say nothing.

It didn't take Seb long to settle on the latter option.

Mark quietened the class down.

"Okay," he said. "Has anyone got a challenge they would like to discuss?"

Alice glanced across to Seb briefly. What was she thinking? Before he had a chance to ask, Alice's hand shot into the air. Seb feared the worst.

"Alice, no," he whispered under his breath. She replied with a little kick under the table.

"Yes, Alice," said Mark.

Before Seb could stop her, she was off.

"I was reading an article about people with anxiety and how they don't always see the world the way it is. They struggle to know what's real and what's not… Like, they see threats where there aren't any. And it got me wondering. Is it possible to get confused between what's real and what's imaginary? Or are real and imaginary actually the same? Like Dumbledore said to Harry Potter, 'just because it's in your head, why should that mean it's not real'. But you probably don't read Harry Potter, because you're a lecturer," she finished sheepishly.

The class burst into laughter.

"Even lecturers read Harry Potter." Mark chuckled. "Well, some anyway."

"It's a very good question," he continued. "It's true. Many people who experience anxiety see threats where others don't. Sometimes the most innocent things can be really scary for them. Bizarrely, they often know that there is no threat… but it doesn't stop them feeling scared."

A couple of hands shot up.

"Yes, Angela," Mark said.

She cleared her throat. "But if they know that something isn't really dangerous, why would they feel scared? That doesn't make sense."

Mark nodded and smiled.

"Good question. Any ideas? Yes, Jonny," he said, pointing to the back of the room.

"My mum's like that," Jonny said. "When my older brother passed his driving test, she was always anxious. If he said he'd be home at six o'clock and he wasn't through the door at like, one-minute-past-six, she'd start thinking he was dead or something.

Dad kept telling her not to be stupid – and she knew she was being stupid – but she couldn't stop. She kept saying it was an irrational fear, so she couldn't get rid of it with a rational argument."

Mark beamed at him. "And what do you lot think?" he asked the class. "Go on, Seb" said Mark, who had spotted his hand in the air.

"Is that the same with paranoia?" Seb asked.

"Great question!" replied Mark, who was clearly enjoying the discussion. "What do you think?"

"I think so. I mean, people who are paranoid start thinking that other people are thinking things they're not really thinking… I think," Seb said.

The class burst into laughter once more.

"You're absolutely right," replied Mark. "Paranoia is a fear of what we imagine others are thinking. Those with extreme paranoia often think that others are plotting against them, keeping secrets from them or even out to get them. As Jonny said, it's not a rational belief, not a logical belief. The big question is: Why do we even care what others think? But that's a question for another day."

Mark paused for a moment and then said, "Remember: Your imagination is powerful. Use it wisely!"

Seb thought back to the conversation with Alice. The pieces seemed to be falling into place. Without really intending it, his hand crept into the air once more.

"Yes, Seb," Mark said.

"It's like fear, isn't it?" Seb said. He wasn't really speaking to Mark. It was more like he was thinking out loud. "Fear is imaginary. We're not scared of the dark, we're scared of what we imagine is lurking in the shadows. We're not scared of the snake, or the spider, we're scared of what it might do to us. I guess, if someone is feeling anxious, they're scared of the pictures in their head… or the voices. Jonny's mum is scared of the *thought* her son might be dead in a ditch. She doesn't actually think he is dead. Paranoid people are scared of what they imagine other people are thinking about them or planning to do to them. And because they imagine it so vividly, it seems real."

"Excellent!" Mark exclaimed. "I'm going to share a concept with you," he said. "Give this some thought. There is often a difference between 'The Reality' and 'Our Reality'." He paused again to let the ideas sink in.

"Think of 'The Reality' as the way things are in the world, and 'Our Reality' as the way they appear to us. Now, you'll find that there's a lot written in psychology about perception – the principle that we all see the world in a slightly different way. For example, if we all look at the same cloud, one person might think it looks like a pig and another might say it looks more like a car. We'll be studying perception in more depth later this year. However, I want to offer you a slightly different way of thinking about it. 'Our Reality' is our life experience. It is the way we experience life. More particularly, it's the way you experience your life, in your mind, through your thoughts and feelings. If it's a gorgeous sunny day, but we're feeling miserable inside, we may not feel the warmth of the sun or notice the bright blue sky. In our internal world, it might look and feel dark and cold. 'The Reality' is that the sun is shining. 'Our Reality' is that life seems dark."

Seb felt like a few more jigsaw pieces had just slotted into place. His hand was back in the air. Mark nodded at him.

"So, Dumbledore was right. The very fact that it is happening in your head means it is real… to you! Whether it is 'The Reality' or not, doesn't really matter. If it's 'Your Reality', it is your life experience. It is real to you."

"That is exactly what I think Dumbledore – or perhaps J. K. Rowling – was trying to express," replied Mark with a very satisfied chuckle. "I'll leave you with this thought before we move on. Often, we can't control 'The Reality'. However, 'Our Reality' is our own territory. It is our lived experience. It's constructed in our mind. And because it's our territory, we can employ the power of choice. Now, that doesn't mean we can simply flick a switch and turn off our fears or just think differently. That's not how it works. Believe me, I know. However, we can start to choose how we experience life.

"So… How do you want 'Your Reality' to be?"

There was a moment of stunned silence in the classroom, which seemed to please Mark immensely. "Right," he said finally. "Who is next?"

"Wow," whispered Alice. "I feel like he's just given me the keys to my own life."

How to Silence Your Demons

Mark says to the class, "Take a few minutes to think about challenges that you're experiencing in your life. Perhaps they are anxieties, doubts or fears that are holding you back". The class share some of theirs.
What are yours?

Mark also shares his understanding of anxiety, 'The Reality' and 'Our Reality'.
What do you think about all this? Does it make sense?
How could this help you with your fears, anxieties and insecurities?

Chapter Nine

THE HEAT

The next few weeks passed in a blur. Seb was so busy with orchestra rehearsals that he barely had time to think about anything else. Most mornings he set his alarm early and walked the three-and-a-bit miles into college for the 7.30 a.m. rehearsal. There were some dark, cold, wet December mornings when he was very tempted to hit the snooze button, roll over and fall back to sleep. But he didn't. This was too important. And the orchestra was starting to sound really good.

It was the final rehearsal before the regional heat and Seb was the first to arrive. The torrential sleet and rain had persuaded him to run most of the way. In fact, as he found a seat and took his bag off his shoulder, a puddle began to form on the floor beneath him.

Sophie appeared a few seconds later and greeted him with a cheery, "Good morning." But as she caught sight of him, she gasped.

"Seb, are you alright?"

He was drenched to the skin and shivering violently. He took off his old coat to reveal a sopping wet jumper and shirt.

"Y-y-y-e-e-a-a-h-h. F-f-f-a-a-n-n-k-k-s," he replied.

"What happened?" asked Sophie.

113

"S-s-l-l-e-e-t-t," he replied.

Sophie wandered over to a small cupboard by the door, keeping her eyes firmly fixed on him.

"Hang on," she said, as she began rummaging in the cupboard. A few moments later she emerged with a slightly scruffy towel, which was frayed at the edges. "It's clean," she said, passing him the towel. She surveyed him as he dried his hair and face.

"Th-thank y-you," he said, as he began to control the shivering.

"Did you walk in this morning?" Sophie asked. Seb nodded. "Don't you live in Cokendale?" Again, he just nodded. "That's got to be three miles, hasn't it?"

"Just over," he said.

"Isn't there a bus? What about your parents? Couldn't you get a lift?"

Seb could hear a mixture of concern and what he thought might be anger in Sophie's voice as she asked.

"The first bus is too late, and Dad leaves really early and..." He paused briefly. "I don't want to bother Mum. She would probably just say I needed to take some responsibility, anyway," he replied.

Sophie sighed. "Do they know you're in the orchestra... or that you've been getting up early for rehearsals?" she asked.

Seb shook his head. He was now staring at the growing puddle on the floor, desperately avoiding Sophie's gaze. The door swung open and several other bedraggled members of the orchestra made their way in. Sophie placed a comforting hand on his shoulder and said, "Wait behind at the end, would you?", before turning to welcome the other students.

As with many of the others, their final rehearsal went well. Even Colonel Walmsley offered a "Well done, everyone" amongst his normal shouts of "Come on, people, focus!" There seemed to be a real togetherness, everyone playing for each other, which Seb loved. Amazingly, he was relatively happy with his solo too.

At the end of the rehearsal, Sophie made a beeline for Seb.

"I know this is the last rehearsal before the regionals, but there's a chance—" she swallowed, "—that we'll qualify for the national final. And, if we do, there will be more rehearsals next term."

She looked at Seb earnestly. "Promise me," she said, "if you need a lift, you'll ask. We can sort something out – even book a taxi. It's not a problem."

Seb felt himself flush but thanked Sophie. He picked up his still soaking wet bag and coat and made for the exit.

Melissa was waiting just outside, her hair blowing gently in the breeze.

"Hey, Seb," she called. His stomach did a little backflip.

Say something cool.

Nothing

Okay then just say something!

Still nothing.

Come on, you dimwit. She looks amazing. You look like a drowned rat. Why do you always look like a charity case? Are you going to answer her or what?

"Uh, hey," he replied rather awkwardly.

"You were great today," she said. "Your solo is amazing. I just know you're gonna win the regionals for us."

They're all counting on you, said the Demon.

"Uh… Thanks," he replied. "You were great too. I mean, everyone's sounding really good."

Melissa smiled. For a brief moment, he completely forgot he was cold and wet. It was like he'd been transported to a tropical beach, with the gentle warmth of the sun and a light breeze blowing through his hair.

"We're having a party," she said with a glint in her eye, "right after the regionals. Do you fancy coming? It would mean a lot to me if you did."

Seb almost choked.

"Uh, yeah… Sounds great," he replied, desperately trying to

sound casual; like he got invited to parties all the time.

Melissa beamed. "Okay. Here's the address," she said, slipping a piece of paper into the chest pocket of his shirt. "Eight o'clock." And with that she blew him a kiss, turned with a swish of hair and walked off in the direction of the car park.

Seb stood rooted to the spot.

Did that just happen?

***

When he arrived home, Seb found his mum in the kitchen reading an email on her phone.

"'I'm sure you're very proud that your son/daughter is representing the college in the forthcoming British Orchestral Championships,'" she read aloud, using the voice she normally reserved for major announcements.

"Well, actually we didn't know. Did we, Seb?" she said, before reading on. "'We are looking forward to seeing you on Saturday evening for the regional heat, which is being held at Rippendale Cathedral. The event will kick off at 5 p.m., but please ensure you arrive between 3.30 p.m. and 4 p.m. It will all be wrapped up by 7.30 p.m. If you require any further information, please don't hesitate to ask. Kind regards, Sophie Burrell.'"

She turned to Seb. "When were you planning to let us know?"

Seb shrugged. His mum stood, hand on one hip, holding her phone aloft, as though it were evidence of a crime. After a few seconds of silence, Seb realised that she wasn't going to accept his shrug as an answer.

"I don't know," he replied sheepishly. "I guess I didn't think it was that important."

A look of exasperation crossed her face.

"I mean, it's just the regional heats," he said.

His mum looked across to his dad. "Doug?" she said in an

unusually shrill voice. "Are you going to chip in here?"

Seb thought he could detect his dad's eyes rolling, but he didn't argue.

"Of course it's important," his dad said softly. "It doesn't matter whether it's the regional heats or Wembley Stadium. Of course we want to know." He smiled and in doing so, took all the tension out of the conversation. "So… How's it going? Is it sounding good?"

His mum huffed, but Seb ignored it.

"Yeah… good. We're sounding pretty tight," Seb replied.

"Excellent. What piece are you playing?" asked his dad as he picked up his mug of tea.

Seb paused for a moment. "'A Hard Teacher… from *The Last Samurai*," he replied. Seb knew that his dad would understand the significance. He'd watched the film dozens of times and knew the soundtrack inside out. He also knew that there was a flute solo. His dad gave him a knowing look.

"Are you happy with your bit?" he asked. Seb nodded. Perhaps his mum realised her husband was not going to support her interrogation. She gave another huff and went back to checking messages on her phone.

***

Saturday arrived before he was ready for it. At 2.30 p.m., he wandered downstairs to see his parents standing in the hallway waiting for him. His mum wore her Sunday best outfit; a salmon pink jacket and skirt suit with her highest heeled shoes. Seb had a feeling that she'd nagged his dad to dress up for the occasion too. As well as the dark grey suit and tie that was normally reserved for weddings, funerals and job interviews, he also wore that reluctant look that Seb knew so well.

Nobody said very much on the journey into the city. The sound of the rain, the rhythmic squeak of the windscreen wipers and mumblings from the radio did a great job of filling the long periods of silence. They pulled into the market square of Rippendale, with its quaint old buildings and cobbled streets. It bustled with late-afternoon Christmas shoppers. Lights twinkled in doorways. Pockets of carol singers and musicians were dotted around the square, and the sweet scent of mince pies drifted enticingly on the breeze.

They joined the steady procession of umbrellas for the short walk down the hill. As they reached the magnificent entrance of the Cathedral, Seb's parents wished him good luck and left to find their seats. Just as they turned to go, Seb caught hold of his dad's sleeve.

"Uh... I've been invited to a party tonight in West Ferrenby, right after this. Could you drop me off?" Seb asked. He thought he noticed a split-second look of surprise flash across his dad's face as he asked the question. Seb hadn't been invited to many parties. The last ones he could remember were birthday parties at primary school. His dad smiled.

"West Ferrenby... Wow. That is an upmarket spot. Is that where your friend lives?"

Seb half shrugged, half nodded, which seemed to appease his dad.

"Sure, no problem," he replied and wandered off to join his wife.

Phew, Seb thought. *That's one less hurdle to cross.*

He found Sophie, Colonel Walmsley and the rest of the orchestra just inside the entrance to the cathedral. There was a real buzz of nervous excitement. Sophie, in particular, seemed to be talking much faster and louder than normal, and Gemma must have said, "G'd luck" to everyone at least a dozen times.

Colonel Walmsley bellowed, "Right, quieten down you lot." He conducted a quick headcount. "I think we've got everyone now," he said, his moustache bristling. "In a moment, we'll make our way into the auditorium. We have a designated area on the right-hand side, next to Harrington College. We will be performing last. The first college are up in just over forty minutes, so you have time to prepare your instruments… and get yourselves focused!" He placed particular emphasis on those last three words.

They filed into the vast nave of the cathedral. Huge stone pillars rose on each side, supporting the enormous wooden beamed ceiling above. Festive tinsel and sprigs of holly decorated the ends of the wooden pews. At the opposite end of the cathedral stood the impressive, stained-glass window, glistening red, blue, green and yellow. In front of it, between the choir benches, was a low raised stage. Seb took a second to drink it all in. There was no doubt, this was an awe-inspiring place. But he couldn't help feeling daunted by it all. He took his seat on the pews with the others, wondering whether their music could do justice to such a majestic building.

But that wasn't the only challenge Seb hadn't anticipated. The problem with going last, he discovered, is that you have to listen to the other orchestras performing. And they were all *really* good! With each passing performance, his confidence eroded. And he obviously wasn't alone.

"OMG… they were like, soooo sick," Gemma exclaimed as Rippendale College completed their piece. As Harrington finished, he was sure he heard Sophie say that they were the best yet. Seb realised that, until now, they had only heard themselves in rehearsal. They had nothing to compare themselves to. Now, everyone was starting to realise the standard of the competition they were up against… and the doubts were starting to creep in.

"You okay?" Gemma asked quietly. "You look like you're gonna hurl."

If he opened his mouth to answer, Gemma may just find out. He took a breath to steady himself.

"I'm okay… little nervous," he replied. "Aren't you?"

"Nah, why should I be?" she asked.

"Are your folks not here?" he asked, a little taken aback.

"Yeah, sure… over there," replied Gemma, pointing them out. Seb had never met Gemma's mum, but he recognised her immediately, with her long auburn hair and wide smile. Her dad placed a loving arm around his wife's shoulder, and she nestled her head into his chest.

"They are soooo embarrassing," she said with a chuckle. "But I'm dead chuffed my dad made it. He's in London a lot this time of year," she explained.

"Work?" asked Seb.

"Yeah, he's a director. West End musicals, mostly."

"Wow!" he said, a little too loudly. "Is he a musician?"

"Yeah. Not as good as Mum, though. She played pro, toured the world. She played with Sophie a few years ago."

"What?" Seb blurted out. "Sophie was a professional musician?"

"Yeah, BBC Symphony, or summat like that," she replied.

What must she have thought of his audition? What about all those times he'd messed up in rehearsals? A professional musician, with a trained ear, would hear all those mistakes… notice all the errors.

"But what if you screw up?" Seb said. "I mean… the expectation."

Gemma shook her head and smiled. "Nah… they're cool. Just enjoy it, that's what they've always said."

As Skipbridge College finished Schubert's *Symphony Number Five* and the applause died down, the master of ceremonies picked up the microphone to announce the final orchestra.

"And last but not least, to conclude this wonderful northern regional heat, please welcome Yeoborough College."

Polite applause rippled around the magnificent cathedral as they made their way onto the stage.

All of a sudden, reality hit him. This was it. His stomach churned. Melissa's words echoed through his mind: "I just know you're gonna win the regionals for us." She was counting on him. Everyone was counting on him. What if he messed up? What if he let everyone down? All those hours of practice would be for nothing. His mum and dad were here. If he messed this up, it would confirm what his mum had always believed – that he was a failure.

He could feel the anxiety building as he walked towards the stage. His mouth was dry... just like the recital... just like his first audition.

Here we go again, said the Demon.

Once everyone was seated on the stage, Colonel Walmsley quietened them down.

"Now then, everyone," he began. "Before I hand you over to Sophie, I'd like you to remember a few things. Firstly, your job right now is *not* to win." He paused to let his words sink in. "It isn't to be better than anyone else or prove anything. All you have to do right now is focus on the music. Just play this piece as well as you can. That's all."

Seb saw looks of confusion spreading through the orchestra. Colonel Walmsley had clearly noticed it too.

"I mean it," he said. "Just focus on the music. Enjoy it. Play the way you've been playing in rehearsals. That's all I ask."

He looked across to Seb and nodded very deliberately as if to say, "That's you I'm talking to, Hall."

Seb thought about it for a moment. Colonel Walmsley was right. Just focus on the music. That's what he'd done in his second audition, after his terrible first attempt. It's what Mark had taught him with the blue pen and the bookcase.

No mind... That's it. Just listen to the music, he thought.

With a hearty, "Good luck," Colonel Walmsley handed over to Sophie and left the stage to take his seat.

"Ladies and gentlemen," she announced. "This afternoon we will be playing a piece called 'A Hard Teacher', by Hans Zimmer. It is from the movie *The Last Samurai*. We hope you enjoy it." She turned back to the orchestra, closed her eyes and lifted her conductor's baton.

As she flicked the baton, Seb heard a smooth, clear note rise from the strings section. He relaxed and began to absorb the beautiful sombre sounds. Note after perfect note, woven together, telling their tale. Each one seemed to pull him into a trace. He saw the fields of Japan and the Samurai warriors. He was walking amongst the tall grasses. He could smell the scent of the autumn breeze. But he wasn't watching the movie. He was in the movie. He was Captain Nathan Algren facing his opponent.

Seb took a breath and raised his flute to his lips. He heard the first soft note take flight and fill the vast cathedral. Then the next... and the next... Like butterflies, one after another, they danced away. He felt the notes flowing through him, rising into the air and blending perfectly with those of the violins. Seb wasn't playing the music. He was the music.

The last note tailed gently away into silence... And the audience erupted into applause.

His eyes snapped open. He'd completely forgotten where he was. In a flash, he was back in the cathedral. The audience were on their feet. He looked around at the rest of the orchestra. Everyone looked stunned. Sophie had tears streaming down her face. With smudged mascara and an enormous smile, she turned to the audience and bowed.

As they filed off the stage, Seb was bombarded with congratulations. He got so many pats on the back, he thought he'd end up black and blue. But why was everyone so overwhelmed? This was just how he played in his bedroom at home. It wasn't anything special. He'd just been doing what Colonel Walmsley said – play like you do when you're rehearsing.

Once the commotion had died down, the master of ceremonies took to the stage, microphone in hand.

"The results are in," he said. "I'll not keep you very long, but I do want to congratulate everyone for the exceptionally high standard this year. The judges agreed that this is the best northern regional heat that anyone can remember, and some of them have been judging a very long time." There was a ripple of laughter from the audience, which seemed to please the master of ceremonies immensely.

"So, without further ado," he said. "In third place... Rippendale College."

The audience broke into well-deserved applause for Rippendale.

"And in second place," he announced, with a short dramatic pause, "Harrington College."

More applause for Harrington. Their conductor stood up and clapped his orchestra enthusiastically, but Seb couldn't help noticing that they all looked pretty dejected.

"And, in first place, representing the North of England in the British Colleges Orchestral Championships at The Royal Albert Hall..." He paused again for dramatic effect. Seb could feel nervous tension all around him. Gemma grabbed his hand and squeezed it so tightly he thought she would cut off the blood supply to his fingers.

The master of ceremonies cleared his throat. "Yeoborough College!"

"Shhuuuuutttt uuuuuppppp," Gemma cried, clasping her hands to her mouth.

Shouts and squeals of delight broke out all around him. The whole orchestra jumped up and down and threw their arms around each other. There were more pats on the back and someone ruffled his hair. Gemma grabbed him and hugged him tight.

"O-M-G… We did it, we did it!" she screamed.

Over the din, Colonel Walmsley tried in vain to restore order. The next few moments seemed to pass by in a blur. Sophie walked up onto the stage to collect the very small trophy and say a few words of thanks. There was more applause and squeals of joy.

After a few frantic moments, the celebrations died down and the audience began to disperse. Seb picked up his things and made his way back towards the entrance to meet his parents. He found his mum in the middle of a crowd of people.

"Oh, yes, Seb is our son," he heard her say. "He's always been a very talented musician. He'll probably take a music scholarship to Durham or Oxford, you know, or maybe the Royal Academy."

In fact, she was so busy addressing her assembled crowd, she didn't notice Seb at all. His dad spotted him straight away.

"That was fantastic," he said warmly. "How are you feeling?"

Seb thought about it for a moment. "Relieved," he replied.

A flicker of concern crossed his dad's face before the smile returned.

"Well, I thought you were brilliant," he said, "and so did your mum."

Seb nodded, not really knowing what his mum thought was brilliant; the performance or that she seemed to have become a minor celebrity. Seb suspected his dad may have been reading his mind.

"Here," he said, giving Seb the car keys. "You put your things in the car, and I'll get your mum. We don't want you to be late for your party."

The drive out to the village of West Ferrenby was just plain weird. His mum couldn't stop talking about how wonderful the whole event was, and what everyone had said.

"Oh, and the conductor from Skipbridge was so complimentary, and the director of music from Rippendale was simply gushing."

Interestingly, at no point did she tell him what she thought.

His dad kept interjecting with "You did a great job" and "As long as you enjoyed it". But, to be honest, Seb was starting to tune out. His thoughts had turned to the party... and to Melissa.

***

As they entered West Ferrenby, Seb demanded that his parents drop him next to the post office, at the far end of the village. The night was clear and cold. The rain had stopped and frost was forming on car windscreens. The tiny village had dressed up for Christmas. Magnificent trees stood in the windows of the enormous houses. Twinkling lights were draped around doorways and cascaded down walls. To his left, the village church was beautifully illuminated against the pitch black of the night.

At the end of the village stood a pair of huge wrought-iron gates, flanked by enormous stone pillars at the top of which sat two wild boars. The engraved sign on the pillars read "The Manor House". He re-read the address Melissa had given him. This was the place. Was this her house? He'd never thought to ask.

He approached the huge gates. On the left-hand pillar was a keypad and button marked "Request Entry". He hit the button. It replied with an indignant buzz. He waited. Nothing. Then a creak. Slowly the gates swung open and he stepped onto the long drive. The gravel crackled beneath his feet. Enormous lawns stretched out on either side of him, illuminated by the moonlight. A peacock strutted away at the sight of him. At the top of the driveway stood a large stone fountain and behind it the beautiful but rather imposing Manor House.

The huge wooden front door stood ajar, emitting a shaft of light across the stone steps. Seb approached the door nervously. He could hear music from the party. Cautiously he pushed open the door and stepped into the enormous hallway. It looked like a medieval castle. Swords and shields hung from the walls. An enormous stag's head stared down from its mounting. In front of him a magnificent staircase led up to a landing, which was packed with people, all drinking and laughing.

He reached the top of the staircase and scanned the landing for Melissa, Sophie and the rest of the orchestra. But he couldn't see them. The room seemed to be filled with the cool kids from the college – the rugby team and their girlfriends, dressed top to toe in designer clothes. Maybe he'd misheard Melissa's instructions. Maybe he'd got the wrong place... or the wrong time. As he turned to leave, Seb heard the one voice he did not want to hear.

"Ah, Hall. So pleased you could make it." Malone appeared over his shoulder. "Mel passed on my instructions, I see. Good."

What? Seb thought.

Now he thought about it, she hadn't said anything about an orchestra party. She had just said, "We're having a party" and that it was after the regional heat. Seb's confusion seemed to please Malone immensely. A smug grin crept across his face.

"You've proved yourself to be surprisingly useful," Malone said. "Jonny there—" he nodded towards Jonny Martyn, "—didn't want me to give you an assignment. Maybe he didn't think you were up to it. I think he was afraid you might usurp him." Malone's grin was widening. "Anyway, why don't you get yourself a drink?" Then he clapped Seb on the shoulder and returned to mingling.

How could he have been so stupid? Melissa would never invite him to a party. What was he thinking? He'd walked straight into Malone's web.

Idiot! he cursed.

This was all a huge mistake. He turned to leave... and came face to face with Melissa.

"Hey, Seb," she said seductively. She looked even more gorgeous than normal. Her hair shimmered in the light as she moved, and her short black dress hugged her figure. Seb was torn. Half of him demanded to know why she'd invited him. The other half was desperately trying to think of something cool to say. Fortunately for Seb, Melissa spoke first.

"You were brilliant this afternoon," she said, edging closer to him. "I knew that you'd win it for us," she whispered.

His heart pounded in his chest. He could smell her sweet perfume and feel her breath on his cheek as she spoke.

"Uh, it wasn't just me," he replied, rather awkwardly.

Melissa smiled. "You're too modest," she said. "It's one of the things I love about you."

She bent her head in closer, so that her hair brushed the side of his face. Each strand sent a burst of electricity through him. It was as if she was casting some kind of enchantment over him.

Snap out of it! he told himself. *Find out if Malone sent her to invite you.*

Just as he was about to ask, Malone appeared through the crowd. But before he could brace himself, Malone shoved him into the wall.

"You little shit!" he spat. "I invite you to my party and this is how you repay me... flirting with my girlfriend."

Seb saw pure hatred in Malone's grey eyes.

"I d-didn't... know," he stammered feebly.

Malone replied with a hollow laugh. "Be warned, Hall. You might be useful, but you're not indispensable. Cross me and you will pay... Got it?"

And with that, Malone shoved him backwards. Seb stumbled down the top couple of stairs and caught the banister to break his fall.

Malone turned to Melissa. "What the hell do you think you're doing? You're *my* girlfriend, remember?" he barked. "Forgotten who gave you this, have you?" he said, swishing the necklace that hung from her neck.

Melissa's eyes flicked to Seb for a split second, then she turned and walked away.

Anger welled up inside him. He marched down the stairs and out into the night. His rage burned so fiercely he couldn't feel the cold air.

How could you have been so stupid? She would never fancy you. She's gorgeous. You're an idiot. Why would she ever like you? said the Demon.

Who are you compared to Malone? Mr Popular, in his posh car, with his huge house, bulging muscles and fancy clothes? You're no one, that's who. Who would ever want you?

On and on he walked into the night. Across fields, along country lanes, through the parkland at the edge of the town and up the steep hill towards his village. With every stride, his anger grew... anger towards himself, for his own stupidity, for daring to dream. He was so caught up in the whirlwind that he didn't notice he'd reached Cokendale.

Through the clear night sky, Seb heard the faint sound of laughter in the distance. It was a mirthless laugh. He knew that laugh. It was laced with evil. With panic rising, he scanned the skies. More laughter... this time closer. Where was it? The sky was pitch back. No moon. Even the stars seemed to have retreated. The laughter grew louder again. There was a swoosh above him and the wind rushed through his hair. He was out in the open. He had no protection.

If the Demon struck now, he was dead.

How to Silence Your Demons

Seb feels under pressure to perform his solo at the regional heat. When have you felt under pressure?
How did you deal with it?
Is there anything you can learn from Seb's experience that might help you next time?

When have you felt under pressure?

How did you deal with it?

Is there anything you can learn from Seb's experience that might help you next time?

Colonel Walmsley gives the orchestra some advice. He told them their job was not to win, or to prove themselves, and just play the way they did in practice.
How do you think it helped Seb and the orchestra?
How could it help you?

How do you think it helped Seb and the orchestra?

How could it help you?

Chapter Ten

THE RECKONING

You are pathetic, the Demon hissed as it swooped overhead. *Thinking she'd like you.*

More laughter. Seb could just about see its outline as it raced past. Standing in this narrow country lane, he was a sitting duck. Panic and terror now dwarfed his anger.

He set off, running through the darkness, with the blur of the hedgerows on either side.

Think you can outrun me? taunted the Demon. *You cannot escape me.*

Through the gloom he saw a gap in the hedge to his left. He sprinted through it, into an open field. A few yards away stood an abandoned old barn. He made a dash for it. The cold air tore at his lungs as he raced across the field. He dived through the entrance and into the shadows. Maybe he'd be safe in here.

There was an enormous crash as the Demon landed on what little remained of the roof. A shower of smashed wood and tiles rained down on him as he cowered on the floor.

There you are! it cried.

Another roar of laughter. It was right above him, peering down through the dust. There was no escape.

How shall I eat him? it said. *Flame grilled? Medium rare? Bloody and juicy maybe?*

Seb's whole body ached. He was covered in cuts and bruises from the falling rubble. However, the pain was eclipsed by his emotion. Anger, sadness and guilt occupied the space where fear had been.

He lay there in the dust, without a hope in the world. He had no chance with Melissa. He was trapped in Malone's web with no idea how to escape. And the Demon had him cornered!

Darkness closed in around him.

Then a thought hit him. A faint glimmer of light in the gloom.

He was tired of cowering. He had been cowering and apologising his entire life… trying to become invisible, hiding in the shadows so that no one would notice him. He was tired of never feeling good enough, tired of feeling like a disappointment, tired of being a failure.

He'd had enough!

If he was going to die now, he was NOT going to die cowering.

From beneath the debris, Seb gathered his strength and pulled himself to his feet. One painful step at a time, he walked out of the derelict building, into the night. The Demon climbed down from the remnants of the roof and faced him… teeth bared… wings flexed… ready to strike.

"Go on then," shouted Seb. "Kill me."

The Demon fixed its fiery eyes upon him.

"What are you waiting for?" he demanded. "I'm unarmed… defenceless… just finish me off."

The Demon took a deep breath. Seb screwed up his eyes and braced himself. In a split second there would be a flash of white-hot flames and it would all be over.

Aahh hahha hahha, roared the Demon. *I'll kill you when I am ready. For now, I'll just enjoy playing with my food. Maybe I'll kill you next time.*

And with a rush of wind, it took to the air.

Seb slumped to the ground. He lay on his back, staring into the darkness. One by one the stars reappeared in the night sky, and he felt the cold air biting his skin. But still, he didn't move. Honestly, he didn't know how long he lay there, it could have been seconds or hours.

You can't stay here forever, he thought.

He rolled onto his side and slowly got to his feet. His life was in tatters but right now there was nothing he could do. With a sigh he trudged back across the field and headed for home.

***

Seb woke late the next morning. Sunlight was already streaming through his bedroom window. Somehow, sleep had given him clarity. The jumbled mass of thoughts seemed to have untangled themselves. He took out his journal. As he reached into his bag to grab a pen, his fingers found the scrap of paper with the words "Find the Demon Charmers".

He stared at it for a moment, then dropped it back in his bag and found his pen.

Dear Jerno,

I've realised that ignoring this isn't going to help. This demon won't just go away. It's getting stronger and, unless I stop it… I'm pretty sure it'll destroy me.

I think I may have taken a step in the right direction.

I made a decision last night. I chose to stand up… not cower in fear. I know that one choice alone won't change anything, but it's a start.

I'm thinking…

What if I keep making these choices… to stand up?

What if I stood up more in the rest of my life too?

What if I stood up to Malone?

Until now, all I've had is questions.

This feels like it might be an answer – maybe the first step along the path.

That's all for now. I'll check in again soon.

His text alert chimed. It was Alice.

> Hey. I heard about the regional heat. Well done. Gemma said you were amazing. Thought you might have let me know yourself though…

He'd almost forgotten about the heat. It was only yesterday afternoon, yet it seemed like months ago. He read the message again. "Thought you might have let me know yourself though." Alice was right. He'd been so caught up in the performance, the thought of seeing Melissa, his unexpected meeting with Malone and encountering the Demon on the way home. He was so embroiled in himself and his own issues, he'd completely forgotten to let her know. Hurriedly, he tapped a reply.

> Hey. I'm so sorry. I got a bit distracted. Ran into Malone again. Then ran into the Demon on my way home.

He lay back and rested his head on his pillow, waiting to see whether she would respond.

Ping.

> You okay? X

He tapped a reply.

A bit battered and bruised but I'm okay. Are you at college tomorrow? I don't have any lectures, but could meet in town? I would love a chat. ☺

Almost immediately, his phone pinged again.

☺ Coffee shop at midday. Xx

And with a smile he lay his head back onto his pillow and drifted off to sleep.

***

Seb stepped off the bus next to the war memorial in the centre of town, just across the road from the coffee shop. The flurry of snow and the small band of carol singers reminded him that Christmas was only a few days away. He'd always loved Christmas, but this year he felt an added sense of appreciation. It felt like an escape. A few weeks when he didn't have to worry about Malone and his "assignments" or seeing Melissa and the constant reminder that she was Malone's girlfriend, not his. Instead, he could hide away from it all. He could slouch on the sofa, using his philosophy homework as an excuse to binge watch movies with his dad.

The bell above the door gave a little tinkle as Seb entered the coffee shop. He spotted a table for two next to the window and pulled up a chair. Outside the snowflakes danced in the wind. He gazed at them, entranced by their hypnotic powers. He was so deeply engrossed that he didn't notice Alice creep up behind him. She blew gently in his ear and he fell backwards off his chair with a crash.

"Oh, I'm sorry," Alice said, chuckling.

Despite feeling bruises on top of his bruises, he couldn't help laughing too. The handful of people in the coffee shop stared disapprovingly as he picked up his chair. But, strangely, he didn't care.

"I feel terrible," she said with a smile, "so I'm buying. Fancy a mince pie too?"

As they drank their coffee and ate their mince pies, he told her all about the regional heat, meeting Malone, encountering the Demon and his latest journal entry. For some reason, though, he left out the bit about Melissa. Alice just sat and listened until Seb had finished.

"I suppose it's right, isn't it?" she said, folding her napkin.

"What's right?" asked Seb, through a mouth full of mince pie.

"The bit about things getting worse if you don't deal with them," she replied. "I mean, it's not just true for demons, is it? It's true in life. Things don't fix themselves or sort themselves out. It's like… I don't know… with people's health. If you ignore things, they just get worse. It's the same if relationships go wrong. They never fix themselves. And if we just leave them, they don't stay the same either. They always get worse."

For a few minutes, they both sat, immersed in their own thoughts until Seb broke the silence.

"I guess I've been avoiding it," he said, wiping crumbs from his mouth, "hoping someone else will give me the answer… hoping that it will go away… enjoying those demon-free moments. I haven't really been dealing with it at all."

Alice looked up at him. "Don't beat yourself up. Most people would do that, don't you think?" she replied.

Seb shrugged. "It's scary. I know I need to do something… I just don't know what," he sighed.

Alice placed her hand gently on his arm but said nothing.

"I guess that's why I've been avoiding it," he went on. "The problem is… the longer I leave it, the scarier it gets."

"Maybe you don't need to know how," she said. "If you know

the first step, you can get started. And, remember, you're not on your own."

Seb smiled. "Thanks. I know. But this is my demon. Only I can do this." He swallowed the last of his mince pie.

"I've got to get on top of my nerves too," he said. "I almost threw up in the cathedral before we played, and yet Gemma was… well, she wasn't bothered by it at all."

Alice gave him a quizzical look.

"I mean, her parents were there," he said. "Her dad's a theatre director, her mum was a professional musician, but she wasn't stressed about letting them down. Why not? I don't get it."

"Nah, they're pretty cool. They don't need her to be their success. They achieve their own success," she replied matter-of-factly.

Seb stared into his coffee cup.

"Sandy would have made her proud," he muttered under his breath.

"Sandy?" replied Alice. "Who's Sandy?"

Seb looked up. He didn't think he'd said that out loud. For a split second he considered saying, "Ah, no one", but he thought better of it. What would that achieve? Maybe it was time he faced up to it after all these years.

"My older brother," he said quietly.

"I didn't know you had a brother," replied Alice.

"He died when I was five," Seb began, his voice distant. "I don't remember much, to be honest. Just images, snippets I've heard from other people. Mum and Dad don't like talking about it. I know we were on holiday, at a campsite in Devon. We were swimming in the pool with a load of other kids. No one really saw what happened. The parents were chatting, reading, sunbathing. We were all playing in the pool. I just remember the screams and the panic… the chaos. And then they pulled him out of the pool. I remember his face… grey… his eyes just staring… Then someone tried to resuscitate him. The rest is just a blur really."

Tears welled up in Alice's eyes. "Oh, Seb," she said as she fought back her sobs. "I'm so sorry."

"Sandy was the smart one," Seb said, "the popular one, the sporty one. He would have been someone, you know. He would have made mum proud. I'll never live up to that." He sighed.

A tear leaked out of the corner of Alice's eye and rolled down her cheek. "She might not think that," Alice said.

Seb's expression was stone. "I'm pretty sure she does," he replied.

"It's not your job, Seb. You don't have to live up to his memory," Alice said. "You don't have to be him. Just be you… that's enough. You are enough. If your mum isn't proud of you for who you are, that's her fault, not yours."

Seb nodded. It all sounded right, but he wasn't feeling it. Alice just looked at him, like he was a wounded animal. For a moment they sat, not really sure what to say. Finally, Seb reached into his bag.

"I found this too," he said, handing her the scrap of paper.

"Who are the Demon Charmers?" she asked.

"Dunno," he replied. "Not sure who wrote it or how it got into my bag either."

"Mmmmm. You never know… It might be helpful."

Alice's alarm chimed on her phone.

"Have you got a lecture?" Seb asked.

"Yeah," she said. "But I can miss it."

"No. Thank you. I'll be okay. I've lived with this for almost thirteen years. I'll see you after Christmas. It's only a couple of weeks and we'll be texting all the time anyway. I'll let you know what I find out from the Demon Charmers."

Alice stood up, leaned over the table and gave him a hug.

"Merry Christmas," she said as she picked up her bag to leave.

"Merry Christmas," he replied, "and thanks for being a great friend."

He sat for a few seconds, alone with his thoughts. He felt like a weight had been lifted. He'd always imagined that talking about it would dredge it back up, and that he'd have to re-live the pain all over again. But somehow talking to Alice was soothing. He no longer felt like he was carrying the burden alone.

His thoughts turned to the Demon. He had to do something, but he had absolutely no idea what. There must be an answer, he just needed to find it. What did Alice say? Something about not needing the whole answer... just the first step. Maybe that was it. If he took the first step, perhaps he could find the next, then just keep going.

He strode through door and out into the snow.

One step at a time.

***

Christmas Day came and went. As always, there was more food than they could eat, presents that no one really needed and more time doing nothing than he could remember. This year, it was all that little bit sweeter. For some reason, his mum seemed happier and less irritated by everything. In past years she would say things like "I just wish we could afford a little more" or "Have you seen the Jones' Christmas tree? Isn't it splendid? Shame we can't have one like that." However, this year, for whatever reason, she didn't feel the need. His dad seemed to be enjoying a few work-free days too. He'd been doing long hours in the build-up to Christmas. Seb guessed they needed the money.

As Christmas faded and New Year emerged over the horizon, Seb whiled away the days watching movie after movie with his notebook in hand. Every now and again he would write down a quote or a thought. Although his dad didn't watch all of them, it was great just having time together, vegging out on the sofa with popcorn and crisps. Occasionally, his mum would join them for a while before declaring that it was "not really her thing" and making her excuses. A combination of rest and an escape from the madness of life seemed to recharge Seb.

He awoke on New Year's Day with his mind firmly fixed on tackling his Demon. It wasn't a New Year's resolution. He just felt ready now… re-energised. It was early and the sun was creeping above the horizon. He wandered downstairs to make himself some breakfast and sat down at the kitchen table.

Find the Demon Charmers, he thought.

He pulled out his phone, typed "Demon Charmers" into the search bar and hit the link.

The Most Secret Society of Demon Charmers.

Beneath the title was a message:

Welcome!
    It's good to see you.
    By now you'll have probably realised that demons don't just go away. It would be nice if they did, but unfortunately that's not how it works. No doubt, you'll have also realised that if you ignore them, they get stronger.
    So, it's time to do something about it.
    Ready?
    Good!
    Then you'll need this…

Beneath this was an image of a book. The title on the cover read:

How to Charm Your Demon; The simple (but not easy) four-step guide, with helpful top tips

Seb scrolled down and clicked the cover of the book.

Simple and easy are rarely the same thing. This is not complicated. However, it's definitely <u>not</u> easy.

We know. We've been there too!

We know that you'll need every ounce of courage you can muster. We know there's a lot you'll need to learn. We know that you'll read this four-step guide and think, "But how the hell am I supposed to do that?"

Remember: we've been there too!

We know it's not easy. But we do know it works!

So, here is the four-step guide:

Step One

Go and face your demon.

Get to know it.

Gain its trust.

We know what you're thinking. "But this thing wants to kill me!" Yes, we know. No one said this was easy. We know it's your greatest fear. You already know you can't outrun your fear. The simple truth is you are going to have to confront your biggest fears and there's no way around it.

Courage is not the absence of fear… it's the ability to step towards it.

Courage has the power to turn even your greatest fear into a friend.

Step Two

Discover its pain.

They all have pain! If they didn't, they would be lovely and cuddly. It's the pain that turns them into a vicious fire-breathing menace.

Their pain usually emanates from self-doubt, lack of self-worth, insecurity, fear, anger, guilt, self-judgement, etc.

If it's fear, you need to find out what they're scared of.

If it's guilt, what do they feel guilty about?

Step Three

Solve the problem.

Work with it. Work together. Help each other.

Yes, that does mean working <u>with</u> your demon, hence why steps one and two are so important. The answers you need are all around you. They are in the books that you read, the movies you watch, the music you listen to and the conversations you have. You'd be surprised just how many people have encountered demons of their own!

Step Four

Keep going!

This is a journey… a process. You won't solve this overnight or in one go. This takes time. Stay patient. Don't expect perfection. It might get tougher before it gets easier. There are no right and wrong answers.

Oh… and keep looking for the lighter shade of darkness!

Top Tips

If in doubt, remember this:

Your demon is like a mirror. It's a reflection of you. And it amplifies you!

If you're calm, it'll be calm. If you're scared, it will be scared… and probably lash out. If you're angry, it'll be angry. If you feel hate, it will hate you (and that will make things <u>really</u> tough!).

It also amplifies you. Anger in you equals BIG anger in your demon.

Okay, that's it. I reckon you're good to go!

Remember: we're here if you need us. Don't be a stranger ☺

PS: Oh… and find Søren. He's often found in his favourite café, on the corner of Vestergade, opposite St. Albani Church in Odense. He can help you.

All the best in your quest.

The Demon Charmers

He'd never remember all this. He swiped his hand across the screen to save the image and a split second later, the book closed.

Seb sat with his mouth open and breakfast dribbling down his chin.

Well, they were right about one thing. He was definitely thinking, *But how the hell am I supposed to do that?*

He wiped the milk and cornflakes from his chin and sunk back in his chair.

Step One, go and face your demon.

Whenever he'd been close to it, that fire-breathing killing machine had tried to incinerate him. Why would he walk back into certain death? How was he supposed to "'get to know it"? Come to think of it, why would he want to get to know it? It hadn't taken Seb long to discover that this particular demon didn't like him very much. As for gaining its trust… he had absolutely no idea where to start.

His little burst of New Year enthusiasm fizzled and died. All those feelings of determination turned to dejection. He got up from the kitchen table, opened the back door and wandered out into the back yard. The fresh snow creaked beneath his feet. It was one of his favourite sounds and yet he barely noticed it. His mind was falling into a tailspin. Why had he put his hopes in these Demon Charmers?

This wasn't a solution... more like a suicide manual.

He picked up his phone and read aloud:

"'Step One. Face your Demon.' What a wonderful idea. I'll just walk in there and strike up a conversation," he said.

He sat on the low wall. It was cold! If he wasn't so angry, he'd have stood up straight away... but anger seemed to have awoken his stubbornness. He read down further, looking for the next ridiculous suggestion.

"It's like a mirror," he scoffed. "What does that even mean?"

Then he stopped and thought, *It reflects and amplifies your anger.*

Maybe there was something to that. The Demon had always been at its most terrifying and powerful when Seb was angry or scared or guilty; when he realised he was a criminal... and as he cursed himself walking home from Malone's party. Bizarrely, it did seem to make sense when he stopped to think about it.

He stared out beyond the farmyard. Normally, sitting here looking out over the paddock and across fields covered by their wintery blanket would fill him with awe. But today it looked distant, like he wasn't really here... like he was viewing it all through a window.

"So to calm the Demon, I have to calm myself," Seb muttered.

Saying it aloud seemed to give it solidity. He realised what he was saying as he heard his own words and understanding began to settle, like the snowflakes landing in his hair. He was closer than he had ever been, and yet still felt miles away. How was he supposed to calm himself in the face of the Demon?

Ping!

He didn't even need to check the name to know that the text was from Alice.

Happy New Year! I hope it's a great one! Text me back when you wake up. X

144

Halfway through typing his reply he abandoned it and hit video call. It rang for a couple of seconds before Alice picked up in a fluster, still in her dressing gown and pyjamas with her hair all over the place.

"Sseeebb," she whispered, pulling the top of her dressing gown closed. "I'm not dressed."

He didn't care. He needed to share this with her.

"Sorry," he said, "but I promised to tell you what I found out. I've been busy this morning. I searched for the Demon Charmers."

He told her everything he could remember about the four-step guide and his little moment of clarity. As he was coming to the end he said, "Now, I just need to figure out how to calm myself so I can calm it." He paused for breath and to allow her time to take it all in. She sat down on the edge of her bed, processing everything he'd just shared.

"Wow," she said at last. "You have been busy. I haven't even had breakfast."

"So, you need a way to calm yourself in order to calm the Demon," she said. "Hmmm… What does calm you down?"

To be honest, it wasn't the answer Seb was hoping for. He'd hoped that she might conjure some brilliant idea or hit him with a blinding flash of inspiration.

"I don't know," he replied, "that's the problem."

Alice looked thoughtful. "Have you asked your parents?" she said.

"My parents?" How they would be able to help? He certainly wasn't going to tell them he'd been having a few problems with a fire-breathing demon.

"I just mean they probably know you best. They must have calmed you down as a baby. I guess they'll probably know," she explained.

Of course. Now he thought about it, it was obvious. He'd

never thought to ask his parents, never considered that this was something they could help with.

"Alice, you're awesome," he cried. "I'm doing it right now. Happy New Year!"

He burst through the back door, bringing a blast of cold air and flurry of snowflakes with him.

"Eurgh," his mum cried, almost spilling her freshly made cup of tea.

"Sorry, Mum," he said. "Can I ask you a question?"

"Uh… Sure," she replied.

"When I was a baby," he said, "how did you calm me down?… You know, if I was crying or scared?" She looked a little puzzled. "It's for my psychology homework," Seb lied.

"Well, I used to rock you in my arms. I think it's what most mums do," she said awkwardly. "Does that help?"

Seb sighed. *Not really,* he thought.

For a split second, the comical image of an almost eighteen-year-old lad being rocked in his mother's arms while facing a monstrous demon flashed through his mind. He smiled.

"Uh… thanks, Mum," he replied.

"You should ask your dad," she offered. "He always seemed to have a way of…" She trailed off and gazed into her cup of tea.

"Thanks, Mum," Seb said softly. He put one arm around her shoulder awkwardly before heading off to look for his dad.

He found him upstairs in the bathroom, with the door ajar, in the middle of shaving.

"Hey, Dad," he said brightly.

"Happy New Year," replied his dad.

"Oh, yeah, Happy New Year… Uh, Dad? Can I ask you a question?"

His dad stopped shaving and wiped his face on a towel. "Of course," he replied. "How can I help?"

"When I was a baby, how did you calm me down? You know, if

I got all angry and upset? It's for psychology."

His dad smiled. "I just followed the advice of The Offspring," he said proudly.

Seb made no attempt to mask his confusion. "The Offspring? The rock band?" he said, trying not to laugh.

His dad beamed at him. "As they said, 'Music soothes even the savage beast'. Music, Seb. That's always worked for you."

"Dad, you're a genius!" Seb said. And with that, he tore off to his bedroom and began rummaging through the piles of sheet music on his desk.

"Music soothes even the savage beast... Whatever works for me, works for the Demon," he kept saying to himself. "Where is it?"

Finally, he saw it. A sheet of music with the opening bars to "Gift of A Thistle" from the *Braveheart* soundtrack. He loved it. He often found himself searching for different versions, by different orchestras and ensembles, just so that he could hear those first few exquisite notes. If there was any melody that could calm him, this was it.

"There... Yes!" he exclaimed triumphantly as he pulled it from the pile and held it in front of him. This was the answer.

All he had to do now was to walk into the Demon's lair and start playing.

How to Silence Your Demons

Alice says, "Things don't fix themselves or sort themselves out" and "If you ignore things, they just get worse".
When have you left something and found it got worse?
Are you avoiding something right now?

Alice also tells Seb that he doesn't need the whole answer. Maybe he just needs the first step so that he can get started.
Is there something that you're stuck on?
What's the first step?

The Demon Charmers said, "Courage is not the absence of fear... it's the ability to step towards it".
When have you been courageous?
Which fears have you confronted?

When you confronted your fears, what happened?
Did they become less scary after a while?

Chapter Eleven

THE MIRROR

That afternoon, Seb pulled on his jacket and boots, picked up his flute and headed toward the woods. It was a cold New Year's Day. It had stopped snowing, but there was a thick white blanket covering the ground. He decided not to tell his parents that he was going out, because that would have meant saying goodbye... and he couldn't bring himself to do it. Although he was trying desperately hard not to think about it, Seb knew that it could be his last goodbye. He looked back at his house and the knot in his stomach tightened.

Ever since he'd found that sheet of music, there had been a tug of war inside his head. Should he practise the tune... trying to perfect it before setting out to meet the Demon? Or, should he just go and do it? In a moment of brutal honesty, Seb realised it was simply procrastination. He could practise for weeks or months. It would never be perfect. And all the while, he would be making excuses to avoid the thing he feared the most.

But that wasn't courage.

So, in a moment of either suicidal insanity or bravery, he didn't know which, he'd decided to just do it. He climbed the gate at the bottom of the yard and crossed the paddock. His footsteps left tracks in the snow. For a moment he imagined the police following the tracks, after his distraught parents raised the alarm when he didn't return.

He turned the corner into the lane. The trees arched over his head ominously. He started up the slope and his feet slipped on the icy surface.

Turn back… the road is impassable. It's too dangerous. Why not try again another day? It doesn't have to be now.

But he knew it wasn't the icy slope his mind was trying to avoid.

Interesting, how his mind conjured up all these justifications to give up. How easy it would be to succumb to temptation. Normally, this was the point he would quit. He'd convince himself that turning around was fine… there's always tomorrow.

But what would that achieve?

He reached the top of the hill, followed the lane as it curved to the left and found the break in the hedge. For a moment he stared across the pristine white field. Beyond it lay the wood; peaceful… silent. Once upon a time that woodland had been his sanctuary but not anymore. Seb's heart pounded in his chest, as if trying to escape. He glanced behind him, back towards home. Maybe this could wait. Maybe he could have just one more night in his warm bed, taste his favourite meal one more time, have one more conversation with Alice. Her face flashed into his mind. There was so much he still wanted to do in his life, so many unfulfilled dreams. And there were the little things. Would he see another sunrise, or hear another dawn chorus?

A lump formed in his throat. He screwed up his eyes. He had to do this.

He fixed his gaze on the edge of the wood, where the path began.

Just do it, he told himself.

He stepped into the field. His foot sank into the snow before hitting solid ground.

Again.

A second step... followed by a third. One after another, each one taking him closer to the thing he feared more than anything. Eventually, he reached the far edge of the field and stepped into the wood. The light faded. The bare branches and leafy floor were covered in a light dusting of snow. Long shadows stretched out through the wood like death's fingers. This place used to feel like a second home... safe and comfortable. Today, all he felt was dread.

A sudden gust of wind blew through the trees, whipping the fallen leaves and snow into the air. It swirled around him like a tornado, leaves and snow obscuring his view, the rushing wind drowning out every other sound. Seb stood still in the middle of the maelstrom. There was nowhere he could run and nothing he could do. Then, as suddenly as it began, the wind subsided.

The mighty Demon's enormous horns glinted in the weak sunlight. Its nostrils flared, its wings flexed. Its eyes narrowed.

You walk in here, bold as brass, it hissed. *Perhaps you are as stupid as you look.*

Seb stood frozen to the spot.

It let out an ear-splitting roar.

You dare to face me!

The Demon advanced, like a tiger stalking its prey.

I taste your fear.

It reared up, ready to strike. A fiery glow emanated from its belly.

I warned you. It said. *Now I will kill you.*

Time slowed and a strange sensation washed over Seb. His own fear and the Demon's anger were rising in sync... somehow entwined. His own anger, fear and self-hatred were reflected in its fiery eyes. His terror was feeding it. He was stoking the Demon's fire.

The cold metal tube slipped between his fingers. His flute. He'd almost forgotten it was there. Slowly, he closed his eyes and raised it to his lips. A beautiful low note rose and glided into the woodland clearing. Then another and another. Gently, the notes wrapped themselves around him.

The Demon struck with a burst of fire. White hot flames engulfed Seb… but he felt nothing. He was shielded in some strange way by the music. On he played, immersing himself in every note. A look of astonishment flashed through the creature's eyes. It let out another roar. Seb felt the rage beginning to subside. It reared again and sent another burst of flames, less ferocious than the first. The Demon seemed confused. It looked to the sky and cried out.

What is this? Some kind of magic?

Seb lowered his flute.

"I suppose it is," he replied. "It's called courage."

For a moment they just stood, fixed upon each other. Seb saw a new look in the Demon's eyes… one he'd not seen before. Apprehensive? Maybe a little curious?

The Demon broke the silence. *Why are you here?*

Seb hadn't thought about what he was going to say when he got here. He'd been so worried about getting killed, he hadn't actually planned the conversation. He tried to think of something clever and then thought better of it. What was it Granddad Bill used to say? Honesty is always the best policy.

"I'm here to help," Seb replied.

The Demon bristled. For a moment Seb sensed the fear and anger building again, but he took a deep breath and continued.

"You're angry," Seb said softly.

Angry? the Demon said. *Yes, I am angry. Angry at you! You, who will always be a failure. You, who will always be a nobody. You, who make us weak and pathetic. You, who humiliate us!*

The words echoed through Seb's mind. *You make _us_ weak and pathetic. You humiliate _us_.* Us. He and the Demon were one. It was his reflection.

"I know you're scared," Seb said.

Scared? Me? bellowed the Demon. *You know nothing. I am fear!*

Fear? Of course.

What had Alice said?

Fear is imaginary.

That's it!

The Demon was fear. The Demon was imaginary – conjured by his own imagination. It was part of <u>his</u> reality, not <u>the</u> reality. This was his self-loathing, self-doubt, fear, guilt and anger amplified and reflected back.

He stared at the enormous beast silhouetted against the gloom. Slowly, its dark outline began to fade. Black became grey. Lighter and lighter, like a mist clearing, gradually dissolving into the background, until he could barely see it.

Then, it disappeared.

The Demon was gone.

How to Silence Your Demons

Seb realises that when things get really tough, his mind offers him justifications to quit... reasons why giving up is okay. What goes through your mind when you're facing a difficult challenge?

Seb realises that his demon is his own anger, fears and guilt reflected back at him. Bizarrely, he has created it.
How are your demons like Seb's?

Chapter Twelve

WITCHES, WIZARDS AND WISDOM

There was a definite bounce in Seb's step as he walked into his philosophy class. He greeted Professor Itsen with a cheery "Good morning" and took his seat. Seb was bizarrely keen to get back to college. Having gorged himself on movies during the festive season, he had pages of notes and a head bursting with ideas to share with Professor Itsen. And morning break would be his first opportunity to tell Alice that he'd conquered his demon.

"Okay, settle down everyone," said Professor Itsen. He was perched on the edge of his desk with his hands nestled in his cardigan pockets. "Welcome back and Happy New Year. Judging by the amount of paper on your desks, I'm assuming you've all been hard at work watching movies during the Christmas break." There was a ripple of murmurs around the room.

"Obviously, you've remembered to watch the films. It also looks like you've taken copious notes but..." he paused for a moment and surveyed the class. "What was the purpose? Why did I ask you all to watch movies? What's the question we're hoping to answer?"

Jeremy Brown's hand shot up into the air with such force, he almost knocked Seb off his chair.

"Yes, Mr Brown," Professor Itsen said.

"You asked us to identify philosophical themes," Jeremy replied breathlessly.

Professor Itsen nodded. "I did… But why? Why watch a bunch of movies to identify themes? Why would that be a valuable exercise? How could it help us?" he asked. This question sparked another round of chatter. "Any ideas?" Professor Itsen asked. Slowly hands began to rise into the air.

"Is it because you knew all our other lecturers would give us boring assignments and you want to be cool?" ventured Grace Perkins.

Professor Itsen laughed. "Well, obviously… But it's not just that. Anyone else? Yes, Andrew, what do you think?"

"Uh… Is it to help us remember the theories better? You know, by linking them to films?" Andrew replied.

"Nice idea, but not quite," replied the professor. "Have any of your other lecturers talked about going 'off-piste' and teaching beyond the curriculum?"

Seb remembered Mark talking about developing them as people, not just as students. He raised his hand slowly.

"Yes, Mr Hall."

"This is to help us *really* understand philosophy. Not just how it helps us pass an exam, but how it helps us as people. There are loads of messages in these stories, things that could help us in our lives," Seb said.

"That's right," Professor Itsen said. "These stories have parallels with real life. In many ways, they reflect our lives and our society. Often, the authors are trying to illustrate real-world issues through the story. They're asking questions and challenging the way we look at our life and our world around us. The characters go through challenges. Theirs might be battling evil wizards, fighting oppression, freeing humanity from a world ruled by machines or saving us from aliens, but when you look below the surface, they have many of the same challenges we have. When we appreciate this, we also realise how much we can learn from them… how they can help us live our own lives."

The class was silent, tuned into his every word.

"So, the question is: What can we learn?"

Seb looked at the pages and pages of notes in front of him. Suddenly he felt overwhelmed by it all. Where do you start with all this? Then he remembered something he'd written while watching *The Lord of the Rings*.

"Professor," he said. "There are some messages about society and our culture… and others about us as individuals."

"Excellent." Professor Itsen walked over to the white board. "Let's look at them through those two lenses. What messages and themes did you find that ran through all of these films?"

After a few seconds, hands began rising into the air as people found ideas to share from their notes.

"Why don't you kick us off, Jennifer?" said Professor Itsen.

"It's all like… good versus evil, dark and light, right and wrong. Like Harry Potter against the Dark Lord and The Fellowship of the Ring against Sauron. It's all morals and stuff, right?" she said.

"On the surface, it is," replied Professor Itsen, "although there are some questions on that too. Did anyone see any shades of grey between light and dark, between good and evil or right and wrong?" he asked.

Next to Jennifer, Rob Franks raised his hand.

"In loads of the films the 'good guys' also do terrible things. It's not just the 'bad guys'. That's the same in real life, though, isn't it? Who are the terrorists and who are the freedom fighters? It depends which side you're on, I guess," he said.

"Excellent, Rob. Throughout history, people have committed many terrible acts by claiming that the ends justified the means.

They will say that what they do is for a good cause. Dropping an atomic bomb on Japan may have brought about the end of World War Two, but does that make it okay?" asked Professor Itsen. "You might remember Immanuel Kant's views on ethics – the means must justify the means, not just the ends. Any other thoughts, anybody?"

"In loads of these films, someone is trying to gain power," said Jeremy Brown. "Voldemort, in Harry Potter… or… or Sauron, trying to gain the ring of power so that he could rule Middle Earth. Voldemort promised a better world for his followers and then ruled them through fear. I was studying how Hitler got voted into power for my history assignment. The German people didn't think they were voting for an evil dictator. Hitler talked about… about building a stronger Germany. Over time he convinced the people to give him more and more power, so that he could build a stronger country. Eventually he had enough power and became a dictator."

"Excellent," said Professor Itsen, who seemed to be enjoying this more and more by the minute. "Why do you think Sauron, Voldemort and many of the other villains in our movies – and indeed Adolf Hitler – all sought power?" The professor scanned the room. "Yes, Justin?"

"Control," said Justin simply. "They wanted control."

Professor Itsen nodded. "That sounds pretty reasonable to me," he said. "So… do any of these movies talk of control in society today? Are there any different views on social control, any modern-day views?"

Other hands were in the air now too. From immediately behind him, Seb heard Rosie's voice.

"In *The Hunger Games*… I know it's set in the future, but the people of the Capitol have all of this over-the-top fashion and make-up. When I first watched it, I thought it just looked ridiculous. But then I thought about it. It's just like our society today. I mean, everyone is so obsessed with how they look and their image, right? Desperate to wear the right labels and the right make-up, be at the fancy parties or seen with the cool people. It looks ridiculous in the film, but it's actually not that different from our lives, is it? And," she continued, "there were some people in the Districts who wanted to be picked for *The Hunger Games*, even though they knew they'd probably be killed. It would make them rich and famous. They would be on TV. I reckon it's a bit like reality TV and YouTube... people desperate for a moment of fame, 'cos society rewards fame and celebrity. They'd do anything for it. Is that a form of control?"

There was a moment or two of stunned silence.

"Very insightful, Rosie," said Professor Itsen. He surveyed the class again before inviting Nick Williams to add to the discussion.

"Is it Roman? I mean, *The Hunger Games*?" asked Nick.

"What do you think?" said Professor Itsen.

"Well, I was studying the Romans at school. The posh people in Rome would eat loads at parties and then puke it back up. And they had gladiator battles, which is just like *The Hunger Games*. Only one would survive and the winner was given their freedom. The gladiator fights were a sport for the people of Rome, like entertainment. And the Romans looked down on anyone that wasn't from Rome. They thought they were barbarians. That's a bit like how the people of the Capitol saw the Districts in *The Hunger Games*, right? Oh... and you asked about power and control. *The Hunger Games* were used to control the Districts through fear. I only just thought about that," he said with a note of triumph in his voice.

"Wonderful," said Professor Itsen.

Seb thought that if Professor Itsen enjoyed this anymore, he might burst.

"Anything else about control?" he asked.

Seb's hand shot into the air once more.

"In *The Matrix*… It shows the world we know and the life we live, like a video game that we're all logged into. We don't even realise we're playing it. The video game has become our reality. The rules of the game have been set for us and we just play by those rules. I wrote down a quote, hang on…" Seb rummaged through his pages quickly and found it.

"'The world has been pulled over your eyes to blind you from the truth.' I know in the movie 'the truth' is that the world is being run by machines. But I was thinking about what that meant in our lives. Maybe 'the machines' are huge companies… the media, advertising, governments, social media. They create the 'game'. It's our real-life matrix. We live in their game. They fill our TV screens, fill our social media and our phones. They decide what we see and hear. They've created the reality that we live."

Professor Itsen clapped his hands together.

"Bravo!" he exclaimed. "Now, we're really beginning to uncover the depth and meaning in these messages. What is real? What's the dream? How free are you in the 'free world', as it's so often called? Your beliefs limit everything. Your choices are governed by what you believe is possible. So… who is drawing those boundaries? Who dictates your beliefs? Who is telling you what's possible and what isn't? Or, more specifically, who are you *allowing* to construct those boundaries for you?"

He picked up a piece of paper from his desk. "Here's a little piece I wrote recently. See what you make of it." The professor began to read:

"'Social Media. The remote control for humanity.

Here we are, slaves to the algorithms and the pixels, entranced by their addictive powers. Polluted. Rendered help-less… thought-less.

Scrolling mindlessly through life, sleepwalking into the arms of our oppressors.

Imprisoned behind invisible bars, unaware that we're captive.

What do we see?

What do we hear?

What do we believe?

Who decides?

We're like baby birds waiting for the next morsel to be dropped into our gaping mouths, consuming everything without question.

How did it come to this?

It's simple.

We invited it in.

We embraced it.

We took the pill, day after day.

We allowed it to surround us, to infect us, to penetrate our inner world and construct our reality.

And we can choose not to!

We can take back the remote!'"

He paused for a moment and then asked, "Are there similar ideas and questions that have been shared in philosophy, by philosophers – maybe some of the people we've studied so far?"

Seb's brain kicked into action and his hand rose again.

"Yes, Seb," said the professor.

"Existentialism," Seb began. "It talks of free will, choice, meaning – of living an authentic life, a life that is genuinely yours. If we try to fit in with everyone else, wear the right clothes or make-up, have the right hairstyle… If we're trying to 'be cool', or be popular, or be what society wants us to be, or if we allow ourselves to be ruled by money or fame, we will never truly be our selves. If we live the life society wants us to live, we are not free."

Seb paused to catch his breath then said, more to himself than anyone else, "Choose life."

The classroom fell into stunned silence. Even Professor Itsen didn't answer. But Seb didn't care. It was as if the fog had cleared in his mind, and he'd found the answer to a question that had been hanging over him for as long as he could remember.

"What do you mean, 'Choose life'?" asked Jeremy Brown.

"What?" Seb said, a little surprised.

"'Choose life'," Jeremy said. "That's what you just said. What do you mean?"

"It's from *Trainspotting*," Seb replied. "I watched both *Trainspotting* movies over the Christmas break too. There are these little poems. They kind of make you question your life choices. There's one in the first movie and one in the second. I can't remember them exactly. They go something like…

Choose life.

Choose a respectable job.

Choose a family and kids.

Choose a big house, a fancy car and package holidays.

Choose electric toothbrushes, consumer goods and expensive junk you neither need or want.

Choose a mortgage and credit card debt.

Choose a slow death on your sofa watching mind-numbing, meaningless, spirit-crushing guff that sucks the life out of you.

Choose prescription medication, type two diabetes, anxiety, chronic-fatigue and depression.

Choose your future.

Choose life."

Professor Itsen grinned from ear to ear. "Well, that's your next assignment, folks. Your challenge is to write your own 'Choose Life' piece. With this one, though, describe the life you want to live… not the prescription life that society dispenses. We have some time left in this lesson to get started, but feel free to finish it in your own time if you need to. Hand them in at the start of the next lecture, please. For now, though… Here endeth the lesson. Go forth and prosper."

***

Seb made his way down to the canteen and headed towards the table in the far corner by the window. He looked at the time on his phone. He was early, so he took out his notepad to finish his philosophy assignment. From across the canteen Seb heard his name and looked up to see Gemma walking towards him. He couldn't put his finger on it, but there was something different about her. Maybe it was the way the sunlight caught her hair, or her mischievous smile. Whatever it was, he liked it.

"Homework?" she asked.

Seb nodded. "Philosophy," he said.

"Eeuuew," replied Gemma, as though she'd stepped in something foul.

"It's not so bad, you know." He smiled. "Our Christmas assignment was to watch a bunch of movies."

"Are you kidding me? That's soooo cooool. Maybe I should've taken philosophy," Gemma replied, grinning. "Is it with that professor dude?"

"Professor Itsen, yeah," he said.

"The one that got sacked by the Uni a couple of years ago?"

"Sacked?" said Seb.

"I know, right… Pretty sure Alice's dad knows him."

Seb was stunned.

"Oh," Gemma said, as if she'd just been remarking on the weather. "Sophie said to give you this." She delved into her bag and pulled out a neatly folded A4 sheet of paper. "New rehearsal timetable," she said excitedly. "There's a meeting, four o'clock. Only a few weeks 'til the national final! It's gonna be unreal!"

He replied with a weak smile. He wasn't sure how he felt about it. Ever since he'd watched *The Last Night of the Proms* on TV as a kid, he'd dreamed of playing at the Royal Albert Hall. So why wasn't he looking forward to it? Surely he should be feeling excitement, rather than the nagging anxiety in the pit of his stomach.

Out the corner of his eye, he spotted Alice wandering across the canteen in their direction and waved. Gemma turned to see who it was.

"Oh, better leave you guys to it." She sighed. As Alice approached, Gemma got to her feet. "Oh, uh… Hi, Alice… uh… Jus' givin' Seb a message 'bout orchestra," she said awkwardly, "Later, Seb." Then she grabbed her bag and hurried off.

Alice watched her go with a slight scowl.

"You okay?" asked Seb. Alice turned to face him and the smile returned to her face.

"Yeah… sure… What was Gemma doing?" she asked.

"Passing on a message from Sophie about orchestra. It's the national final in a couple of weeks, so we've got a new rehearsal timetable," he said, less than enthusiastically. Seb unfolded the piece of paper. He didn't have to look closely to see that it was a packed schedule. There was a practice session almost every day for the next three weeks. He pushed the piece of paper across the table towards Alice.

"Wow," she said. "That's a lot of practice! You don't seem very excited about it, though."

"I am," he replied flatly. "It's just that… well… everyone's going to expect heroics from me after the regional heat and I won't be able to…." He trailed off and gazed out of the window. Alice waited for him to continue. "It's just that… the piece we played at the regionals. Sophie picked it because I played it in my audition. I know it inside out. I play it all the time. I'm pretty sure she was trying to make it easy for me. But we're bound to get a different piece to play in the national final, and if they all expect me to play that perfectly, I'm just going to let them all down." He hadn't really realised what was gnawing away at him until he said it out loud.

Alice smiled at him. "So you don't know what piece you're playing for the final?" she asked.

Seb shook his head.

"Then maybe we should cross that bridge when we come to it. But now… tell me about this demon."

"Okay," he said. "But first… What do you know about Professor Itsen? Gemma said he was sacked by the Uni and that your dad knows him."

A wry smile crossed Alice's face. "Did she? "Well, yes, it's true. Mum and Dad both know him. They all worked at the Uni together until he was… 'released'."

"Your parents work at the Uni too?" Seb asked. He was impressed.

"Dad is a cardiac surgeon. He spends most of his time in the hospital but does some research and teaching at the Uni. Mum kinda does the same thing, but she's a lawyer."

"Wow," he said, a little dumbstruck. "So what did he get sacked for?"

Alice's expression hardened. "Because he dared to think for himself," she said.

"Why was that a problem? He's a philosopher. That's what they do, isn't it?"

"The university were bidding for research grants from governments and big global businesses," she began. "Professor Itsen started asking how ethical the research was and whether the university should be involved. The grants were worth a fortune. The chancellor knew that if Professor Itsen kept asking awkward questions, they would never get the money. So the chancellor gave him a choice: keep quiet and keep your job… or not. Professor Itsen spoke his mind and became 'surplus to requirements'. I think that's the way he described it. I remember him telling my dad one night at our house. He was devastated."

"Blimey… poor bloke. Well, good on him, sticking to his guns.

I reckon their loss is our gain," Seb said.

Alice replied with a sombre smile. "So… tell me about this demon!"

He told Alice everything he could remember about his encounter on New Year's Day. How he'd realised it was imaginary and how it had faded to nothing.

"You did it, then?" she said. "It's gone?"

Seb shrugged. "I guess so."

For a couple of hours they sat sipping drinks and chatting about nothing in particular. He could not remember feeling this comfortable in anyone else's company. Conversations with other people were such an effort. He was constantly trying to think of something cool to say or desperately avoid saying something stupid. But with Alice, he could just be himself.

They completely lost track of time until Alice caught sight of her phone. She let out a little squeak and cried, "I'm going to be late," then snatched up her things, said a hurried goodbye and headed out the door. Seb checked the time. It was a few minutes before the orchestra meeting, so he slung his bag on his back and set off.

As he emerged into the entrance hall, he spotted Jonny Martyn loitering at the bottom of the stairs. Seb knew him as a polite mild-mannered member of his psychology class, who also doubled as Malone's lieutenant. He remembered what Malone had said at the party: "Jonny didn't want me to give you an assignment. Maybe he didn't think you were up to it." Was the "nice Jonny" from the classroom just a front to hide the more sinister side of his personality?

As Seb headed up the corridor, Jonny followed, keeping a few strides behind. Seb quickened his pace to put a few more metres between them. But before he could reach the corner, he heard a low voice over his shoulder.

"Seb," Jonny said, almost in a whisper, "I've got a message for you. He wants to see you."

Seb spun around.

"What if I don't want to see him?" he replied angrily.

"I'm just passing on the message, Seb," said Jonny, looking a little startled. "Tonight, five o'clock at the sports hall. Of course, he said 'Don't be late'. I don't really need to tell you that, but he told me to tell you anyway... You know what he's like."

With that, Jonny gave Seb a weak smile, turned and set off the way he'd come, leaving Seb feeling like he'd been punched in the stomach.

How to Silence Your Demons

What do you think about the ideas that were shared in Seb's philosophy class?

What makes sense?

What doesn't?

What do you agree with?

How do you think these ideas could help you live your life?

Seb shares a version of the 'Choose Life' poem from Trainspotting. Then Professor Itsen says, "Well, that's your next assignment, folks. Your challenge is to write your own 'Choose Life' piece. With this one, though, describe the life you want to live... not the prescription life that society dispenses". What would you write in yours?

Chapter Thirteen

EVEREST

The orchestra meeting didn't last long. Sophie looked like she might burst with excitement as she announced that the national finals were a little over three weeks away. The organisers had set some conditions on the piece of music they could choose. All pieces had to be composed by a "non-classical" composer.

"That means no Beethoven, no Mozart, no Bach, or anyone else we'd normally choose... and no movie theme tunes by composers such as Hans Zimmer or Howard Shore either," she said, looking towards Seb. "We're going to have to think outside the box."

After a little discussion and a few people sharing tunes from their phones via Sophie's bubblegum-pink Bluetooth speaker, it was agreed that they would play "Exogenesis Symphony Part 1" by the rock band Muse. The only problem was that it featured an electric guitar and a vocal, neither of which they had. Sophie and the others seemed to find a solution to this alarmingly quickly. Gemma would play the guitar piece on her electric violin and Seb would play the vocal part on the flute.

Gemma seemed to embrace the whole idea with real enthusiasm. Seb, on the other hand, failed to make anyone take his protests seriously. No one listened when he said, "I don't think I'll be able to do it justice", "Maybe we should pick another piece" or "I really don't want to let you all down". Instead of hearing, "Okay, Seb, we'll do something else," all he heard was, "You'll be great! You're a natural! You're too modest. You can do it."

He left the music block with a head full of doom and a lead weight in his stomach. All he wanted was to get home, crash out on his bed and feel sorry for himself. Then he remembered... Malone. His heart sank. It was a couple of minutes to five. He turned towards the sports hall. But then he stopped. He didn't have to do this. He had a choice. He could simply walk down the hill, get on the bus and go home. He was in charge of his own legs. He could point them in whichever direction he wanted.

But at what cost?

He wouldn't be much use to the orchestra with a broken neck. Although, maybe it would get him out of playing this stupid vocal piece. He mulled it over. Then, he turned and marched down the hill towards the bus stop. Malone could do his own dirty work.

***

Seb lay on his bed gazing at the ceiling. What had he done? Malone wouldn't let this go unnoticed. He was sure to exact revenge, make an example of Seb to show his band of cronies that no one crosses Michael Malone. And he'd make it painful. Hot acid bubbled up in his chest. He bounced up from his bed, ran into the bathroom and threw up.

Pathetic. Weak, said the Demon.

Seb stared into the porcelain abyss, his mind racing, imagining how Malone might torture and humiliate him. Visions of the Japanese disembowelling sword flashed through his mind. Then the scene changed. He was back playing that nightmare first audition. This time it was in front of thousands of people at the Royal Albert Hall. He saw Sophie and the orchestra; anger and disappointment etched on their faces. Doubts and fears flooded his mind, spiralling out of control, each one taking him deeper into despair.

You can't play this, the Demon taunted. *It'll be a disaster. You're going to lose and it'll be your fault.*

He trudged across the landing to his bedroom and slumped face down on his bed. He buried his head in his pillow and began to sob. Raindrops hammered on the windows.

Darkness descended.

Wind whipped through his hair. Cold rain stung his face. He could smell the damp forest floor around him. He opened his eyes and stared through the darkness. Only the shadowy outline of the trees stared back. The Demon was somewhere close by, he could sense it… but where? He tried to run but was rooted to the spot. Why couldn't he move? Panic rose like a monster within him. Then, through the trees came that merciless laugh.

Oh look… the little boy can't run away.

"B-but… I th-hought," Seb stammered.

That I was gone? said the Demon.

It's horned skull appeared through the darkness, its eyes glowing like embers.

"You're not real," Seb protested. "You're imaginary."

Yes, it said. *I am. Here, deep inside your mind. You will never outrun me. There is no place you can hide. No escape. For too long have you failed us. Now you must pay.*

Everything seemed to happen in slow motion. The Demon's mouth opened and a lizard-like forked tongue appeared between its lips. The tongue reached out into the night towards him, tasting the air. Closer and closer, right up to his face. Then it transformed. Flesh became flame. The fiery tongue licked Seb's cheek. He yelled out as it blistered his skin, fighting to escape the invisible bonds… but to no avail. The tongue began to wrap itself around him, consuming him in flames. Searing pain ravaged every fibre of his body. Everything was fire. In the distance he heard the Demon's triumphant roar of laughter.

Seb woke with a start, his heart pounding, drenched in sweat. He rolled onto his back gasping for air. It was just another dream... or was it? He didn't know. He couldn't tell... and he didn't care either.

***

The bus meandered its way through the country lanes towards Yeoborough. The sky was blue. Sun streamed through the windows. And yet, all Seb could see was gloom. Today, no doubt, he would come face to face with his nemesis. Malone was bound to send one of his henchmen. Seb would be summoned and then executed without trial, for daring to disobey. He'd half considered not going into college. Why walk straight into Malone's trap? There seemed no point going to orchestra rehearsal either. He'd never be able to play that piece. But, he also knew he couldn't stay in bed and hide under his covers forever. Sooner or later, he'd have to face the music. And the longer he left it, the worse it would be.

But that wasn't all. The Demon was back. He pulled out his phone and re-read the Demon Charmers' instructions. He'd done what it said. He'd faced it. He'd walked into the Demon's lair, and he discovered its pain. But the next step just didn't make sense. Solve the problem with your demon? It was impossible. He read to the bottom of the page.

Oh… and find Søren. He's often found in his favourite café, on the corner of Vestergade, opposite St. Albani Church in Odense. He can help you.

Who the hell was Søren and where was Odense?

I guess that's one question I can answer.

He typed it into the search bar on his phone. His heart sank. Odense, it seemed, was a small city in Denmark.

"Denmark?" he exclaimed out loud. "What the…?"

The woman in front of him turned and gave him a disapproving look. This was getting ridiculous. How on earth was he supposed to get to Denmark? Why had he placed his hopes in the Demon Charmers? How stupid could he be?

The bus pulled up next to the college and he stepped off. He looked around for Malone's welcoming committee, but there was no one else in sight. Come to think of it, it was probably too early for them. They didn't have to get out of bed for him. They could take their time, hunt him down at their leisure and then drag him through the corridors like an animal ready for slaughter.

There was no point going to the rehearsal either. He was just going to screw it up. What were they all going to think? Sophie would realise she'd made a massive mistake at the audition. His first attempt was the real Seb, before she let him play his favourite tune. She, and the rest of the orchestra, were about to realise what kind of a musician he really was.

He wandered mindlessly through the campus until he reached the music room. Most of the others had arrived and were setting up their instruments. There was a buzz of excitement, which only fuelled his feeling of dread.

"Good morning, everyone," Sophie said. "You'll find sheet music on your seats. Have a quick look through it. We'll get started in a few minutes."

Seb stared at the collection of dots and lines on the page… but no music played inside his head. Slowly and deliberately, he started reading the notes and deciphering a tune, while piecing his flute together.

"Right," Sophie said. "Let's give this a try. Okay, on three. One… two…"

The first tentative notes rose from the strings. They seemed to be hitting most of the right notes, but not quite at the right time. Nevertheless, he could make out the tune. Then the brass section began to build in the background, finally joined by the rest of the violins and the drums. His moment was drawing near. He raised his flute and panicked. Which note was he supposed to play first?

Uhhh… pick one.

He played a note.

Was that right?

It didn't sound right. His eyes scanned the sheet in front of him.

What's next? Think. Think! Quick!!

A second note followed, but that didn't sound right either. Then a third. It was better but now he was behind the rest of the orchestra. Perhaps he could shorten the next few notes by a fraction and get back into time. Or maybe he could manage if he didn't take a breath at the end of the next bar? He decided to give it a go. He gasped for air between two notes that he was supposed to blend. It sounded awful. He took another breath and gradually built towards the higher notes. As he reached the top, Gemma struck up and took over. He had a few seconds before he needed to come back in. It was a long section and he'd need full lungs. He gathered himself, found the next few notes, took a breath and played. He heard his notes and Gemma's jostling with each other clumsily, like two dancers tripping over each other's feet. It was a mess.

Their last notes faded away, replaced by an awkward silence. Finally, Sophie spoke.

"Well, we're not going to get it perfect first time, I suppose," she said. "We have a lot of practice ahead of us. Why don't we start by breaking it down into sections and then build it back up?"

The rest of the rehearsal wasn't much better, but there were a few small signs of progress. At the end of the session, Sophie called Seb and Gemma to one side.

"I'm wondering whether you two would benefit from a little rehearsal time together... just the two of you," she said. "Your pieces seem to be like a conversation, particularly towards the end. If you can get the timing right, I think it will really help. What do you think?"

"Defo... right Seb?" Gemma said.

Seb couldn't think of any reason not to and, to be honest, anything was worth a try. "Uh... yeah... sure," he replied.

"Great!" said Gemma. "Let's do it."

He nodded along, not quite knowing what he was agreeing to. In truth, his mind had drifted to his imminent encounter with Malone.

Seb left the music block and headed towards the canteen, hoping that he'd strike lucky and see Alice. He crept cautiously down the long corridors, checking every corner and stairwell for one of Malone's brutes. However, as he turned towards the main entrance, he was met by an entirely different sight. Melissa, leaning casually against a wall. Her dark hair blew gently in the breeze.

"Hey, Cutie... He's not happy with you," she said, as if remarking on the weather. "You'll have to go and see him. The longer you leave it, the worse it will be."

Seb said nothing. Melissa moved in close. Her trailing hair caught the side of his face.

"And I wouldn't want him to make a mess of your boyish good looks," she whispered. Then she winked, blew him a kiss, turned and walked off. "You'll know where to find him. In the sports hall, as always," she called back over her shoulder.

Seb was dumbfounded. He'd expected to be jumped by two muscle-bound lunatics and dragged through college. But instead,

Malone had sent Melissa to taunt him; whispering in his ear and blowing kisses. Then the penny dropped. Of course Malone wasn't going to cause a scene in a corridor. He wanted Seb to walk into the sports hall alone, out of sight. The knot tightened in his stomach. What on earth did Malone have in store for him?

Well, thought Seb, *it can't be any worse than facing a demon. Malone might have terrible breath, but he can hardly incinerate me.*

And with that, he hitched his rucksack back onto his shoulder and set off towards the sports hall.

***

The sports hall door opened with a creak. Seb stepped into the tired and gloomy entrance way. For a moment he wondered whether anyone was there and then WHAM. It was like being hit by a truck. His face slammed into the noticeboard, smashing the wooden frame. His shoulder shattered the pane of glass. He bounced off the wall and landed in a heap on the floor.

"You little shit," spat Malone from behind him.

Seb struggled to get up. He reached for the bannister on the stairs, but Malone kicked Seb behind the knee and he crumpled to the ground again. A warm sticky liquid ran down the side of his face. Seb caught his reflection on a broken shard of glass. There was a deep gash above his right eye.

"No one defies me… No one!" yelled Malone. "Especially not some scrawny clarinet player."

Seb staggered to his feet. He wiped his sleeve across his forehead. It was covered in blood. He looked directly into Malone's grey eyes.

"It's the flute, actually," he said.

"What?" said Malone.

"Flute, not clarinet," Seb replied.

"Who cares anyway?" Malone barked. "Listen to me, Hall. I have a job for you."

Seb felt his anger rising. He clenched his fist tight. He had never punched anyone in his life and he knew he'd never win. Malone could break every bone in his body, but he didn't care. He just wanted to lash out.

"What if I don't want to?" he said with as much strength as he could muster.

Malone scoffed. "I don't care if you want to or not. You're doing it!"

"I'm not your slave, Malone," said Seb, looking him straight in the eye.

Malone glared at him. "We'll see about that." He pulled a parcel out from a nearby locker. "You're going to take this. Give it to a bearded man. He'll be in a red BMW in the far corner of the main car park, ten o'clock tonight. Go up to the driver's window. He'll exchange this package for an envelope. You bring the envelope back to me. Here. Tomorrow morning. Eight sharp. Got it?"

Seb said nothing.

"And just in case you're thinking of doing something stupid, failure will see your little friend Alice involved in a nasty 'accident'. Are you getting this, numbskull?"

Seb nodded.

Malone thrust the package into his chest. "You'd better not fail… for her sake." Then Malone turned on his heels and stormed out.

***

It took Seb almost an hour to stem the bleeding before he left the sports hall. For a moment he wondered whether to go to his next class. He checked his reflection in a car window. What a mess. As well as the gash, his eye was puffy and swollen. The mottled purple shadow of a bruise starting to appear. There was no way he could walk into a classroom without a barrage of unwanted questions. So, he pulled the hood of his jacket over his head, stowed the package in his bag and headed for home.

Thankfully, his parents were out when he arrived. He went straight to the freezer and took a bag of frozen peas with him upstairs. Then he sunk his head into his pillow and laid the ice-cold bag over his swollen eye. The cold seemed to awaken his mind and thoughts began to flow. How could he stand up to Malone now? If Malone's only threat was to beat him to a pulp, he could handle that. But now… now he'd threatened Alice. Seb wanted nothing more than to crush Malone's precious package into a thousand tiny pieces, but that would put Alice in danger. He was trapped. Whichever way he tried to think his way around it, he came back to the same conclusion. He had to go through with it.

Just as he'd resigned himself to the inevitable, a bizarre thought stuck him.

Maybe the Demon could help.

He burst out laughing. That was probably the most ludicrous thought he'd ever had. Then he stopped.

Remember what the Demon Charmers said: Get to know it.

He lay there for a few seconds wondering what on earth his mind was doing. Was it really suggesting he should meet the Demon now? He scoffed at himself and flipped over the bag of peas.

Got any better ideas?

Come to think of it, he didn't.

Well? Are you going, then?

"Fine," he huffed as he got to his feet. He threw the bag of peas on the floor, pulled on his shoes and headed for the woods.

The sky was sapphire blue and the winter sun cast long shadows across the fields. The light wind carried a chill, which persuaded Seb to zip his jacket up to his chin. He had an unusual sense of purpose. While he had no idea why he was doing it, it seemed strangely right. The same few thoughts rattled around in his head.

Got any better ideas? What have you got to lose anyway?

He stepped beyond the trees and made his way towards his thinking spot. This time, there was no strange wind or mist to blind him, just the odd fallen leaf dancing carefree on the breeze. Ahead he saw the huge frame of the Demon lying on the path ahead of him, seemingly asleep. As he approached, it woke from its slumber.

How brave you are, it said with a sneer, *to walk in here without your little music stick.*

It hadn't even occurred to Seb to bring his flute.

"I've come to ask for your help," Seb said.

Why should I help you?

"We have a problem," Seb replied.

We have a problem? How do we have a problem?

"You hate it when I fail, when I humiliate us," said Seb.

That's not my problem, said the Demon. *It's yours.*

"Not really," Seb replied. "It's ours. You hate it. It's what you fear most. You said so yourself. Burning me… punishing me… taunting me… It isn't helping, is it? Be honest. Am I getting any better? Am I failing less?"

The Demon smouldered for a moment.

No, it muttered softly.

"Then help," Seb said with a rare note of conviction.

With what? asked the Demon.

"Malone."

The Demon examined Seb closely. *You want to know how to wriggle out of this assignment.*

Seb nodded. "I'm not worried about me. Malone can do his worst to me. It's Alice I'm worried about."

The Demon let out a deep rumbling "Mmmmm".

You're a curious individual, aren't you? Maybe there is more to you than meets the eye, it said.

Seb couldn't think of a decent reply, so he remained silent. The Demon filled the void.

It looks like you're stuck for now. However, this is just one battle… it's not the war.

Seb was puzzled. "What do you mean?" he asked.

The Demon lifted its head. *It's not the first job he's given you and I suspect it won't be the last. You might have to go along with this one. But, if you're expecting another, you can be ready. Plan for it.*

A smile crossed Seb's face.

"I like it," he said. "But what? What plan?"

The Demon looked very pleased with itself.

We'll figure that out when the time comes, it replied.

"Thank you," said Seb as he turned to leave. "Hang on… I don't even know your name."

For a split second, he thought the Demon looked emotional.

They call me Timidis, it replied softly. *Timidis Autem.*

"Thank you, Timidis," said Seb. "I will return."

I believe you will, it replied.

***

The alarm on his phone chimed. It was nine o'clock; one hour until his meeting with the bearded man in the red BMW. He picked up the package. It was the first time Seb had really examined it. It was a large, sealed courier bag. Inside it, he could feel five individual boxes. Each one was about the size and shape of his hardback A4 notepad. However, he suspected this was not a consignment of notepads. It was probably best not to think too much about it. He shoved the package into his bag, slung it over his shoulder and crept down the stairs. His parents were back from work. From the overdramatic screams echoing up the staircase, he suspected they were watching one of their murder mysteries on TV.

He reached the front door and carefully turned the handle.

"Seb… Is that you? You're not going out at this time of night, are you?" his mum shouted.

He closed the door behind him and ran towards the bus stop. He felt slightly guilty for not answering but concluded it was for the best. He could hardly tell them that he was about to deliver a package of stolen goods to a dodgy bloke in a car park. So, he could either lie… or pretend he hadn't heard. The latter seemed best.

Unsurprisingly, Seb was the only one on the bus. He began to imagine the driver being questioned by detectives who were solving his murder. His body had been discovered in a deserted corner of the college car park and the police were trying to establish the victim's movements in the preceding hours. They'd found CCTV footage of a youth matching Seb's description near the college bus stop, so assumed he'd taken the bus. But why was he going to college at nine o'clock at night? His distraught parents heard him leave the house but had no explanation as to where he was going or why. After checking his belongings, all they knew was that his rucksack was also missing.

Seb snapped out of his daydream as the bus pulled up at the bottom of the hill. His eyes followed the dimly lit path up the slope towards the college. The huge concrete grey building stood lifeless and abandoned. He stepped off the bus and made his way up the dark path. The bushes to his left rustled with the scurrying of unseen creatures. It was surreal. The campus, which normally bustled with students and staff, was empty and silent. The only light was the eerie green glow of the exit signs above the doorways.

He passed the octagonal music block and followed the path until he reached the car park. In the far corner, amidst the shadows, sat the red BMW. Seb checked the time on his phone. It was two minutes to ten. *Better get it done.* As he approached the car, a wisp of cigarette smoke rose through a narrow gap in the driver's window.

"Package," demanded a gravelly voice from behind the tinted window. Seb dutifully produced the courier bag from his rucksack. The window slid down to reveal a tanned man with a closely shaved beard, dark glasses and a black baseball cap. He didn't turn to look at Seb; his eyes remained resolutely forwards, staring out across the car park. He extended a tattooed hand out of the window to receive the goods, then grabbed the package and pulled it inside the car.

"Stay there," he said.

The window slid closed while the man inspected the package. Then the window slid open a fraction and an envelope emerged through the slit at the top. As soon as Seb took the envelope, the engine fired up and the car screeched off into the night.

Seb stored the envelope safely in his jacket pocket. The last bus back to Cokendale had long gone. He began walking home.

***

It was three minutes past eight when Seb arrived at the sports hall the following morning. Another unspectacular orchestra rehearsal had overrun.

"You're late," said Malone as Seb burst through the door into the dingy entrance way. The noticeboard was still hanging off the wall; splintered wood and shattered glass littered the floor. There were droplets of his own blood tracing the path he took to the toilets the previous day.

"Envelope," barked Malone. Seb looked at him defiantly and

slowly reached into his jacket. As soon as Malone caught sight of it, he snatched it out of Seb's hands, ripped open one end and peered inside. He gave a brief nod; all must be in order.

"Well, looks like your little friend is safe for now," said Malone. He drew a deep breath, puffed out his already sizeable chest and took a step towards Seb.

"Remember: there are two ways to do this. One is a very painful way. For your sake, I suggest you choose the other one. If you want the pain-free way, for you and your friends, stop being a dick and do what I tell you. Got it?"

And with that, Malone barged past, knocking him into the vending machine as he went. Seb clenched his fist tight. Now, more than ever, he was determined to put a stop to this. He needed to break free. But it was more than that. He was determined to stop Malone... for good. He had no idea how, but surely being on the inside gave him some advantage. His mind began to churn through ideas as he wandered down the hill towards the canteen to meet Alice.

There must be a way, he kept telling himself as a stream of equally idiotic suggestions flowed through his brain.

He was so consumed in his own thoughts, he didn't see Alice creep up behind him.

"Boo!"

Seb spun around.

"Alice... you almost gave me a heart attack!" he said, catching his breath.

"Sorry," she replied, not sounding particularly apologetic at all. Then she caught sight of the gash on his forehead and the bruising around his eye. "What happened?"

"It's nothing really," he said, unconvincingly. "Come on, let's grab a cuppa."

"That's not 'nothing', Seb," she insisted.

He couldn't bring himself to look her in the eye. She had

warned him not to get mixed up in it in the first place.

"You know me... clumsy," he said, even less convincingly. Alice looked as though she was about to reply and then thought better of it. Then, she pulled a piece of paper from her pocket.

"Have you seen these?" she asked, holding out a small poster.

THEFT IN COLLEGE

Regrettably, there have been a recent spate of thefts at college. During the last few months, a number of valuable items have been stolen. Before Christmas, an expensive watch was taken from a lecturer's car. Another lecturer's handbag, containing a mobile phone and credit cards, was stolen from her classroom. Most recently, five brand new iPads were taken from the sports hall office.

If anyone knows anything about the disappearance of these items, please inform a member of staff, college security or the police.

Rest assured, the police have been informed and security across the whole campus has been stepped up. Every effort is being taken to apprehend those responsible.

He stared at the poster.

"Are you okay?" she asked, concern ringing in her voice.

Seb nodded weakly. "Let's find a seat," he said quietly. He spotted an empty table standing alone in the far corner and led her over to it, checking to make sure they wouldn't be overheard.

"That job I did for Malone before Christmas... It was that lecturer's watch, wasn't it?" he said in a hushed voice. Alice clapped her hands to her mouth.

"Oh my God... Seb!"

He waved her down. "There's more," he continued. "Yesterday... well... Malone gave me another 'assignment'. It was the same sort of thing. I had to give this package to a dude in a car, in exchange for an envelope." He could see the look of anguish starting to form on Alice's face, but she said nothing. "At first I didn't know what it was. The package felt like notebooks or something, but…" He stared at the table. "I think it was these iPads."

There was a moment of silence. It was Alice who spoke first.

"Is that how you got this?" she asked, pointing to his eye. He nodded slowly while inspecting a small patch of the table. "You have to say something. Go to the police… or security… or tell Mark!" she begged. Seb looked up at her.

"No… I can't," he said.

"Then I will," said Alice firmly.

"No! Alice, you promised!"

"Why not?"

He felt cornered. He knew that if Malone found out, which he surely would, it was Alice who would suffer. But there was absolutely no way he could tell her that.

"Y-you…" he stammered, trying to think of a way to explain it. "You wouldn't understand."

As the words tumbled out of his mouth, Seb knew that they were probably the worst three words he could have chosen. Alice stood up, sending her chair clattering. Behind her horn-rimmed glasses, tears glistened in her brilliant blue eyes.

"Really?" she said, her voice cracking. "After everything… You think I wouldn't understand?" She snatched up her bag.

"I didn't mean it like that," he said. "Please, Alice… Please… trust me." He didn't know how much she heard as she stormed out.

Seb stared at the upended chair. What had he done? He only wanted to protect her, keep her out of all this. The last thing he wanted to do was hurt her. She was his best friend… probably his only real friend. Without her, he was completely alone.

How to Silence Your Demons

Seb often feels intimidated by Malone.
Why do we let people get to us and intimidate us?
Why do we give them the power to control how we feel?

How do you think Seb could start to take control back, and not feel intimidated?
How could you do the same if someone is trying to intimidate you?

Chapter Fourteen

A TOUCH OF GENIUS

Seb trudged out of the canteen and across the sparse grey entrance hall towards his philosophy class. Ordinarily, he would have been really looking forward to the lesson. He was fairly pleased with his "Choose Life" assignment and had been re-reading his movie notes ready for part two. But the argument with Alice left a dark cloud hanging over him. He entered the classroom, plonked his assignment on top of the pile and took his seat.

"Well, good morning everyone," said Professor Itsen cheerfully. "Let's pick up where we left off, unravelling some of the messages and lessons from these movies. As you may remember, last session we looked at the social and cultural messages. Today, we'll be looking at the individual and personal lessons we can draw from them. To help us, I've invited a friend and colleague from the psychology department to join us. Please welcome Mark Charmers.

"Those who study psychology will already know Mark. And, since psychology and philosophy share a lot of common ground, we decided that it would be good to deliver this session together. So," said Professor Itsen as he surveyed the class intently. "Who would like to kick us off?"

There was a nervous murmur and shuffling of papers. "Come on… just because we have a guest, there's no need to be shy," said Professor Itsen. Mark looked across to Seb and gave him a nod of encouragement. Slowly, Seb raised his hand. "Ah, wonderful. Yes, Mr Hall," said Professor Itsen.

"Uh… I noticed in all of the stories… It's not the strongest, the most powerful or those with the greatest wealth that win. Instead, it's the ordinary people who are fighting for a cause," he said.

"Excellent," replied Professor Itsen. "Have you got any examples?"

Seb nodded. "In *Harry Potter*, Voldemort was a far more powerful wizard than Harry. He knew more magic. I mean, other than Dumbledore, he was one of the most powerful wizards of all time. But he lost. The same is true of Katniss Everdeen, taking on President Snow in *The Hunger Games*. Or a small band of dwarves and a hobbit a taking on Smaug the dragon. Or the Fellowship of the Ring taking on the mighty Sauron in *The Lord of the Rings*. There's that quote from Gandalf," he said, rifling through his notes. "Here it is: 'Saruman believes it is only great power that can hold evil in check, but that is not what I have found. I've found that it is the small everyday deeds of ordinary folk that keeps darkness at bay.'"

"Very good," said Professor Itsen. "And are there echoes of this in real life?"

A number of hands shot up.

"It's like the civil rights, the anti-apartheid and the suffragette movements, isn't it?" Barney Jacks said from the back of the room. "They were just ordinary people who had a cause too. They didn't have power or money. They were all taking on governments… and whole societies. It's the same, right?"

"Good point, Barney," said Professor Itsen with a grin. "And history is littered with similar examples. Okay, what else did you find in these movies? Yes, Jonny."

"I found that none of the heroes and heroines started out being heroic," said Jonny confidently. "And they didn't become heroic overnight."

Professor Itsen clapped his hands together. "Bravo, Jonny," he said excitedly. "You're absolutely right. Let's think about the heroes and heroines in these stories for a moment. Harry Potter was not capable of defeating Voldemort until right at the end of the story. Katniss Everdeen grew into a heroine through the course of her story too. It was the same with Frodo and Sam in *The Lord of the Rings*. They were not heroes when they set out on their quests. Whichever example we look at, the lesson is the same. The heroes and heroines all had a journey. It took a long time and a lot of hard work. They all faced huge trials and challenges and multiple failures along the way. They all had moments of doubt and self-doubt, times when they didn't believe they could do it."

Professor Itsen turned to Mark. "Is this true of real-life heroes and heroines too?" he asked. Mark nodded and took a step towards the centre of the room.

"Absolutely," he replied in his melodic Scottish accent. "Take Albert Einstein, for example. Most people think of him as a natural genius. Did you know that he wasn't granted a full-time position to study his PhD at Zurich Polytechnic, because he wasn't one of their brightest students? He took a job in the patent office. He researched his general theory of relativity in his spare time. And, even after publishing it, it was eight years before his work was finally recognised.

"Equally, Martin Luther-King was not a great leader at the start of the Civil Rights Movement. In 1955, he was a pastor in a church who led some non-violent protests against racial inequality. Gradually, he began to lead and organise marches and rallies. It wasn't until 1963, eight years later, that he spoke at the March on Washington. That's where he delivered his famous 'I have a dream' speech.

"And did you know that Amy Johnson started as a typist who loved aeroplanes? She began her journey in aviation by spending her spare time at airfields. She became a ground engineer first. Then her father, who was a fisherman, paid for her to have flying lessons. We now celebrate her as the first person to fly from Britain to Australia.

"So, as you can see, none of these people were born heroes either."

Professor Itsen stepped forwards again. "Has anyone noticed another very interesting phenomenon here?" he asked.

The class was silent. What could he be referring to?

"It's the same with the villains, isn't it?" Seb said. "Most of them weren't born evil… or they didn't become evil just like that," he said, snapping his fingers. "It happened quite gradually."

Professor Itsen's face lit up. "Exactly, Seb, exactly!" he said wagging his finger excitedly, "So… which characters show this most clearly?"

"Well… when Dumbledore met the young Tom Riddle in the orphanage, he didn't think he'd just met one of the most dangerous wizards in history. I don't think the young Tom Riddle was very nice, but he certainly wasn't evil. It's the same in many stories where people turn from good to evil or from light to dark. It's a journey too."

Again, Professor Itsen turned to Mark. "What does this tell us about ourselves?" he asked.

Mark turned to face the class. "Sirius Black said in one of the Harry Potter films, it might have been *Order of the Phoenix*, that everyone has both light and dark inside them. The question is: Which do we choose to follow? There is an old Cherokee Indian tale of a tribal chief telling a youngster about two wolves that are fighting inside him. One is evil – it is anger, envy, greed, arrogance, self-pity, resentment, dishonesty, false pride, superiority and ego. The other is good – it is joy, peace, hope, humility, honesty, sincerity, kindness, compassion, truth and love. The youngster thinks for a moment and then asks which wolf will win the fight. And the chief replies, 'The one you feed.' As Professor Dumbledore tells Harry Potter, it is our choices that make us who we really are, not our abilities."

Mark paused for a moment to allow his words to sink in, then asked, "What does this tell us about how we've become the person we are… and who we are becoming?"

The room fell silent. Slowly people began whispering and chattering. Seb's mind cranked into gear. He'd never really considered that he had become the person he was, or that he was becoming the person he would be. He'd always thought he just *was* the way he was. He'd concluded he was probably born that way. He was just a shy, insecure, uncool, nerdy kid who wasn't popular or particularly good at anything. It's the way he'd always been and the way he'd always seen himself. But now he began to wonder *how* he'd become the person he was.

As Seb was pondering all this, he noticed Jeremy Brown raising his hand.

"Is it… choice?" he asked.

"That's right," Mark replied. "These stories illustrate how we develop our character. If you look beneath the surface, *Harry Potter*, *The Lord of the Rings*, *The Last Samurai* and *The Hunger Games* are all stories about character. There are a few characteristics that feature quite heavily in these particular stories; for example, courage, humility, honour. Importantly, these stories also show us that character has a moral dimension, as well as a mental dimension. Our heroes and heroines' get tested. More specifically, their moral compass gets tested. They need to make choices between right and wrong. Do they choose what's right or what's easy? Those two are rarely the same thing! What about if they need to choose between doing what's right and being popular? They are often different too! What do they do when they have power? How do they treat those around them?

"Knowing the difference between right and wrong, and having the courage to follow the right path, is often not easy."

Mark paused and took a breath before continuing.

"Importantly, these stories also show how character is developed. We develop our character through challenge. To be honest, they're often the tough challenges! And it is the choices that we make when we hit those challenges that really shapes our character. What happens when you get scared? Do you step away from the thing you fear or approach it? That choice shapes your courage. You'll see that the characters in these stories are constantly presented with challenges and choices. That's how they become heroes and heroines."

Seb's hand rose into the air again. "Does that mean that every single choice we make takes us towards who we are becoming… one little step at a time?" he asked.

Mark beamed at him. "That's exactly what it means! In some cases, the characters in our stories took steps towards courage and honour. In *The Last Samurai*, Captain Nathan Algren chose honour. He chose to be someone he could be proud of. In other cases, they took steps towards the 'dark side'. In many cases, they became obsessed with power. Interestingly, when people take steps towards the darker side of their character, they often do so by justifying their actions. In *Harry Potter*, Voldemort justifies acts of cruelty and murder. If you remember, he says something like, 'there is no good and evil… only power… and those too weak to seek it.'"

Seb's hand was in the air again. "I also noticed that when characters in films change… I mean really change as people… their name changes too."

Mark smiled. "You're right, of course. Tom Riddle becomes Voldemort. Smeagol becomes Gollum in *The Hobbit* when he finds the ring of power. It corrupts him. It changes him. Then there are characters who could have changed… but chose not to. On the eve of the first Hunger Games, Peeta tells Katniss that he doesn't want it to change him. Bizarrely, he seems less concerned that he might die. He just doesn't want to become a piece in the Capitol's game. He doesn't want to abandon his principles and become a ruthless murderer. He doesn't want it to change who he is. And, importantly, this sheds light on another huge lesson. Can anyone think what that might be?"

Again, there was silence in the class while everyone digested the question. Rebecca Sansom, who was also in Mark's psychology class, spoke up. "Is it something to do with identity?"

Mark looked like he was about to burst with pride. "It absolutely is!" he said. "Identity is who we believe we are. *The Matrix* illustrates this when Morpheus tells Neo that the way you appear in the matrix… the way you appear in the video game… is based on the way you see yourself. Can anyone see a direct reflection of that in their own life?"

Next to the window, Amy Palmer raised a hand. "Uh… social media?"

"Go on," Mark said.

"Well, the way people present themselves on social media is often like… like a projection, a picture of how they would like to be. It's like presenting yourself as a character in a video game like the matrix. The video game is not real. Nor is social media. It's like a virtual world. It's just a collection of pictures people post to show how they want to appear."

Professor Itsen threw his hands into the air. "Fantastic!" he said. "Mark, why is this really important for us?"

Mark took a breath and surveyed the sea of faces before him. "Our identity drives everything," he said. "There's a famous quote by a man called Henry Ford, who founded the Ford Motor Company. Henry Ford said, 'Whether you think you can, or you think you can't… either way, you're right'.

"What does all this mean in our own lives? What happens if you think of yourself as a stupid person? How do you think you will respond to a tough assignment? What happens if you start to struggle with it? Will you believe you can do it? Will you give it everything you've got? Or will you conclude that you'll never be able to do it and give up?

I give up, Seb thought, *That's exactly what happens.*

"Of course, this doesn't just apply to college work. This applies to every part of your life. If you believe that you're ugly and uninteresting, are you likely to approach the person you fancy and ask them out? Or will you tell yourself that they'll never like you anyway, so there's no point?

Seb looked intently at Mark. Was he reading Seb's mind?

"What if you believe that you're rubbish at everything? How will you respond when a really tough challenge comes your way, like learning a new skill in sport or playing a new piece of music?"

Mark's eyes flicked towards Seb as he said the last few words.

"Unfortunately, social media encourages people to compare themselves to others. The problem is, we compare ourselves to pictures that aren't real. These pictures don't show people as they are but how they would like others to see them.

"That's why people portray themselves as beautiful, successful, popular. It's all driven by ego. Our ego is the part of us that cares what other people think. And ego is a path to darkness!

Seb thought about it for a moment. He'd never considered himself to be egotistical, but he definitely cared what other people thought.

"I heard a rabbi on a radio show. He was delivering a 'thought for the day'. Mark went on, 'Don't compare your insides to other people's outsides'. If you compare yourself to these pictures, you are comparing yourself to a fantasy. You compare your reality to their fantasy. You all know your own imperfections. Most people not only know their imperfections – they magnify them and amplify them!"

The words magnify and amplify echoed through Seb's mind.

"Imagine comparing all your imperfections with the unrealistic, photo-shopped, filtered, picture-perfect lives that other people present. If you do that, you'll end up feeling like you're not good enough, and that will become part of your identity. Our identity perpetuates and compounds, like a snowball rolling down a hill, gathering pace and power.

"If you don't feel like you're good enough, everything you hear will sound like a criticism. Regardless of whether it is a criticism or not, that's the way you'll perceive it! And if you always hear criticism, you will feel like you're not good enough. And so, the cycle continues. Unless you break it. Unless you control it. Remember: our identity drives everything."

There was silence as the gravity of Mark's words began to hit home. Seb imagined the possibilities. If he could choose who to become, if he could shape his own character and sculpt his identity, how different could his life be?

Professor Itsen now walked towards the centre of the room and addressed the class.

"During the last few sessions, we have shared some profound and potentially powerful ideas. I suspect your minds are spinning right now. So, I'd like to help pull all of this together for you. During the last session we talked about free will, choice, being authentic and the importance of meaning".

He twisted his grey beard to a point.

"What does all of this mean in our lives? It means that the path to peace and happiness requires three things. Firstly, you need to *be* yourself, which the existential philosophers refer to as 'authenticity'. Secondly, you need to *know* yourself, which Socrates calls 'self-knowledge'. And thirdly, you need to *accept* yourself, like yourself, be proud of yourself."

Easier said than done, thought Seb.

"These ideas are central to a lot of fictional and real-world teachings. When we have these three, we aren't driven by ego, jealousy, or a thirst for power, because we don't need them. When there is an absence of self-knowledge, authenticity and self-acceptance, people often attempt to fill that void by trying to feel successful, or show themselves as successful. Ego tries to fill the hole where self-worth should be.

"When ego is in the driving seat, people crave popularity, wealth, power and control. This, as we have seen, is the path to darkness. It could mean that people become evil but not always. It could mean they experience an inner darkness."

Seb looked around the room. There was a mix of awe and confusion on the faces of his classmates. But, for him, the pieces of the jigsaw seemed to be slotting into place.

"So," Professor Itsen continued, "your next challenge, and the subject of your next assignment, is to answer this question: How can all of this help us uncover the meaning of life?"

There was a collective gasp.

What? Seb thought. *Has he just asked us to decipher the meaning of life? And I thought demon charming was hard.*

"Before you go," Professor Itsen said, with a smile, "to help inspire you, I'm just going to share one person's Choose Life assignment, at random, anonymously, from the top of the pile."

Professor Itsen lifted the A4 sheet that Seb had folded into quarters from the stack. He slid lower into his chair, trying desperately to dissolve into the floor.

Professor Itsen cleared his throat and began.

"Choose Life.

Choose to walk in the woods.

Choose sunrises, sunsets and a glorious dawn chorus.

Choose coffee and cake, and meandering conversations about

nothing in particular with your best friend.

Choose melodies and symphonies.

Choose adventure and challenge and things that scare you.

Choose to laugh.

Choose to live!

Choose meaning and purpose.

Choose to feel proud and to make a difference.

Choose your own path.

Choose demons.

Choose life."

Seb waited for the roars of laughter… but there were none. Instead, someone muttered, "Wow, that's pretty cool!" and a hushed voice asked, "Who wrote that?" He slowly sat back up in his chair as Professor Itsen addressed the class once more.

"Okay, everybody. Please help me thank Mark," he said extending his arm towards his colleague. The class dutifully gave Mark a round of applause.

"Right," said Professor Itsen. "Here endeth the lesson. Citizens – go forth and prosper."

At these words, the class collected up their papers and filed out.

Seb pulled out his phone and texted Alice.

> I didn't mean it how it sounded. Let me by you a cuppa and I'll explain what I meant.

Nothing.

> Please, Alice, don't blank me.

Still nothing.

That hollow feeling returned to the pit of his stomach.

Chapter Fourteen and a half

Dear Jerno

Dear Jerno,

I feel like so much has happened, and yet so little has changed.

I thought the Demon was gone, but it's not gone.

I'm no closer to escaping Malone's web.

I can't play this solo piece and the national finals are looming.

And I think I've lost Alice… and I don't know how to get her back.

I don't know what to do. I followed the Demon Charmers' instructions. I went out to meet it. To be honest, I don't know why I thought it would work in the first place. It's ridiculous!

"Go and meet it.

Get to know it.

Gain its trust.

Solve the problem together."

They don't know what they're talking about!

And who is this Søren bloke?

And how the hell am I supposed to get to Denmark?

I'm not yet 18. I don't have the money. It's not like I can just hop on a plane and disappear off to another country for a few days.

Let's face it… I need a bloody miracle!

By the way, if you have any ideas, let me know.

How to Silence Your Demons

There were loads of ideas that were shared in Seb's philosophy class.
Which ones, in particular, made most sense to you?
How do you think they could help you?

Mark asked the class... "How have you become the person you are?"

What do you think? How have you become the person you are? What choices have you made that have changed who you are today?

Mark also says that we develop our character one choice at a time.

How can this help you become the person you want to be?

Chapter Fifteen

THE BREAKTHROUGH

The next few weeks passed in a blur. With the constant stream of orchestra rehearsals, college, assignments, his own practice sessions, more orchestra rehearsals and late finishes, Seb barely had time to catch his breath. He wasn't making great progress on his own piece, but at least the orchestra was sounding better. Yet he detected a growing sense of frustration. With just a few days to go before the final, Seb found himself struggling in yet another rehearsal.

"Okay, let's take it from the start of that section again," Sophie said, amidst the sighs and moans. Seb could tell that, like everyone else, she was starting to get nervous. The orchestra struck up once more and he counted himself in. He raised the flute to his lips and tried to follow the little path of dots and lines on his music sheet. He knew the notes by now, but somehow it just didn't sound right. The harder he tried, the worse it got. As they finished the piece, one of the clarinet players behind him muttered, "He's not supposed to get it wrong. He's supposed to be a natural."

Seb spun around to face them and the room fell silent.

"You don't get it, do you?" he said, fighting back the emotion. "I'm not a natural. I never have been. I'm not gifted or talented.

This doesn't come easily to me. The truth is, I find this hard."
There was a moment's stunned silence. The trio of clarinet players just looked at each other, as if trying to identify the culprit.

Then Sophie spoke. "But you play so beautifully with so much feeling."

Seb stared at the floor. He may as well tell them. He'd already admitted that he wasn't the amazing musician they all imagined.

"It's just… practice," he replied. "I just keep playing until I get it right." And, ordinarily, he could just keep practising until it came good. He could take as much time as he needed. Normally there were no deadlines. But, as they all knew, time was running out.

"I think that'll do for today, don't you, Sophie?" Colonel Walmsley boomed from the back of the room. "Why don't we take the morning off and come back for our final rehearsal tomorrow evening?"

A little reluctantly, Sophie agreed, and everyone began packing up.

As the room emptied, Gemma wandered over to Seb. He couldn't put his finger on it, but there seemed to be something different about her. Maybe it was the light, but her skin seemed brighter, and her hair shone. The confusion must have been etched on his face.

"You 'kay, Seb?" she asked as she drew closer.

"Uh… yeah," he replied. "It's just… your hair."

Gemma looked horrified. "Wos wrong with it?" she asked.

"Oh, nothing wrong," he replied at once. "It's nice."

Gemma's face lit up. "Oh… fanks," she said, smiling. For a moment, their eyes met and Seb found himself transfixed by their greeny-blue depths.

"I just wondered, like, now we're not rehearsing in the morning, how 'bout you and me, y' know, use that time together?"

"Uh… What?" Seb replied.

"Like Sophie said – practise our duet," she said, as if explaining something to an old person who was losing their marbles.

"Oh, yeah, sorry," he said, as his ears turned crimson. "Yeah, good idea. How about eight o'clock, here?"

"Deal!" she said with a smile and bounded up the steps towards the door.

He stepped out into the cool early evening. The sun had just dipped below the horizon, leaving the trees perfectly silhouetted against an exquisite turquoise-blue glow. There was a gentle whiff of wood smoke on the breeze, from a bonfire on one of the allotments nearby.

In the distance he saw Mark walking down the path towards the music block. He remembered Mark offering to help if he ever needed it and, right now, he needed something. Mark had helped when he'd had his panic attack. Maybe it was worth a shot.

As he got closer, Seb called out, "Uh, Mark?"

Mark looked up and pulled the headphones from his ears. "Ah, Seb," he said. "What a glorious evening!"

"Uh, yeah. Uh… You know you said your door was always open, if I needed it…" Seb didn't quite know how to finish the sentence.

"Sure," Mark replied. "The canteen shouldn't be closed just yet. If you give me a couple of minutes, I'll meet you in there. Mine's a double espresso," he said with a wink.

Seb bought the drinks and wandered over to an empty table as Mark entered the canteen. He placed his coat and scarf on the back of the chair and sat down.

"Well, I probably won't sleep tonight," Mark said. "I don't usually drink coffee this late in the afternoon but… well, you have to fracture the odd rule from time to time. Now, how can I help?"

Seb stared into the murky depths of his own coffee. He wasn't entirely sure how to explain it. He didn't fully understand it himself.

"It's my nerves," he said. "They're getting worse. The national final is at the weekend and I'm nowhere near ready. I'm gonna screw this up, at the Royal Albert Hall, in front of everyone… and I have no idea what to do."

Mark took a sip from his miniature coffee cup. "Can I share something with you?" he asked.

Seb shrugged. "Yeah, sure," he replied.

"I've failed too, a lot, and in public," Mark said. Seb looked up from his coffee cup and caught Mark's gaze. "Once upon a time, many years ago, I was an athlete. I know that might be hard to believe," he said, smiling. "To be precise, I was a fencer. I even made it into the Olympic squad once. But I never achieved my potential. My coaches told me that I could have been a world champion. My fencing was good enough, but my mind let me down." Mark paused and took another sip from his miniature cup.

"Is that why you became a psychologist ?" Seb asked.

"Exactly," Mark said. "I wanted to know how to control my mind and my emotions, rather than allowing them to control me. And I wanted to help other people to control theirs too. I may not have achieved my potential as a fencer, but perhaps I can help other people achieve theirs."

"What are you most nervous about?" Mark asked.

"Failure," said Seb.

"I can remember feeling this crushing sense of pressure," Mark said. "Weirdly, it didn't come from my parents, or coach, or anyone else. It was all self-imposed. I was petrified of failure. At the time I didn't fully understand what was behind it all. Now I can see it all more clearly. The problem was, fencing was the only thing I had ever been good at. So, if I failed at fencing, I thought I had nothing left – there was nowhere to go. I couldn't see a way to be successful. I've learned that there's a huge difference between failing and failure. Failing is what happens if we try something that doesn't work. Failure is how we see ourselves. We don't say 'I am a failing'. We say, 'I am a failure'. It tells us that failure is linked to our identity. That's the bit we're really scared of. That's why I felt the pressure."

"What did you do about it?" asked Seb.

"I learned to see myself as more than just a fencer. I needed to know I wasn't defined by my performance with a sword. It meant knowing myself as a person, not just as an athlete. It took a while, but I got there," Mark said.

"That's pretty much what I'm feeling. I think," Seb mumbled. He steadied himself. He hadn't planned to share any of this, but maybe it would help. "And I'm scared that I'm going to run out of time. I need more practice, I'm not ready, I'm going to let everyone down," he said quietly. "I'm trying so hard, but the harder I try, the worse it seems to get."

Mark gave Seb a wry smile. "I know that feeling too," he said. He took a final sip of his espresso and then pushed the tiny cup and saucer to one side. "That's the irony. We think that trying harder will help. Sometimes it does. Sometimes it doesn't. I learned this the hard way, believe me. Our natural response when we're making mistakes and things are going wrong is to think more and try harder. However, sometimes we need to think less and just… do."

Seb thought about it for a moment.

"You mean I need to stop trying and just… play?" he asked.

Mark nodded knowingly. "For years, I didn't truly understand what that meant," Mark said.

"No mind," Seb whispered to himself.

"Go on," Mark said.

"Oh… I did it in my audition. I just let go and played. But… how? How was I able to just let go and lose myself in the music?"

"How much do you love this piece of music?" Mark asked.

Seb sighed. "It's a great piece but, to be honest, I'm not really connecting with it."

"Then that would be my invitation to you," Mark said. "Connect with this piece, find meaning in it, make it yours, fall in love with it! Have fun… Enjoy… Play!"

Perhaps Mark was right. He'd been taking this all very seriously. He'd been practising so hard. He was desperate not to let anyone down. Maybe he had lost the enjoyment. It seemed that Mark sensed this too.

"I use the word 'play' very deliberately," Mark said. "I'm inviting you to *play*… not *perform* this piece. Play like you did when you were a child. Play like no one is watching or listening. Play with freedom. Fall in love with *playing* again."

Mark was right. The pieces that he played really well, with real passion, were all tunes that he loved. Mark checked his watch.

"I'll leave you with that," he said as he got to his feet. As Mark stood up, a torrent of thoughts flooded Seb's mind. Malone… the Demon… getting to Denmark… finding this bloke Søren … Alice… It was overwhelming.

"How can I control the voice in my head?" Seb blurted out.

Mark stood for a moment considering the question. "Who does the voice belong to?" he asked.

"The Demon," replied Seb immediately.

Mark looked earnestly at him and asked again, "Whose voice is it really?"

Seb stared into his coffee cup.

"I hear my mum's disappointment. I hear my teachers at school, telling me I'll never amount to anything… and the football coach who laughed at me… and Buster Johnson bullying me in year eight… they're all in there. So, it must be their voices, right?"

"What do you think?" Mark asked.

Seb's brain was beginning to ache. Why couldn't Mark just give him a straight answer?

"Do you hear *every* comment that has *ever* been said to you echoing back through the voice in your head? Do you hear *everything* your mum has ever said, or *everything* your teachers have said?" Mark asked.

"No," Seb replied. "Just a few things… just the things that stung."

"So it can't be their voice. Someone must have selected certain words or phrases and started replaying these back through your mind. Someone has given these thoughts and memories a voice. Who does the voice really belong to?"

Seb examined his coffee cup once more.

"Me," he whispered as understanding enveloped him. "It's my voice… The Demon is imaginary, but it's like a vivid dream. It appears real but it's part of *my reality* not *the reality*… so I can control it."

There was a moment's pause.

"What about the other voice, then?" Seb said.

"Which voice?" Mark asked.

Seb looked at him, a little surprised. He hadn't realised he'd asked that question out loud.

"The quiet one," Seb said, staring at the last dregs of his coffee.

"What does it say?" asked Mark.

"It's kinda the opposite to the Demon. A bit of advice, encouragement," Seb said.

"And when do you hear this voice?"

Seb paused to think.

"When all the noise has died down… and the chattering stops," he muttered.

Mark smiled. "It sounds very much like your inner wisdom," he said. "In my experience it's always there, trying to guide us, but its voice is easily drowned out by the chaos in our heads. Only when we find stillness and peace do we hear it."

Seb nodded to himself as he tried to digest it all. He'd never thought of it like that, but now that he did, it all seemed to make sense.

"You'll go far, Seb Hall," Mark said.

***

Seb lay on his bed, in the dark, staring at the ceiling. How was he supposed to fall in love with this piece of music? He'd been playing it over and over for weeks. In fact, because he'd been struggling, he'd even started to resent it a little. Mark was right. He needed to connect with it. He needed to fall in love with it. But how?

He was just about to give up, when his mind offered him a rather bizarre suggestion.

Why don't you ask your demon? It worked last time.

Seb smiled. What is a demon going to know about playing in an orchestra? It didn't even know what a flute was. On the other hand, what did he have to lose? He remembered the Demon Charmers' four steps and sighed.

I suppose this qualifies as 'getting to know it', he thought as he rolled out of bed and rummaged on the floor for his shoes.

He stepped into the chilly night air. The moonless sky was now inky black. He strode up the lane and across the field, marvelling at the millions of stars shining down. When he was a boy, his dad had explained how each one was a sun, just like our own sun, that had been burning for millions of years. Some of them were so far away that they'd actually burned out, but their light was still travelling towards us. He remembered being amazed that the light he was seeing right now left those stars millions of years ago. And how, as he looked at these tiny dots in the sky, he was actually looking back in time.

He passed into the woodland. It was almost pitch black and his foot slipped as he stepped onto the muddy path.

Mmmmm… No mist, he thought. *No sudden gust of wind.*

Seb picked his way carefully along the winding path through the wood until he found his thinking spot. He climbed upon the smooth rock and sat motionless. What now?

He closed his eyes. Nothing.

"Timidus. Are you there?" he asked.

I'm always here, in your head, came the response. *I'm not sure why you come all the way out here to find me.*

"Good point," Seb conceded.

There was something different about the Demon's voice. It was not the vicious growl he was used to. It sounded more like his own voice… like he was talking to himself.

"I need your help again," Seb pressed on.

With the bully? it asked.

"No, with the orchestra," Seb replied. "There's this piece I need to play at the national final. It's a huge deal for everyone – they've worked so hard for it. I've got this duet to play with Gemma and I'm just not getting it. The final is only a few days away and… I'm scared. I just know I'm going to let everyone down."

Hmmmm, came the reply. *So… you're not scared of the bully who could beat you to a pulp, but you are scared of letting your friends down.*

"Uh, yeah," Seb replied. "I hadn't thought about it like that."

So, what's the problem with this music? Timidus asked.

"I've got to play a vocal piece on the flute. It's a bit tricky. I can play the notes, that's not the difficult bit. I also need to play with Gemma, which is a little more difficult, but we can do that if we spend a bit of time practising together. The problem is, I need to connect with it… to fall in love with it. I mean, I do really like it, it's a great piece, but at the moment I'm not feeling it. When I play well, I don't just hear the music, I don't just play it with my flute… I feel it. I play it from my soul," Seb replied.

Seb now saw the faint outline of the Demon in his mind's eye. Gradually it became clearer. Horns, skull, eyes. Then, its fiery eyes fixed him with such intensity that Seb felt he was being X-rayed.

What does it mean? asked the Demon.

"What does what mean?" Seb replied.

The Demon shook its head in frustration.

You said it was a vocal piece. What does the lyric of the song mean? What is the singer singing?

He'd only been so worried about the tune. He had no idea what the lyrics were, or what they meant.

"That's it!" cried Seb in delight. "You're a genius!"

A broad smile crossed the Demon's face and it disappeared from view.

Seb's eyes snapped open and he jumped down from the rock.

"Thank you," he said slightly breathlessly. "That's the answer. I need to sing this through the flute. When I know the lyrics, I can play it with meaning."

***

He was barely through his bedroom door when he pulled out his phone and began searching for the lyrics to "Exogenesis Symphony Part 1". He hit the link, scrolled down the page and began reading them aloud.

As he heard his own voice reading the words, something stirred deep within him. These lyrics meant something to him. They talked of freedom, breaking the grip of oppression, creating your own path and of discovering who you truly are. He thought of Malone, his fears, disappointing his mum. He yearned to be free, to just be himself. He felt it too. All of a sudden understanding rose within him. The philosophy lectures with Professor Itsen and Mark, his Choose Life piece… it was all coming together.

He found the tune on his phone and hit play. Notes filled the room. He heard the emotion in the vocal, the cries of confusion, desperation, pleading and anguish, all mirroring his own emotions. A tear rolled down his cheek. It was not a tear of sadness but of understanding.

He truly felt this piece of music. He had connected.

With a broadening grin, he picked up his flute and began to play. On and on, into the night, connecting his notes with the meaning and the emotion of the music. His parents must have banged on his bedroom door a dozen times, but he didn't care.

At some point in the early hours, he placed his flute back on its stand and slumped into bed.

***

He woke to the sound of his name echoing up the staircase.

"Seb... SEB!" his mum shrieked. "Aren't you supposed to be at a rehearsal this morning?"

Slowly, his dazed mind began to process the question.

"Uh… it's okay, Mum. We've got the morning off," he replied, yawning.

He rolled over to catch sight of the time on his alarm clock. The large green numbers stared at him from behind their dusty screen: 07.14. Seb plumped up his pillow and laid his head down. He'd just started drifting back to sleep when his eyes snapped open, and he sat up with a jolt.

"Gemma!" he yelled.

"What?" came his mum's voice from downstairs.

"I've got to meet Gemma!"

His mum's footsteps echoed up the stairs. "Who is Gemma?" she asked from the other side of his bedroom door. Seb knew that tone. This was no innocent enquiry.

"My duet partner," he replied flatly.

"Ahhhh," she said, sounding thoroughly unconvinced. "Well, if you want a lift in to meet this Gemma girl, you'd better get your skates on. I'm leaving in six minutes."

Seb jumped out of bed, threw on some clothes and thundered down the stairs just in time.

At two minutes past eight, he burst through the door into the music room. He looked a mess. His jacket was falling off his shoulders, his bag hanging off his arm, his hair all over the place and he was gasping for breath. Gemma turned to greet him. She looked immaculate, like she'd just stepped out of a beauty salon. Her sheet music was propped on its stand. Her electric violin was plugged in and ready to play.

"Hey Seb, I was just gonna text. You 'kay?" she asked as she caught sight of him. He nodded, still trying desperately to catch his breath.

"Sorry… slept in… practising 'til late… two seconds," he muttered between breaths. Hastily, he pieced together his flute. He could have sworn that as he did so, Gemma's eyes kept flicking across to him. No… he must have imagined it.

"Okay, ready," he said after a few moments of fumbling.

Gemma looked at him serenely. "I'll count you in," she said. "One… two…."

Seb lifted the flute, closed his eyes and began to play. He imagined himself singing the lyrics, living every word, feeling the anguish. As he reached the climax of his first section, he heard the deep growl of her electric violin. For a few seconds their notes blended before Seb tailed off and Gemma took over. He stood, eyes closed, absorbing each vibration, sensing the moment when he would re-join their musical conversation.

He raised his flute… and sang.

For a split second, he didn't realise that he was actually singing. The high clear note in his head sounded very different from the tuneless croak that left his mouth. Gemma's bow slipped on the strings and her violin screeched indignantly. His eyes opened with a start. Gemma stood open mouthed. For a moment neither of them knew what to do or say.

Then he burst out laughing. A relieved smile broke across her face and they both melted into a fit of giggles.

As he laughed, all his stress seemed to drop away, like shackles he was shaking off. He felt free for the first time in as long as he could remember.

Gradually the laughter subsided. Seb opened his eyes and caught Gemma's gaze. He was lost in their bluey-green depths once more. She was beautiful. For a fleeting moment he imagined himself kissing her.

Don't be stupid. Why would she want to kiss you?

There was a moment of silence. He gave an awkward half-smile.

"Uh… Let's try that again," Gemma suggested. Seb's brain was frozen, and his gormless expression seemed to convey this. "Seb… Shall we play that section again?" Gemma asked.

"Oh, yeah, sure," Seb replied, as the cogs in his head began turning again.

They played the piece a few more times. Something had just clicked. It sounded like a duet, played with feeling.

"I think we're ready, don't you?" he said with a blend of satisfaction and relief.

"Yeah, I reckon we are," she said a little sheepishly.

Seb smiled. Something had changed between them in that moment. It was like they'd crossed a threshold and could not go back.

The final rehearsal was the best they'd had. The piece was really coming together. It was not only Seb's vocal piece, or the duet with Gemma. The whole orchestra sounded much better. The opening bars from the strings were more elegant. The brass was deeper and darker. The whole piece just seemed to have more depth and purpose.

As they finished the final rendition, Sophie looked out across the orchestra.

"Thank you, everyone," she said. "Thank you for all your hard work. This has not been easy, I know, but you sound really good.

All we can do now is play to the best of our ability on Saturday...
and leave the rest to the judges. The coach leaves for London at 6
a.m. Don't be late!"

How to Silence Your Demons

Mark shares his experiences of feeling under pressure. He realised that the pressure he felt was self-imposed.
When do you feel under pressure?
Where do you think it comes from?

Do you have a 'quiet voice'?
What does yours say?
How could you tap into it more often?

Chapter Sixteen

THE FINAL

Hundreds of students, each laden with musical instruments, ascended the steep stone staircase in front of the Royal Albert Hall. On either side of them, rows of majestic wrought-iron street lamps stood guard. At the summit, the jet-black statue of Prince Albert, his cape draped from his shoulders, surveyed the scene. Behind him, the immense, domed building rose like a Roman amphitheatre, its regal colours shining in the morning sunlight. Deep earthy red walls. Gold window and door frames.

Beneath the huge glass domed roof, there was a story being told in pictures. It reminded Seb of the Bayeux tapestry he'd once seen on a school trip to France. Gold figures stood against a terracotta canvas. Farmers bringing their livestock to market. A peasant kneeling before a nobleman and the bustle of daily life a time long ago.

The sea of students flowed behind the statue. Seb and the others were swept along with the crowd. They passed between the great pillars, through the huge arched entrance and into the auditorium.

As the scene unfolded, his heart stopped. He stood, awestruck, in the middle of a huge oval arena. Row upon row of opulent red seats rose on all sides, broken only by the tiered stage at the far end. Above these seats were two layers of grand boxes, with their majestic golden dressings. These, as Seb knew, contained the most expensive seats in the house. The circle towered above them. And finally, beneath the magnificent glass domed ceiling, the gallery seats nestled high in the rafters.

"Wow... How many people does this place hold?" Melissa asked.

"Over five and a half thousand," said Seb.

"Wait... what?" said Gemma, who'd just appeared by his side. "Did you say five and a half thousand? That's insane!"

Imagine screwing up in front of that many people, came the echo through Seb's mind.

Seb gulped. Judging by the looks of trepidation on the faces of a few others, he was not alone.

"Right, this way," Colonel Walmsley boomed over the hubbub. He pointed out a sign bearing the words "Yeoborough College – North Region" and led the students over to their seats. Gradually, the melee began to subside. Seb found a spot on the end of the row and sat down. Through the crowd he noticed Gemma and Melissa jostling as they walked over. As they got closer, Gemma pushed her shoulder in front and made for the seat next to him.

"Hey, Seb," she said slightly breathlessly. Melissa shot her an evil look. "This place is e-pic," Gemma continued.

"Uh, yeah," he replied, still puzzling over what he'd just seen. "What's going on between you two?"

"Oh, nuffin'," she replied, slightly unconvincingly. "Not important."

"Right... Calm down everyone," Colonel Walmsley called over the din, his moustache bristling. "There are seven regions here today. We're representing the north, obviously." He was interrupted by a cheer from the brass section. "There are colleges from the south, east and west of England, plus Scotland, Wales and Northern Ireland," he continued. "We have been drawn last.

So, as the sixth college takes the stage, we'll need to start getting ready. Until then, relax and enjoy the other performances."

Seb cast his eyes around the vast auditorium. It was filling fast. The mass of red seats were replaced by thousands of people, all dressed in their finest attire and chattering excitedly. It seemed that none of them shared his growing sense of dread.

To his right, the first orchestra took the stage, followed by the master of ceremonies, a very small gentleman wearing a smart black suit, crisp white shirt and black bow tie. He adjusted his small round spectacles and tapped the microphone. This was it. All of a sudden, it was starting to feel very real. His stomach churned ominously.

"It gives me great pleasure to welcome you all today," the master of ceremonies said, "especially the orchestras. Well done for having made it this far, it is a wonderful achievement. However, as you know, there can only be one winner. The honour of representing the United Kingdom at the world championships, in Copenhagen, awaits the successful college."

There was a collective gasp from the audience.

Did he just say Copenhagen? The capital of Denmark?

A cauldron of acid boiled in the pit of his stomach. Not only was he carrying the hopes and dreams of the college but, he now realised, this was his only route to Denmark and a meeting with Søren. He sank into his seat.

"It gives me great pleasure," announced the master of ceremonies, "to introduce the southern regional winners, performing a piece entitled 'Victory', written by their own musical director. Ladies and gentlemen, please welcome Anchester College!"

Following a polite ripple of applause, Anchester struck up and played their very powerful, almost triumphant number with real enthusiasm. They were followed by Sedwell, representing the west, then the Welsh Champions, Llangellen . College after college delivered their brilliant performances. With each one, Seb's small glimmer of hope faded. How on earth were they going to win? They'd have to play better than ever. They needed a miracle. Somehow, he needed to conjure some magic from somewhere. But how? The colour drained from his face, and he began to feel sick.

"You 'kay, Seb?" asked Gemma.

"Fine," he mumbled.

"You got this," she said. Unfortunately, that really didn't help.

Everyone expects you to be great. They're all relying on you.

The words rumbled like thunder, trapped in his skull.

As the fourth college finished their piece and received their applause, he croaked, "Gents," then dashed up the stairs towards the toilets.

He raced up the corridor, pushed open the door and dived for the nearest sink. He felt sick, but nothing seemed to be moving. He ran the cold tap and splashed some water over his face. As he did so, Seb saw the weirdly distorted image of himself, staring back from the gleaming surface of the taps. He could see the fear in his own eyes. And then reality hit.

This fear was imaginary. It had all bubbled up inside his own mind. What was he scared of? There was no monster out there… no fire-breathing demon waiting to incinerate him. What had Colonel Walmsley said at the cathedral all those weeks ago?

Your job is not to win, it's just to play this piece as well as you can.

That's it. All he had to do was play his flute. He'd dreamed of playing here for as long as he could remember. And here he was… at the Royal Albert Hall… in the toilets… staring at a tap.

He had to focus on the process and let the outcome take care of itself. That was exactly what Mark would be saying. His job was not to win, or to produce some miraculous solo, or to impress everyone. He just needed to play the way he played in his bedroom, and the way Gemma and he played in the music room. Oh… And enjoy it! Enjoy the moment. Immerse himself in his surroundings… and the music… and the meaning. Play! That's where the magic comes from.

Seb smiled. Maybe he was starting to get the hang of this. He closed his eyes and felt the smile grow somewhere deep within him.

Okay… Let's go do this!

The next college were in full flow as Seb returned to his seat. He was met by Gemma's anxious expression.

"You 'kay?" she mouthed at him when she caught his eye.

He winked and smiled. "Ready!" he mouthed back.

On Colonel Walmsley's cue, they made their way to the stage. Seb glanced across at Gemma, who looked like he felt a few moments earlier. She had an almost ghostly look and he half expected her to decorate the stage in vomit. He leaned towards her and said quietly, "It's just you and me. Just you and me in the music room together." Gemma looked up, her eyes glistening, and thanked him with a smile.

Sophie climbed onto the rostrum and the enormous room fell silent. The master of ceremonies took the microphone and cleared his throat.

"And now," he announced with a squeak, "to cap off this magnificent event, representing the North of England and playing a piece entitled 'Exogenesis Symphony Part One'… by a rock band, called… Muse," he said, as if not quite believing it, "Please welcome, Yeoborough College."

He stepped from the stage to another round of polite applause. The lights faded. Sophie raised her baton and counted them in. The sharp high notes of the violins and violas rose gradually, breaking the silence. Then the rumble of the drums and the growl of the brass in the background. And finally, the rest of the strings, cellos and double bass, their deep voices carrying across the vast auditorium, wave after wave. Seb was carried along. In the distance he heard the beat building, announcing his arrival. He raised his flute.

A sweet solemn note rose into the air, followed by another. He heard the lyrics in his mind. He felt their meaning and the emotion echoing through the notes... their anguish... their confusion... lost and alone... yearning and pleading. As he reached the peak, Gemma's notes joined his; embracing and entwining, they danced their tragic duet. He lowered his flute, eyes still closed, as Gemma took the lead. He thought ahead to the next lyrics. "I can't forgive you. And I can't forget." The feeling changed. Anguish and confusion morphed into anger and resentment. He lifted his flute and translated emotion into sound. Gradually the waves began to subside, and the piece came to its smouldering finish.

As his last note trailed away, there was a moment's stunned silence. No one dared to breathe. Seb looked up, not quite knowing what to make of it. Five and a half thousand stunned faces looked back across the expanse of the auditorium. Then it began. A small smattering of applause that grew. It built, louder and louder, until the whole of the audience was on its feet clapping and cheering.

Seb exhaled, quite unaware that he'd been holding his breath. He looked around at the rest of the orchestra. Relief seemed to have crashed like a tsunami over them. Sophie looked like a puppet whose strings had been cut, slumped over the lectern with a huge smile on her face. Colonel Walmsley stood at the side of the stage, applauding. The rest of the orchestra were on their feet. There were high fives and fist pumps and hugging. He saw Gemma, eyes swimming with tears, and was hit by that surge of electricity again.

What is this feeling? Could it be...? No, surely not.

The master of ceremonies stepped back up to the microphone and asked Yeoborough to retake their seats. There would be a short recess while the judges made their decisions and then they'd announce the winner.

As they dutifully made their way back to their seats, Melissa whispered into his ear, "Hey, cutie."

She was so close, he felt her breath on the back of his neck. He spun around in surprise, almost knocking the pair of them off their feet. Melissa looked mildly amused.

"That was some performance," she continued, her voice hushed. "Fancy celebrating later?"

She gave him a seductive look, which left him in little doubt what she meant by the word "celebrate". He stood gawping in response, which seemed to fuel Melissa's amusement.

"See you later, then," she said, gliding off to her seat.

The master of ceremonies reappeared on the stage, just as the last of the students took their seats. He needlessly straightened his spectacles and stared down at the small piece of card in his hand, which can't have carried more than a handful of words.

"This has been a truly fantastic event," he said. "The standard has been phenomenal. As I said at the outset, there can only be one winner. However, it gives me great pleasure to recognise the supreme performances of the colleges in second and third places as well. So, in third place, representing Northern Ireland… Balleymowen College!"

The audience applauded generously and Balleymowen took a bow.

"And in second place," continued the master of ceremonies, "representing the East of England… Kings Markham College!"

Seb noticed the cocktail of pride and disappointment etched onto the faces of the Kings Markham students and teachers. He'd never finished second. Before the regional heat, Seb couldn't remember finishing anywhere above dismal… in anything. He'd always thought of second place as a fantastic achievement. Now, though, he could see why they would have mixed feelings.

"And our winners… who will be representing the United Kingdom at the world championships next month…" he announced, pausing for dramatic effect, "… Yeoborough College!"

The Royal Albert Hall disappeared behind a mass of bodies and squeals of joy. Gemma grabbed Seb and pulled him tight. With a little effort, he freed his arms and wrapped them clumsily around her. The chaos and the din of the celebrations seemed to recede into the distance. He could smell her hair and the subtle aroma of her perfume. And for a glorious moment, all became peaceful and still.

"Ha ha ha," came the burst of laughter in his ear as the brass section engulfed them both. He'd watched footballers on the TV celebrating when they scored a goal. He'd always thought it must feel amazing, to be in the middle of it all, receiving the congratulations. Ironically, now he was here, all he wanted was to be alone with Gemma.

Eventually he emerged from the mass of bodies and regained his senses. Then it hit him.

He was going to Denmark.

He was going to meet Søren.

How to Silence Your Demons

Seb and the others feel overwhelmed when they walk into the Royal Albert Hall.
Have you ever felt like this?
If you were in a similar situation, how would you deal with it?

Seb remembers the advice he got from Colonel Walmsley and Mark. He just has to stay in the moment and focus on the process.
What does this mean to you?
How could the same advice help you?

Chapter Seventeen

THE MEANING OF LIFE

"Good morning, philosophers," said Professor Itsen as the classroom door swung closed behind him. "Those of you with good memories may recall the small challenge that I set at the end of the last session… to explore the meaning of life," he said as he walked to the front of the room. But, far from relishing the prospect, Seb was starting to feel rather daunted by it. Judging by the expressions on the faces of his fellow students, he wasn't alone. Perhaps Professor Itsen had noticed too. He assumed his customary half standing, half sitting position on the edge of the table.

"Towards the end of the last session, we talked about the reason many people seek power and control," he began. "Typically, it is a result of their own insecurities. Some of you may have seen this reflected in your own lives. If you've ever bullied someone, or been bullied by someone, it is likely that you've experienced exactly this. Bullying in its various forms, whether it's physical, verbal or emotional, is often one person's attempt to make themselves feel superior by making someone else feel inferior. It's an attempt to feel power and control. And, as we have discovered, the reason many people *need* to feel powerful, successful, popular or in control is because there is a hole inside them. They don't feel like they are enough… they don't feel good enough… they are not happy with who they are.

People also use bullying to create a sense of belonging. Bullies often target someone and ostracise them. They create a little hate club… something to belong to. They become the leaders, so they can be right at the heart of it. But, why do they do it? Why do have this overwhelming need to belong, that drives them to do this? Maybe, without their little gang, they would feel like a sheep without the safety of a flock. Which brings us back to insecurity."

Professor Itsen paused, before continuing.

"Today, I'd like to build on this understanding, as we start exploring the meaning of life. You have all read books, watched movies, met interesting people, had conversations, seen things, done things and lived a life full of experiences. So… what do you think so far? What is the meaning of life?"

You could hear a pin drop in the classroom. Beyond the fifth-floor window, Seb heard the rumble of traffic on the main road at the bottom of the hill. A crow cawed from the canopy of a nearby tree. But no one spoke. Professor Itsen didn't break the silence either. It was a few moments before anyone ventured a thought.

"Professor," said Dan Lewis, "I read a book by the Dalai Lama once. He says the meaning of life is to be happy. It made sense to me."

"That's a very good start to our discussion," Professor Itsen replied. "Would anyone agree… or disagree? Does that sound reasonable?" A few hands crept into the air. "Yes, Robert."

"I heard some dude on a YouTube clip once talking about how we all go towards pleasure and away from pain. He was, like, some kind of personal development dude that my mum was watching. She's a bit sad like that." Robert's revelation was met with chuckles from around the classroom.

"It seems reasonable on the surface, doesn't it? But can anyone see where this might not work… Where humans actively approach fear and pain?" Professor Itsen said.

Seb thought for a moment about his decision to walk back into the woods, to face a demon that had tried to incinerate him on several occasions and threatened to eat him. He wouldn't describe that as "approaching pleasure and avoiding pain". In fact, it was the opposite. But, unsurprisingly, he didn't feel like sharing that particular example with his philosophy class.

"War," came the familiar voice of Jonny Martyn from the back of the room.

Professor Itsen nodded his approval. "Go on," he replied.

"Well… people go to war knowing that they are walking into hell. They know they're likely to be killed or injured. They know it will be painful… and yet they do it willingly," Jonny explained.

"You're absolutely right, Jonny," said Professor Itsen, beaming at him. "But why?" The professor stood up, slid his hands into his cardigan pockets and began pacing in front of the white board.

"Why throughout the course of human history have we done this?" he asked. Again, there was stunned silence, while the gravity of the question sunk in. Slowly, Seb's hand began to rise. Professor Itsen nodded his invitation.

"It's for the cause for freedom. People fight for their freedom, whether it's fighting in a war or… or for a civil rights movement. People sacrifice happiness for freedom. So… is that it? Is that the meaning of life… freedom?" Seb asked.

"Splendid! Now we're starting to think!" Professor Itsen said. "Take a moment and consider this. Ask yourself why we humans do the things we do. Why do people strive to gain money and wealth? What's it for? What do they believe money will bring them? Why do people seek power? What do they believe it will do for them?"

Now Seb's mind was whirring. He started to see jigsaw pieces falling into place. Without really thinking, he began to answer Professor Itsen's question aloud.

"It's the illusion of freedom. We think that wealth and power and control will give us freedom. We imagine that if we had more money, we would have more choice to buy what we want, go where we want, whenever we want. We imagine that power will give us the freedom to control the world around us. Perhaps people think that having power means they won't have to answer to anyone else. Maybe that's why some people become obsessed with the idea of ruling the world. Maybe they think they can design the world the way they want it, wipe away all those things they hate about life, change the rules in their favour. Or maybe people think they can design *their* world, I mean, the world around them, the way they want it…"

Seb paused to take a breath and allow his thoughts to catch up with him. Professor Itsen seemed quite content to let him keep going. Perhaps he could sense the lightbulbs that were beginning to illuminate inside Seb's head.

"But it doesn't work," Seb continued. "In fact… it's the opposite. The lust for wealth and power and control imprisons us. Is that why kings and queens lived in fortified castles, and why multi-billionaires have mansions with huge walls and gates? Instead of feeling free, they become scared… scared of losing their wealth, scared of losing the power." He paused as the full impact of his words hit him. "People fear losing their power. Freedom comes when we let go of the need for power and let go of those things we're scared of losing," he said quietly.

Professor Itsen looked towards Seb and smiled.

"Such wisdom from one so young," he whispered. "Here's a thought for you," Professor Itsen said to the class. "There are people in prison who are free. And people who wander the earth but are imprisoned. What do you think I mean?"

Silence. Then Jeremy Brown raised his hand.

"Does it mean people have stopped choosing, stopped thinking for themselves?" he asked. "They live their lives like they're asleep... or on autopilot... like some kind of zombie."

"That's very insightful indeed, Mr Brown," Professor Itsen replied. Out the corner of his eye, Seb saw Amy's hand go up.

"I was thinking about this," she said breathlessly. "I think it means they're, like, you know... trapped inside their own heads. Not trapped by, like, walls or bars or whatever. It's like they are imprisoned by their own fears, or insecurities, or something. I reckon they make their own boundaries, set their own limits. It's like we were talking about last time. This is their prison and until they break out, they will never be free."

Professor Itsen looked like he might burst with pride. "Superb!" he exclaimed, clapping his hands together. "Let's take a moment to consider some of the really profound messages in the stories we have been studying. For example, when Harry Potter becomes 'master of death', he does so not by owning the Deathly Hallows, but by choosing to face death. In *The Lord of the Rings*, Lady Arwen did something similar when she chose a mortal life, rather than immortality, so that she could be with the man she loved. She chose to really live and to love, which meant that she would die rather than remain immortal."

He walked over to his desk and picked up a small book. On the cover was a small bird perched on barbed wire.

"In, *Man's Search for Meaning*, Viktor Frankl talks of 'the last of our human freedoms', the freedom to choose how we think and feel in any circumstance. He found freedom in one of the most horrific prisons ever created – Auschwitz. If it's possible there, I suspect it's possible anywhere. These stories also tell us that when we do find this freedom, we unlock our true potential. In the movies, our heroes and heroines discover their superpowers. In *Captain Marvel*, Carol Danvers needs to find her true self and refuse to be controlled in order to release her superpowers. It's the same for Neo in *The Matrix*. But it's not just true in these stories. Heroes and heroines in real life often have the same challenge. Think back to the lives of Nelson Mandela, Marie Curie, Martin Luther-King and many others. They had a similar challenge. They all needed to step beyond their boundaries, fears, doubts and insecurities to find true freedom and unlock their potential – their superpowers."

Professor Itsen resumed his position on the edge of his desk.

"I'm going to give you time to let all of this sink in. By all means, take a few minutes to chat amongst yourselves before beginning your next challenge. Feel free to use the time remaining in this session as well as your own time to answer the following question: What does all of this mean to you and your life? How can *you* find freedom? How can you unlock your superpowers?"

And with that, Professor Itsen gave them all a broad smile and left the room.

***

Seb turned out of the main building and headed to the music block for the first world championship rehearsal. The whole thing still seemed quite surreal. His mind could not compute that they, Yeoborough, a very modest college from a small market town in North Yorkshire, were going to play at the world championships. As he turned the corner and walked up the small flagstone path toward the music department, he came face to face with Melissa.

"We never did get to celebrate, did we?" she said in that dangerously seductive voice. "Shame," she said, her dark hair gleaming in the afternoon sunlight. "Looks like we might have missed our chance. He wants to see you. Straight after this. You know where."

For a moment she considered him. Her eyes searched almost every line and shadow of his face. Her intense glare, a cocktail of lust and hatred. Seb didn't know whether she was preparing to slap him or kiss him. She did neither. With a flick of her hair, she turned and marched towards the music room door, leaving him utterly perplexed.

There was a palpable crackle of excitement in the music room. The brass section warmed up with a few bars of "We Are the Champions" by Queen, which was very well received by the rest of the orchestra. Sophie let the exuberance continue for a few minutes.

"Okay, okay, that'll do now," she called over the hubbub. "Thank you," she said, as the noise finally subsided. "Does anyone want to know the brief for the world championships?" Her words sparked another round of excited chatter.

"Calm down, everyone," Colonel Walmsley said loudly from his usual spot at the back of the room. Sophie gave a weak smile and continued.

"We have been challenged to perform," she began, looking down at the notes in her hand, "a medley composed of at least three pieces, lasting between six and ten minutes, and not written by a classical composer."

Her words were met by audible gasps.

"Now," Sophie continued, "we don't have very long to get this all together. The world championship is in less than five weeks' time. So, I suggest we decide upon the music today. Colonel Walmsley and I will get your sheet music together overnight and we'll start working on it all tomorrow morning." She paused, looking around the room.

"Does anyone have any ideas?" she asked. Her question was met with silence. "It's a tough challenge, I know," she said, "but it's the world championships, so I guess that's to be expected." More silence. Then Gemma raised her hand.

"Yes, Gemma," said Sophie with a note of relief.

"Can we play show tunes... ya know... like, from West End musicals?" she asked.

Sophie shook her head. "No, I don't think we'll get away with show tunes or movie themes," she replied.

Seb wracked his brains. An idea began to form and his hand rose into the air.

"Seb?" Sophie asked, without hiding the surprise in her voice.

"My dad used to play this dance music... I think he called it 'trance' or something. He used to listen to it when he was at Uni, so I'm guessing it must be ancient." There was a ripple of laughter that seemed to break the tension in the room. "He played it once in the car when we were on a long drive together and, while he was embarrassing himself doing all this dad dancing behind the wheel, I started wondering if an orchestra could play it. I remember a remix of Barber's 'Adagio for Strings'. It was a dance version of a classical tune. I wondered if you could... 'de-mix' these tunes. You know, do the opposite – turn dance tunes into classical pieces." He looked up at Sophie, who seemed to be either confused or disappointed in his answer. "It could be a shit idea, though," he said quickly.

"No!" replied Sophie hastily. "No, it's not a bad idea at all. You might be onto something there."

Hurriedly, she pulled out her phone, connected it to the Bluetooth speaker, selected a tune and pressed play. A series of rhythmic electronic bleeps issued from the speaker, gradually building into a tune.

"This is called 'Resurrection'. Use your imagination for a moment. Slow it down by half, hear the tune that sings from beneath the beats. See if you can turn electronic notes into the notes you would play," Sophie said. "This part... violins and violas," she said as the tune picked up momentum. "Brass provides the background. Percussion pick up the beat. Cellos, those rhythmic waves." Sophie picked up her baton and began conducting an imaginary orchestra in front of her. As she did so, she brought each section into the piece. As it played on, comprehension began to dawn on a few of the faces around him. Others, however, seemed completely lost. This hadn't escaped Sophie's notice either.

"Okay," she said after a little while. "Have a listen to these two pieces." She searched on her phone for a moment and then hit play. "This is called '1998', by a dance act called Binary Finery." They listened to the complex blend of beats, with an unmistakeable melody in the background.

"Now," Sophie said as she selected a different track from her phone. "Listen to this… This, too, is '1998', by a rock band called Peace," she explained. "It's essentially the same tune, but interpreted and presented differently." He could see people nodding as the idea began to sink in.

"Oh, and this," she said excitedly. "This is a classical interpretation by Lowland." Judging by the nods and muttering from around the room, it seemed that understanding was starting to dawn on everyone now.

Lost in her own thoughts, she grabbed her phone again and began rifling through tracks, playing them through the bubblegum pink speaker. One after another, the beats pumped out into the room. Occasionally, she would skip one saying "No, not that one" or "Mmmmm, maybe" or "That's a keeper". At the end of a frantic half-hour, she turned back to the orchestra and said, "Okay… I think three or four tunes will be enough for around eight minutes of performance. What does everyone think?"

She looked like an astronomer who had just discovered a brand new planet. Even if anyone did have reservations, Seb was pretty sure it would have been washed away by Sophie's enthusiasm. She answered the few nods and murmurs by saying, "Great… We'll see you all in the morning. Sleep well!"

And with that, they filed out.

With all the excitement, Seb had almost forgotten about his impending meeting with Malone. But his smile soon faded as he trudged towards the sports hall. What had Malone got in store for him this time? A sinking feeling began to grip the pit of his stomach. And then he caught himself.

There's no point in worrying about it. I'll find out in a few minutes anyway.

As he turned the corner at the bottom of the design block and headed up the shaded alleyway to the shabby sports hall entrance, another thought hit him. This was his opportunity. This is what Timidus had been talking about. It was a chance to set a trap for Malone.

But how?

Without realising it, he quickened his pace. He pushed open the tatty old sports hall door and stood tall in the doorway. Malone looked around in surprise. It took him a moment to recognise Seb, perhaps because he was silhouetted in the doorway. Or, maybe, because he actually looked taller. Malone puffed out his chest.

"Get in here," he barked. Seb stood in the doorway motionless. For a second or two, Malone seemed unnerved by his lack of response.

"Or have you forgotten about your accident-prone little friend, Alice?" he sneered.

A wave of anger rose within Seb but he forced himself to quell it. He could not do anything to endanger her. Reluctantly, he walked towards Malone.

"No, I haven't forgotten," he replied through clenched teeth.

"Good," said Malone as he squared up to him. When Seb stood to his full height, there was not a lot of difference between them. And while Malone was a lot more muscular, Seb had obviously begun to fill out since their first encounter in the corridor all those months ago. All of a sudden, he felt that he was genuinely looking Malone in the eye.

"I have an assignment for you," Malone announced. "You will be my lookout on a job. There are a few valuable items that I wish to… liberate from this waste of space they call a college. Things that I can put to better use elsewhere. It's not a complicated task. All you need to do is to look inconspicuous and raise the alarm if you see anyone coming. Think you can do that?" he asked in a condescending tone.

Seb's glare remained resolutely fixed on Malone. "I can do that," he replied.

"Good," said Malone. "Six weeks today, 10 p.m. in the alleyway outside. And remember: don't be an idiot. You don't want your friend's pretty little face to be rearranged, now do you?" Malone didn't wait for Seb to answer. In his customary style, he barged past him and strode through the door. It swung closed behind him.

***

Seb wandered up the path towards college the following morning. It was the first proper rehearsal for the world championships, and he was exhausted. He felt like he'd had about twenty minutes' sleep. His mind seemed to flip constantly between Malone, the world championships and missing Alice. As he reached the top of the path, he heard Mark's mild Scottish accent a little way behind him.

"Ah, Seb," Mark called.

Seb turned around to greet him. "Hi," he replied. "You're in early."

"Orchestra rehearsal. I gave Sophie a lift in this morning," Mark explained. "Are you free afterwards? We need to do a one-to-one before the end of the year… it's like a progress check meeting to see how you're getting on."

Seb nodded. Normally, he would have hung around in the canteen whiling away an hour or so before his next lecture. It was the time he used to spend with Alice, but he'd hardly seen her during the last couple of weeks, never mind spoken to her.

"Yeah, sure," he replied.

"Great," said Mark. "I'll be in the classroom. Grab us both a coffee on the way up. Mine's a double espresso." And with that, Mark handed him a five-pound note, turned and strode through the huge glass doors into the main building.

"Good morning, everyone," Sophie announced as he walked into the music room. "You'll find your sheet music on your chairs. Now, before we begin, I'd like to play the medley of the three tunes we've chosen. I asked my DJ friend to mix this last night. It's a little rough and ready, but hopefully you'll get the idea."

She picked up her phone and hit play.

"This is called 'From Russia with Love'. I've picked the Alaska mix, which is quite chilled," she said as the first few bars built into a melody. They all listened intently. Some were following the tune through their sheet music to see how their piece slotted in. Seb didn't need to look at his sheet of music to know he'd be playing the vocal, so he closed his eyes and began to feel the emotion.

As the first tune wound down, the second piece kicked in.

"You heard this one yesterday," Sophie said. "This is '1998'. We've decided to adapt the rock version. Listen closely to the way the tune builds to a climax. Now, we're only incorporating the vocal from the chorus," she said looking directly at Seb. He listened hard to pick up the lyric, without much success. Perhaps he'd need to search for that later.

"And finally," Sophie said, as the third tune kicked in, "this is called 'Protect Your Mind' by DJ Sakin and Friends." As the first bars filled his ears, Seb began to smile.

Behind him, someone muttered, "Where have a I heard this

242

before?" Seb knew exactly where he'd heard it before. It was based on "Gift of a Thistle" from the *Braveheart* soundtrack. It was the tune he played in the woods to calm the Demon. It was a favourite.

But, it was a movie soundtrack.

It's a classical tune. You'll get in trouble.

He started to raise his hand, then stopped. He knew this tune. He knew he could play it. It was one less thing to worry about. Surely, Sophie must have recognised it too. If she thought it was okay, that was good enough for him. And if she hadn't recognised it, the judges were sure to miss it too. Everything would be fine.

"So, as you'll see, this is a step up from anything we've done before," Colonel Walmsley announced as he descended the tiered steps. " We'll need to up our game. There are some signature pieces, so a few of you will find it more challenging." He turned to face them, moustache bristling. "We have five weeks. Let's give this everything we've got!"

***

Seb nudged the classroom door open with his shoulder, careful not to spill their coffee. Mark sat at his desk reading from his laptop. As Seb entered, he closed the lid and turned to face him with a smile.

"Ah, thank you," he said as Seb handed him the comically small espresso cup. "Now… I know that you're progressing very well in psychology. I have no concerns with that at all," Mark began, "but how do *you* feel it's going?"

Seb half shrugged, half nodded in response. "Uh, good I think," he replied. "I'm enjoying it."

Mark smiled. "Good. Any questions or concerns?" he asked.

Seb shook his head and took a sip of his own drink.

"And what about college life in general?" Mark asked casually.

243

Seb felt his stomach tighten. A terrifyingly distorted picture of Malone's face swam in front of his eyes. Should he tell Mark? Should he mention the forthcoming break-in... admit to the thefts? And if he told Mark, would he be endangering Alice?

But maybe this was his opportunity. Maybe Mark could help. Questions raced through his mind. Could he trust Mark? Would Mark be duty bound to call the police? And... what would Mark think of him? Right now, Mark seemed to like him, perhaps even respect him a little. What would he think if Seb confessed to being a criminal?

Seb swallowed hard.

"There is something," he began, his voice trembling slightly. "Something I'm not proud of."

Mark's expression didn't change. He just sat gazing at Seb over the top of his miniature coffee cup.

He told Mark about his first meeting with Malone in the corridor, about how he'd come across him in the alleyway while hiding behind the rusty car... how Malone had sent him to meet the woman with the pink hair... about the package he'd passed through the window of the red BMW... and how he'd pieced it together with Alice when he saw the "theft in college" notices. Mark simply sat and listened.

As he finished, Mark said, "It's very brave of you to tell me."

"W-what?" Seb spluttered. Those were not the words he was expecting! He'd braced himself for a volley of "I'm so disappointed" or "How could you be so stupid?".

"Many people don't step forward or get help because they are scared of being judged, scared of what people will think. So they keep themselves locked in a destructive cycle. It's far braver to open yourself up to judgement than to stay locked in that cycle," Mark said.

Bizarrely, it seemed to make sense. Even though he desperately wanted to escape Malone's grasp, the fear of judgement had stopped him telling his lecturers, his parents or the police. As he was now beginning to realise, these people would probably respect him more because he stepped forward, not less.

"That's not everything, though," Seb said. "There's something else, but I don't know what to do about it." He looked at Mark, who calmly returned his gaze. "If I tell anyone, Malone says he'll hurt a friend," Seb said.

Mark took a final sip of his coffee and placed his cup on the desk.

"I'm not going to ask you to share something you're uncomfortable with, but I can assure you that I will do my very best to help… and to protect your friend," Mark said earnestly.

Seb swallowed hard. In his heart of hearts, he knew that Mark wanted to help. But how could he be sure that Alice would be safe? Whichever way he looked at it, this was going to be a leap of faith. He was just going to have to trust Mark.

"Malone is planning something… a robbery, I think. He described it as 'liberating some valuable items' from college. I don't know where exactly. I've just been told to meet him… six weeks yesterday, at 10 p.m. in the alleyway outside the sports hall. I'm supposed to keep lookout. That's all I've been told," he said. "But… I need to find a way to stop all this. Somehow, I need this to end." Seb was staring at the table, deep in his own thoughts.

"Have you got any ideas?" Mark asked quietly.

Seb nodded. "My De— I mean, a friend," Seb corrected himself at once, looking up to see whether Mark had registered his slip. Mark's eyes narrowed very slightly.

"Go on," he encouraged.

"A friend gave me an idea," Seb said, "to set some kind of a trap. But I'm not sure how. I mean, if I go to the police now, it's my word against his. But if there was a way to catch him in the act…." He trailed off, not quite knowing where his thoughts were taking him.

"I think I can see where you're going with this," replied Mark. "Leave it with me. Can you share your location with me via your phone?" he asked.

Seb nodded.

"Okay, that's all you need to do. Let me take care of the rest. And you don't need to worry about your friend," he said with a knowing smile. "By telling me all this, you have invested a great deal of trust in me. I take that very seriously. I will not abuse your trust," he said, looking Seb deep in the eye. The glimmer of a smile crept into the corner of Seb's mouth, and he began to feel a weight that he'd almost forgotten he was carrying begin to lift.

All he had to do now was figure out how to play the most difficult piece of music he'd ever seen and how to win back Alice's friendship.

How to Silence Your Demons

Professor Itsen shares a few ideas about what drives people to bully others. He shows how bullying, in its various forms, is often fuelled by insecurity.
What do you think?
Does it make sense?
How could understanding this help you?

Professor Itsen talks about 'the last of our human freedoms'; the freedom to choose how we think and feel in any circumstance. When would you like to think and feel differently?
How could you start to choose how you think and feel more often?

Professor Itsen also says that when we find this freedom, we unlock our true potential... our superpowers.
Which superpowers have you started to unlock?
How can you unlock more of your superpowers?

Chapter Eighteen

SØREN

Five weeks later…
Copenhagen Central Station.

Seb stepped from the packed train onto the platform. He was surrounded by a sea of students and lecturers, all laden with luggage and musical instruments. On one hand it seemed rather daft to have this amount of baggage for just a couple of days, but, in their wisdom, the organisers of the World Colleges Orchestral Championships had decreed that everyone must wear "evening dress." This had caused no end of panic. Ever since the announcement, he'd heard more talk about what they'd all be wearing than about the music they were playing. Fortunately, he didn't have much choice in the matter. He'd been presented with his dad's old dinner suit which, according to his mum, had only been worn once. And, since he and his father were almost exactly the same shape and size now, it made things pretty straight forward.

"This way, Yeoborough," came Colonel Walmsley's booming voice above the commotion. "Follow me."

They followed Colonel Walmsley along the platform, packed with people boarding the various scarlet trains, and towards the escalators. The enormous roof arched above them, held up by a web of crimson steel. As they reached the top of the escalator, the huge concourse spread out before them. It was bathed in the orangey-yellow light that reflected off the brickwork and the vast domed roof. Seb and the others wove their way through the myriad of little shops and stalls selling delicious freshly baked breads and sweet-smelling pastries, and headed for the grand entrance.

They emerged into the warmth of the afternoon and the bustle of a busy city. The road to and from the station was packed with people and taxis. Across on the main city street sleek trams glided past, sunlight glinting from their windows. To their right stood a hotel, towards which Colonel Walmsley seemed to be leading them. Just before entering, he stopped.

"Right, you lot," he bellowed, his voice carrying over the hum of the city. "Before we all check in… Breakfast is at seven o'clock in the morning. We have a rehearsal in the hotel conference room at eight. Don't be late! After that you will have time to relax and wander around the city. Go in groups. You are all responsible and we trust you to be sensible. We leave the hotel at 4 p.m. for the concert hall. Please be in reception fifteen minutes early, wearing your evening dress, with your instruments. Any questions?"

Unsurprisingly there were none, so they all checked in and headed to their rooms.

***

At a couple of minutes to ten the following day, Sophie called their final rehearsal to a close.

"Well done, everyone," she said. "That's sounding really good. We're as ready as we'll ever be. Enjoy your free time. See you at a quarter to four." Hastily, Seb stowed his flute in its case, shoved the case in his rucksack and sped out of the door. He had a train to catch.

After settling into his room, the previous evening, he had contacted the Demon Charmers. He'd realised he had no idea how to get to Odense, who Søren was, or how to recognise him. He also knew that he had a little over five hours in which to get from Copenhagen to Odense, meet Søren, get back and change into his dinner suit, before boarding the bus.

According to the Demon Charmers, Søren would be wearing a crisp white shirt, with the collar turned up, and a fawn-coloured jacket. Apparently, this is what he always wore. The instructions were very clear. He could be found in his favourite café on the corner of a street called Vestergade, right opposite St Albani's church.

The train Seb needed would pull away from the platform in just five minutes. He tore out of the hotel, wove between the taxis and dashed through the station entrance. He slowed slightly to read the departures board and then sped off again. He leaped onto the slowly moving escalator. The train was already standing at the platform. He pushed past a few people, apologising, jumped the last four steps and sprinted for the train. He ran for the nearest door, hoping beyond hope that this was the right train, and dived through it as it closed. He'd made it… just.

Step one, done. He slumped into a nearby seat.

It was an hour and forty-five minutes to Odense; plenty of time to listen to the recording of this morning's rehearsal. He pulled his phone from his pocket and plugged in his ear buds… but hesitated before pressing play.

Alice.

How dearly he'd love to talk to her right now. For a brief moment he thought about texting but concluded it was probably pointless. She'd ignored every message he'd sent since storming out of the canteen all those weeks ago.

He closed his eyes and hit play.

***

Seb skidded to a halt at a pedestrian crossing in the centre of Odense, completely out of breath. The navigation app on his phone told him that the imposing church to his right with the tall spire was St Albani's. Diagonally across the street was a café. That must be the place. The figure on the crossing turned from red to green and he trotted across the road, trying to calm his breathing. As he drew closer, Seb saw a magnificent display of cakes and pastries in the window; every conceivable shape and size, all set out in immaculate rows. Many of them were topped with custard, cream or icing and laden with fruit and berries. Some were so tall, he wondered how anyone could bite into them. It was a sight to behold.

He pushed the glass door and peered in. There was a small queue at the counter and a handful of people seated at tables, sipping coffee and chatting. In the far corner, on his own, sat a man in a white shirt and fawn jacket reading a very old book. Nervously, he wandered up to the table.

Søren was a lot younger that he had expected. Rather than a venerable old man in his late eighties, Søren seemed to be in his mid-thirties. In Seb's view, that still made him old, but not quite as old as he had imagined. His slightly greying wavy hair was pushed back off his slender face. In addition to his old-fashioned white shirt and fawn jacket, he wore grey trousers and chestnut brown shoes. If Seb didn't know better, he would have thought this man had just stepped out of the nineteenth century.

"Søren?" he asked.

The man looked up and smiled.

"Ah… You must be Seb," he replied in a light Danish accent. "Sit." Seb pulled up a chair and sat down. "Would you like something to eat and drink?" he asked.

"Uh, yes… please," replied Seb, now realising that his stomach was growling.

Søren waved a waitress over and ordered something in Danish. Seb recognised the word "kaffe" but not much else.

Then Søren fixed him with his electric blue eyes. "So… how can I help you?" he asked.

For a moment Seb was stumped. He had been so worried about getting here and finding Søren, he hadn't given a moment's thought to the conversation.

"Uh… I'm not really sure," he said weakly. "The Demon Charmers said I needed to meet you."

Søren didn't look at all surprised by this reply. His gaze drifted to the kindly middle-aged waitress who appeared over Seb's shoulder. She placed a cup of black coffee and a delicious-looking open sandwich onto the table next to him and left with a smile.

"For you," Søren said, gesturing towards the food. "The Demon Charmers have a habit of knowing who needs help. Tell me… What do you find is your biggest challenge?"

Seb thought for a moment. "Self-doubt," he replied simply.

"What do you doubt you can do?" asked Søren.

"Anything… everything," replied Seb with a sigh.

"Everything? Really?" Søren asked.

"Okay, not everything," Seb admitted. "I know I can play the three pieces this evening. And, now I think about it, I did learn to play the solos and duets for the regionals and the national final." He paused for a moment. "But there are things that can't be solved with a flute," he said.

"Go on," Søren said.

"Like the Demon and Malone and getting Alice back," he said.

"And how have you been getting on with those?" asked Søren.

"What do you mean?" he replied.

"What progress have you made?" Søren asked.

To be honest, he hadn't really stopped to think about it, but now he did...

"Uh, I suppose things have changed," he said. "I've learned the pieces, which I didn't think was possible. Not so long ago I was terrified of the Demon. It hunted me and I ran. But now it's different. The Demon, Timidis, is not so much a monster now – almost a friend."

"And Malone?" asked Søren.

"Yeah, that's a bit more of a challenge." Seb sighed. "I just want to stop him."

"Stop him from doing what?" Søren asked.

"Making me miserable," Seb muttered.

"Interesting," Søren said.

"Interesting?" Seb repeated, his voice rising. "How is it interesting?"

"Because there are two elements. One which you can control and one that you cannot. And you're trying to change the one you cannot," Søren said calmly.

"How do you mean?" asked Seb, trying to compose himself.

"You cannot control what he does or what he says, but I think you would like to, yes?" Søren said.

Seb simply nodded.

"However, you can control whether he makes you miserable," Søren said.

Seb remembered Viktor Frankl's words. "The last of our human freedoms", he muttered, "to choose how we think and feel."

"Exactly!" said Søren. "Nobody can *make* you feel afraid. This Malone person could put a gun to your head and threaten to pull the trigger, but he can't make you feel afraid. Only you can decide if you feel the fear. Think of the fear like a dagger. He can offer you the dagger. Only you can plunge it into your own chest. He can never invade your thoughts and feelings, unless you let him. He only has control if you give him the remote."

Seb thought about it for a moment. He imagined Malone holding a gun to his head. He didn't have to cower in fear or beg for his life. He had the choice. He could tell Malone to do his worst, to pull the trigger. Søren's words echoed through his mind.

He only has control if you give him the remote.

"At least I have a plan now. I guess that's progress," said Seb with the glint of a smile.

"You have done all of this," Søren said. "You conquered your nerves in the orchestra. You conquered your fear of the Demon. You have taken steps to deal with Malone. You have done all of this… and yet you still doubt yourself." Søren paused to let his words sink in.

"Yeah, I s'pose," replied Seb as his brain grappled to make sense of it all.

"I suspect you already know that belief is an expression of confidence, and that confidence comes from evidence," the Dane continued. "However, the evidence alone is not enough. You must also recognise it and appreciate it. You already have the evidence. But you're not seeing it because you don't look."

"I guess I have faced some pretty scary stuff," he replied, as he stared into the depths of his coffee cup.

"The self-belief that you seek emanates from your *identity*," Søren said, placing great emphasis on the final word. "It comes from who you believe you are. You might think of it as a state of being, rather than doing."

Seb thought for a moment. For as long as he could remember, he had thought of himself as a failure… as incapable… as someone who always screwed up and disappointed people. And, even though he had overcome some extreme challenges during the last year, it hadn't really changed the way he saw himself.

"I suspect that your identity has not yet caught up with reality," Søren said.

"You're probably right," replied Seb.

"Doing is good," Søren said, "but most people have a narrow view of what they can do. By playing one piece of music, you might believe you can play another. But, could you climb a mountain, or run a marathon, or defeat a mortal enemy? Could you become someone that others would respect? Or, more to the point, could you become someone that *you* respect? This is where we step beyond doing and into being."

Seb looked at Søren, who smiled warmly. How could he know this? These were things that Seb barely understood about himself, and yet this man, whom he'd met just minutes before, seemed to have figured him out almost instantly.

"How do you do that?" Seb asked.

"Are you asking how I can know this about you? Or are you asking how to build self-belief?" Søren replied.

"Uhh, both. But the second one… How can I build this self-belief?" Seb said.

"Ahhh. Well, that's simple," said Søren, "We start by knowing our self. This is our foundation. It is the foundation of peace and meaning. We must learn to know ourselves before knowing anything else."

Seb took a mouthful of coffee and tried to make sense of it all.

"Look at who you are, not just what you do. Most people do not reflect on who they are. They are too busy being busy. They look only at what they do and never stop to think about who they are. They measure their success by their achievements: what they have done and what they have attained," Søren explained. "But you don't have to do that. There is another way. You could choose a different measure for your own success."

"What kind of measure?" asked Seb.

"Be proud of who you are, not just what you do," replied Søren, "Imagine three interwoven strands of rope. One is knowing yourself. The second is being yourself. And the third is accepting yourself, liking yourself, being proud of yourself. You cannot have

256

one without the others. You need all three. How can you know yourself if you aren't being yourself? How can you be proud of yourself if you don't know who you are? Why would you want to be yourself if you weren't proud of who you were?"

"That's all easy to say," replied Seb. "But how can I build these three strands? Where do I even start?"

Søren leaned forwards in his seat and fixed Seb with his gaze. "Self-reflection," he said simply. "This is a life-long quest… a journey, not a destination."

Seb thought for a moment.

"I guess it makes sense," he replied. "But what if I just don't see it? What if I look at myself and just see failure?"

Søren looked Seb in the eye once more, as though connecting with his soul.

"We always see what we look for. We see what we expect to see, not what is there. If you don't see it, it's because you're not *really* looking. Look with honest eyes," Søren said.

"I understand what you're saying, but how can that help me right now… with this demon, with the world championships, or with Malone, or getting Alice back? It all just seems… impossible," he said.

"Good question," Søren replied. "So many people fail before they ever get started. To answer your question, we need to challenge a long and widely held belief. Do you have to believe, before you can achieve? Many people think that you do. But I would question it. Most people need to believe before they commit. Why can't we commit anyway, whether we believe or not?"

Søren took a sip of his own coffee before continuing.

"What if you were to combine your lack of belief with fear?" he asked. "Fear, as I'm sure you know, is something we imagine. And what we imagine tends to be far worse than reality. If you asked yourself, 'Do I believe I can overcome the terrifying monster I've created in my imagination?', I suspect the answer will be 'No', and so you won't even try. And, if you do that too many times, you will probably see yourself as a person who cannot, rather than a person who could. Eventually, you will conclude you are a failure. It will become part of your identity."

Seb thought for a moment. Søren was absolutely right. He remembered back to his childhood, to the time just after Sandy had died. He'd always looked up to his older brother and marvelled at the things he could do. When Sandy died, he desperately wanted to fill that void, to be everything that Sandy had been, to make his parents proud. But he couldn't. Nothing he did ever seemed good enough, it never seemed to match up to Sandy. So he'd always felt like a failure.

Maybe that's where it all began. Maybe that lack of self-belief had stopped him from fully committing.

Søren pushed his empty cup to one side.

"There is a word in Scandinavia: Lagom. It means 'enough'. So many people today are searching for more, striving to be more, to have more. They are forever hungry. It doesn't matter how much they have, they always need more. When we understand 'lagom', we realise that we have enough, we are enough. It means we can be content with our life. That doesn't mean we can't improve. I think we can always improve. But we can still be happy knowing we are enough."

Seb simply nodded while his brain tried to process it all.

"Remember: We shape our character one choice at a time. Your character is the culmination of all the choices you have taken, like your choice to step towards your fears. And we sculpt our identity one belief at a time. Your identity is the culmination of all the beliefs you hold about yourself. If you want to evolve these, you simply do it one choice and one belief at a time. Now... I think maybe you have a train to catch?" Søren said.

"Train?" He hurriedly checked the time on his phone. The

train back to Copenhagen was due to leave in twelve minutes.

"Oh, shit! Sorry!" he spluttered. He looked down at his uneaten sandwich.

"Take it with you," said Søren. Seb hastily wrapped the sandwich in a napkin and gulped down the last mouthful of coffee.

"Thank you," he said.

Søren smiled. "It is my pleasure. Now go, before you miss that train."

And with that, Seb got up and ran.

How to Silence Your Demons

Søren shares a lot of ideas with Seb during their conversation.
Which ones make most sense to you?
How could they help Seb?
How could they help you?

Which ideas make most sense?

How do you think they could help Seb?

How could they help you?

Søren points out that Seb has made loads of progress... with overcoming his nerves, learning the pieces for the orchestra and developing his courage. But Seb hasn't really stopped to reflect on this or feel proud of himself.

What have you done that you could feel proud about?

If you were Søren, what advice would you give Seb, to help him with his challenges?

Chapter Nineteen

THE FINALE

Seb looked out the window in awe as the coach pulled up outside the DR Koncerthuset. The huge blue cube stood proudly on the water's edge, shoulder to shoulder with the other ultra-modern buildings.

"Okay, everyone," Sophie called from the front of the bus. "Please collect your instruments and music, and follow Colonel Walmsley. Just to let you know, we are one of eight colleges and, as seems to be the luck of the draw, we'll be playing eighth."

Her words were met with a collective groan.

The students followed Colonel Walmsley through the impressive entrance way and into the auditorium. It was enormous. Lights reflected off the wood that lined the vast room from floor to ceiling, giving it a soft golden-brown glow. Right in the centre was the tiered stage, above which hung an impressive tubular chandelier. The stage was surrounded on all sides by jet-black seats. Unusually, though, the seats were not laid out in a smooth oval or circle around the stage. Instead, they were arranged on wooden platforms, in a variety of angular shapes – triangles, squares, diamonds – all set at different heights. The highest of these nestled beneath the vast wooden ceiling. Towards the top were two groups of seats, set out in interlocking triangles. From a distance, it looked a bit like an upper-case A and V, positioned high above the stage to the left, with the flag of the United Kingdom draped over the seats. Flags of other nations adorned more clusters of seats. Seb spotted the Danish flag immediately to their left. To their right, the black, red and gold of Germany. There were also flags for France, Italy, Canada, the Czech Republic and Brazil. Colonel Walmsley led them up the steps to the seats beneath their flag.

They sat and watched as the auditorium filled with hundreds of people, all dressed in their finest attire. The men looked like James Bond, with their dinner suits and bow ties. The women wore elegant evening dresses in a dazzling assortment of colours.

Once everyone was seated the lights dimmed. A spotlight picked out a very attractive middle-aged lady in a flowing emerald dress at the front of the stage. Her blond hair shone in the bright light, giving her an angelic appearance. She welcomed the audience in the eight languages of the competing orchestras and then invited the French national champions to join her on stage.

One after another, the orchestras lit up the arena, each one performing almost faultlessly. The orchestras from Denmark, France, Germany and the Czech Republic played pieces they had composed themselves. The Brazilian orchestra performed a rousing compilation of patriotic national tunes. The Italians adapted and interpreted pop music, while the Canadians played a tribute to the rock band Queen.

As the orchestra from Canada exited to a standing ovation, the hostess in the emerald dress took to the stage once more and announced the final performance of the evening. This was it. They made their way down the countless steps and out into the middle of the arena. For perhaps the thousandth time, Seb checked the notes he'd scribbled on the back of his hand. He would be playing the vocal pieces that would open and close their performance. It was all in his head. He knew it. He'd practised it over and over again. But it didn't stop him from glancing down to check one last time.

They were starting with Matt Darey's "From Russia with Love", followed by "1998" and finishing with "Protect Your Mind", the piece with the *Braveheart* melody.

Isn't that a classical tune? I'm sure they're not allowed, said a dark voice from the far recesses of his mind. *You should have told them!*

Not now! Seb thought. *This is not the time. Concentrate!*

You can't shut me out, said the Demon, it's voice growing louder.

Watch me! Seb replied.

Sophie stood before them in a fitted black satin dress. She had an air of calm that seemed to radiate out across the stage. With a smile, she raised her baton and, simultaneously, Seb raised his flute to his lips. As the baton swept through the air a pure note filled the silence, followed by another. A clear, lone, haunting voice drifted through the vast auditorium. Slowly, the percussion added their rhythmic beats. For a few moments, they played together in perfect harmony before Seb's flute tailed off and the plucked strings of a single cello took over. Ten exquisite, crisp notes emanated from the stage. Then Seb picked up again, the notes from his flute weaving in and out, in perfect unison. The cello died and woodwind took the lead, their soft notes filling the cavernous hall.

As the last breath of the woodwind faded, the strings picked up, smooth and serene. As before, Seb entwined his sombre, forlorn voice with theirs. Like the woodwind before them, the strings delivered ten perfect notes. Then the brass section took the baton: gentle and melodic. And as their last note faded, Seb took the flute from his lips, leaving the percussion section with the beat. This was the point where they needed to blend one tune seamlessly with the next.

The plucked notes of a lone double bass led the orchestra into "1998". Then the violins. Quickly the tune built. More violins and violas. Faster and faster, louder and louder. In came the woodwind and Seb on the flute. Finally, the brass section, adding their power. The piece rose to its crescendo and…

Sophie held her baton. There was a split second's silence, like a sharp intake of breath. Then… CRASH! The whole orchestra picked up as one, perfectly synchronised on the same beat.

Gradually the tune spiralled down. Each section peeled off, leaving the lone double bass with the percussion once more. It was time to blend into the final piece. The faint low notes from a single violin paved the way for his entrance. He closed his eyes. He'd played this tune so many times on his own. It meant something to him. Not through the lyric, but through his own emotion. Whenever he played it, the voice of his flute was lonely… lost… desperate to belong. He'd known that feeling for as long as he could remember… ever since Sandy had died.

He raised his flute to his lips and feeling became sound as he told his tragic but beautiful tale.

In the far distance he heard the strings and the deep choral voices of the brass adding their weight. Wave after wave, it built.

Again, the voice of his flute sang out, each note laced with emotion.

Then came the power. Strings, brass, woodwind, percussion, all in perfect harmony, united in one voice. Emotion flooded over him. He felt a lump building in his throat and tears welling up in his eyes. The loneliness he once felt had gone. He did belong. He belonged to this orchestra. He belonged here.

Gradually, the brass section fell away, the strings died, and the woodwind gave their last breath. All that remained was Seb's lone voice. He held his final note, then allowed it to fade gently into nothing… leaving only silence.

For a split second, he stood encased in a perfect bubble of his own emotion. Then it burst.

The audience erupted into applause. Sophie was in floods of tears at the front of the stage. The rest of the orchestra were crying, hugging, high fiving. Through the crowd, he saw Gemma. She raced over to him and threw her arms around him. He pulled her into a tight embrace. He could smell her hair and feel her breath. Her hot tears ran down his neck. It felt like they were melting into each other. He honestly didn't know whether that moment lasted seconds or hours. Finally, she released her embrace and their eyes met… then their lips.

He was kissing her… her soft lips locked to his.

For a moment, Seb was lost in a moment of pure bliss.

Suddenly, there was a roar of whoops and cheers, gasps and laughter. He had completely forgotten where they were… standing on a stage… in the middle of an auditorium… with the whole orchestra, and almost two thousand people, now staring at them.

"Well," said the blond woman in the emerald dress. "That was quite a finale."

Gemma smiled at him. "That was some first kiss," she whispered.

***

Seb barely noticed them exit the stage and climb the steps back to their seats. He didn't hear the shouts of congratulations or feel the pats on the back. He, and his irremovable grin, were lost in *that* moment.

It took a little while for the commotion to subside. Gradually, Seb became aware of his surroundings again. He heard Colonel Walmsley telling Sophie, "It was the best performance of the night. We're in with a great chance." The lady in the emerald dress resumed her position in the spotlight and took the microphone from its stand.

"Well done, everyone. It has been a wonderful competition," she said. "It's time to announce the results."

Seb felt the tension all around him. There seemed to be an air of excited expectation. The whole orchestra were poised, like a canon full of confetti, just waiting to explode. For a split second, he imagined them down on the stage, picking up that trophy. How amazing would that be? Little Yeoborough College... world champions. And maybe another kiss with Gemma...

"In eighth place," she began, "despite an amazing performance... the United Kingdom."

"What?"... "No!"... "That can't be right."... "There must be some mistake."

"Unfortunately," the lady continued, "their final piece was taken from a movie soundtrack by James Horner, a classical composer, so it didn't meet the criteria. But, it was such a great performance – maybe good enough to win. So please give a very big round of applause to the United Kingdom."

Darkness fell as the applause rang around the enormous concert hall. In the far distance, Seb heard the protests and cries of his fellow orchestra members. On stage, the lady in the emerald dress went on to announce those in seventh... sixth... fifth... and so on. The winners received a large trophy. But Seb barely noticed. He felt like the ceiling was caving in.

This is your fault, came the angry growl of the Demon. *You should have told them.*

He screwed his eyes up hoping that it would all disappear... that he'd wake up from this.

You can't pretend it's not happening, the Demon said. *Even if they don't know, you do, and you can never escape that!*

***

Seb climbed the steps of the coach. He was the last on. He looked down the long aisle half expecting a sea of accusing faces staring back at him. But they weren't. Most people seemed lost. Some stared out of the window, others at the floor, many seemed to be looking for some kind of comfort in their phones.

The Demon was right. This guilt would erode him, it would eat him from the inside. Bizarre as it sounded, he needed to apologise. He had to tell them it wasn't their fault... it was his. He knew he'd be an outcast again, back to being alone. He'd be giving up the only real sense of belonging he could remember. And Gemma would hate him. But it was the right thing to do.

"Are you okay there?" asked the driver.

"Uh, yeah," replied Seb. "Can I use this?" he asked, pointing towards the microphone resting in its holster. The bus driver nodded a little uncertainly. Seb picked up the microphone.

"I'm sorry everyone," he began. " I'm so sorry. This is all my fault." Now he saw the faces. But they weren't angry. They were confused.

"No, Seb," Sophie said. "It's not your fault. You played beautifully... everyone did."

Seb shook his head. "No, you don't understand," he said. "I knew... I knew our third tune was taken from *Braveheart*. I recognised it when you first played it in rehearsal, but I didn't say anything. It's a favourite. I play it all the time. It's one I'm confident with. You know, one less thing to worry about, one less tune to learn. I guess I thought... I don't know... Maybe I hoped no one would notice... Maybe it would all be okay."

There was a sizeable lump forming in his throat. If he said any more, there was a very good chance he'd burst into tears. He'd humiliated himself enough already, without crying in front of everyone... in front of Gemma.

He handed the microphone to the driver and walked through the stunned silence towards an empty seat.

"Wow," said Will Janes, the trombonist, from the back seat of the bus. "I don't know many people who'd have the balls to do that. Respect!"

Seb looked up, astonished.

"Bravo, Will," boomed Colonel Walmsley's voice from behind him. "Well said."

"Seb," Sophie said, her voice cracking with emotion. "We should have checked. I don't think I've ever watched the film, but I thought I recognised the melody. I just couldn't place it. I had this nagging little doubt, but I got so carried away. I didn't stop to think. It's not your fault."

Seb opened his mouth to argue but Sophie beat him to it. "Seriously!" she said. "It's absolutely not your fault."

For the briefest moment Seb considered replying, then thought better of it. He was exhausted. He slid into the empty seat and stared out of the window. The lump was still in his throat, but the knot in his stomach was loosening.

How to Silence Your Demons

Seb managed to block out the demon's voice in the concert hall this time.
How did he do it?
Why do you think it worked this time?

Sometimes it takes real courage to do the right thing. Have you ever been in a situation like this?
What did you do?
What would you do if you were in a similar situation again?

Chapter Twenty

THE SUMMIT

The sound of his phone alarm snapped Seb out of his daydream. It was time! He had been imagining the break-in that Malone had planned. It's amazing how time races by when you don't want it to. It didn't seem like six weeks since he'd been given this latest "assignment". It had always seemed a long way away, the other side of the world championships. But now it was here.

The world championships. It was only a few days ago, but it seemed like something that had happened in another lifetime, or to someone else. Maybe he should have stayed in Copenhagen… taken a new identity… started a new life. But he'd missed his chance. Instead, here he was, sitting on a park bench in the gloom, about to walk into this nightmare.

He thought for a moment of Alice. More than anything, he just wanted someone to talk to, someone who might understand.

He checked the time. He had fifteen minutes. With a feeling of impending doom, he slid his phone back in his pocket. Then he remembered… Mark. He needed to share his location. With a little prayer, he hit share and set off towards the sports hall, keeping a keen ear out for his text alert.

But there was nothing.

The light was fading as he walked up the hill towards college.

The imposing grey concrete wall of the main building towered above him.

You need to make sure he's caught in the act, said a voice deep inside his mind.

But what if Mark didn't pick up the message? Malone wouldn't be *caught* doing anything... he'd walk free.

Maybe he should just turn back now. Maybe all of this was pointless. Or maybe not. This was his shot. It was a chance to escape this poisonous web. He had to go through with this. It was the only way to break the cycle, stop Malone and make sure Alice would be safe. He quickened his pace.

Seb turned the corner of the alleyway. Shadowy figures gathered in the gloom ahead of him. Malone and his cronies had already assembled by the sports hall entrance. Their hushed voices echoed between the high walls as he approached.

"Ah, Hall. You're almost late." Malone sneered. "Right... Listen up! The plan is simple enough. Not even you lot can screw this up," he said. "The items are in the art block. There's a storeroom off the main classroom. The door has a key-code lock. The idiots here think that's enough to keep it safe."

A large, ape-like lad to Seb's right gave a nervous laugh. Maybe Seb wasn't the only one who was feeling it.

"Shut up, Crowe," barked Malone. "There are CCTV cameras and an alarm on the outer door. Jonny takes care of the CCTV cameras. I've got the alarm for the door. Hall is going in to get the stash."

"What?" cried Seb.

Malone turned to him slowly and deliberately, then drew so close they were nose to nose.

"Yes, Hall," he spat. "You got a problem with that?"

The gigantic frame of Crowe and what looked like his twin brother bore down on Seb.

"Fine," he replied between gritted teeth.

"Good," said Malone, with a look of pure hatred. "There are twelve identical boxes piled on the shelf. As you open the storeroom door, they will be right in front of you. Not even you can miss them." Malone turned to the rest of the group. "The rest of you are on lookout duty. Same drill as always. You know what to do. Now, follow me," he ordered.

Seb watched as they all obeyed, like remote-controlled toys. Reluctantly, he trudged on behind. They turned right behind the design block and headed towards the art department. It was a plain rectangular building. Behind it was a lawn dotted with a few trees and the moonlit sports fields beyond. Jonny had pulled on a mask and raced on ahead to place covers over the security cameras. After a few minutes, Jonny gave the all-clear and the others followed.

Malone reached the front door of the building, tapped a code into the keypad and entered. Once inside, he flipped down the cover on the security alarm and punched in another code. The flashing red light on the outside wall extinguished.

"Hall," Malone hissed.

Seb walked slowly towards the doorway. The others began to disperse to their various lookout points. That cocktail of nerves, anxiety and fear that Seb knew so well began to bubble up in his stomach once more.

"That's the main classroom," Malone said, pointing down the corridor to their left. It was illuminated by a single security light that cast an eerie green glow. At the end of the corridor was a solid grey door.

"Not even you can get lost," Malone said. "The storeroom is to the left of the desk. The code is five-seven-three-one . Twelve identical boxes. Bring them to me... for the girl's sake."

Seb gave Malone a look of pure loathing, then turned and walked down the corridor. Acid was rising from his stomach into his chest.

Hold it together, he told himself. *And think!*

This was not going to plan. How on earth were they going to catch Malone in the act if it was he, Seb, who was carrying the stolen items? More to the point, if Mark had received his message and called the police, it was Seb who'd be caught with the stash. He needed a plan, and he needed it fast.

Keep it simple, said the Demon. *That way, less can go wrong.*

Yeah fine, but what exactly am I supposed to do? Seb thought.

Keep calm, came the reply.

Seb took a breath. Somehow, he needed to get Malone into the classroom and make sure it was Malone who carried the boxes out. Seb reached the classroom door. It stood before him, like an impenetrable wall. But it wasn't impenetrable at all. All he had to do was turn the handle. He placed his hand on the cool metal and pressed. The door gave an unnerving creak as he pushed it open. He stared around the dark room. The storeroom was exactly where Malone had described it. Cautiously, he walked over to it and stood before the locked door.

Don't leave any fingerprints, he told himself.

Carefully, he pulled his sleeve down over his hands to cover his fingers and punched in the code. With a click, the door unlocked and he pushed it open. There were the boxes – two piles of six, all identical, sat on the shelf in front of him. From the labels on the boxes, they contained state-of-the-art laptops. So this is what Malone wanted to steal.

Then the idea hit him.

What if they weren't where Malone thought they were?

Malone hadn't said what was in them. If they weren't on the shelf, Malone would have to come in and look for them himself. Quickly, he took the boxes from the storeroom and stacked them in a nearby cupboard. Now he had to ensure that Malone walked out with them. And he needed to get out of this room without walking back through the front door.

He scanned the room, looking for an escape. The windows…
of course! They were quite high up, and narrow, but he was pretty
sure he could squeeze through. He ran back to the door and
called down the corridor, "There's nothing there."

"What?" Malone snapped.

"No boxes in the storeroom," Seb said.

"Aaarrrgh!" Malone cried. He stomped up the corridor and
burst through the door.

Seb pointed at the empty shelf in the storeroom. "No boxes,"
he said simply.

Another cry of anger and frustration from Malone. Even
though the classroom was dim, Seb saw colour rising in Malone's
face.

"They must be somewhere," Malone said. "Get looking!"
Malone tore around the classroom, flinging cupboard doors
open and pulling the contents onto the floor.

"There are six laptop boxes over here. Is this what you're
looking for?" asked Seb calmly, holding six of the boxes in front
of him and obscuring the remaining six from view.

"Give me those," said Malone.

"Okay, you take these and I'll find the others," said Seb. Malone
snatched the boxes and headed for the door. As soon as he'd
turned out of sight, Seb leaped up onto the workbench to open
the window. He pulled down on the handle and pushed. Nothing.
He pushed again and it squeaked open a fraction. Malone's
footsteps echoed in the distance.

Maybe if he gave the window one last push it might open.
Perhaps he could squeeze through it. What if he was stuck halfway
through when Malone came around the corner? He remembered
how Malone had pulverised him in the sports hall just a few
months ago. He'd need little excuse to do the same again.

He drew his arm back, ready to force the window open… and
then stopped.

A bizarre thought struck him.

This was one of those defining moments... like his decision to walk into the woods and face the Demon. That night, when he'd been cornered in the derelict building, he'd decided to stand up, not cower in fear.

Courage is not the absence of fear, said the quiet voice.

What if he just decided not to run? What if he stood up to Malone? What if he told him to do his own dirty work? Obviously, there was a very good chance that Malone would beat him to a pulp. Maybe that was a price worth paying. But what if he turned his anger on Alice? Had Mark got the message? Was he keeping her safe?

Yes, said the quiet voice.

Seb climbed down from the workbench and stood facing the door, with the six boxes stacked on the workbench behind him. His heart was pounding. Acid bubbled up in his chest once more. Malone stormed through the door and into the classroom, his eyes fixed on Seb.

"Where are they?" he said.

"Just here, where I left them," Seb replied. Slowly he stepped aside to reveal the boxes.

"Where you...? What...?"

As if in slow motion, Malone's expression changed. Confusion became comprehension. "You little shit! You pick up those boxes now!"

Seb stared back, resolute. "No," he replied.

It all happened so fast. Malone crossed the room and shoved him into the cupboard door, all in one motion. The force must have knocked Seb off his feet, because Malone got hold of his sweater and dragged him up to standing again. Seb saw Malone draw his fist back, but the punch was so fast, there was nothing he could do to avoid it. It slammed into the side of his face with such force that Malone lost his grip and Seb slid to the floor. Lights popped in front of his eyes. For a moment he felt nothing. Then the pain swept in. He screwed his eyes up. This was only pain. He'd felt worse.

Malone stood over him, as if he didn't quite know what to do next. Seb smiled to himself. Søren was right.

He only has control if you give him the remote.

Slowly, Seb looked up at him. "Or what? You'll beat me up?" Seb wiped the blood that tricked down the side of his face. "Go on, then. I'm past caring."

"I'm gonna kill you and your pathetic little friend," Malone yelled.

In the far distance Seb heard the unmistakable sound of sirens. He needed to buy some time.

"She's safe," he replied simply. He gathered his strength and slowly pushed himself to his feet. "You could kill me, but then you'll just have a dead body to take care of as well. I'm not carrying those boxes anywhere. So, it seems you have two choices. You either take them yourself or leave them here."

For a second, what looked like panic flashed across Malone's eyes. Why did he need these boxes so badly? Why couldn't he just leave them and walk out?

"You wouldn't want to disappoint your buyer, would you?" Seb said. There it was again – raw panic. "There's always a bigger fish," Seb whispered.

"Shut up!" yelled Malone.

The sirens were getting closer. Malone looked from Seb to the boxes and back to Seb. For a moment they stood in deadlock. Seb searched Malone's eyes. Panic had turned to fear. He was looking at a small boy, lost and afraid.

Through the open doorway came the faint glow of blue flashing lights.

"Looks like you're running out of time," said Seb.

"Give me those," said Malone. He shoved past Seb, grabbed

the stack of laptops, pelted through the classroom door and sped down the corridor. In the distance, Seb heard another voice.

"Police! Stop right there."

Seb climbed back onto the workbench. He gave the window one more shove, squeezed through the gap and jumped down onto the moonlit grass. He paused for a moment to check he was alone, then silently rounded the corner of the art block to get a glimpse of the entrance. The flashing blue lights of three police cars illuminated the scene. Half a dozen officers were leading Malone and his cronies away in handcuffs. A few yards away he saw Mark looking around anxiously.

Seb pulled out his phone.

There was the reply from Mark:

Got it. Leave it with me. Mark.

How long had it been there? Never mind.

I'm okay. You might want to close the window at the back of the classroom ☺ Seb.

Mark checked his phone, then wandered into the art block. After a few moments, the police cars pulled away with Malone and his gang. All was quiet.

Seb leaned back against the wall and breathed in the cool evening air.

He was free.

⁕⁕

It was a perfect spring morning. The sun sat in a pristine blue sky. Blossom petals, like confetti, floated past on the light breeze. The buds on the trees were beginning to unfurl and, in the distance, Seb heard the last chattering of the dawn chorus. Dew lay on the grass like a carpet of tiny diamonds. As he strode across the field it coated his boots, leaving tracks behind him. He took a lungful of the fresh morning air and smiled to himself.

The woodland floor had begun to take on a green tinge as young nettles, flowers and brambles pushed their way through the mass of leaf litter, waking after their winter's nap. He wandered along the path to his thinking spot. He knew he didn't need to come all the way out here to meet Timidus, but somehow it made more sense.

He climbed onto the smooth rock, sat down and closed his eyes. All was quiet but for the rustle of the leaves and the chirping of the birds.

Why have you come here? Asked the Demon as it appeared through the trees.

"To apologise," replied Seb. "You were right about the compilation for the world championships. You told me we shouldn't have played that tune. You tried to warn me, and I ignored you. I know the others don't blame me for what happened, but I should have said something to Sophie. If I had, who knows what might have happened?"

It seems I was wrong about you, came the reply.

This time, it was not the demonic growl he was used to. It wasn't laced with hatred… or even disappointment.

"How do you mean?" asked Seb.

You may have lost the world championships, but you're not a loser. You're not Sandy. You're not perfect, but you don't need to be. I used to hate you... I hated being humiliated by you. But recently I've come to see you differently. You're not the blithering idiot I always thought you were. You work hard. You're courageous. You do the right thing, even when it's far easier not to. I respect that. You're a good person, Seb. I'm proud of you.

And with that, the Demon bowed its head and faded into nothing.

How to Silence Your Demons

When Malone announced that Seb would be going in to get the stash, he needed to stay calm, think fast and change his plan. What has he learned so far, which helped him do this?

Seb realises that he's facing a 'defining moment'. For him, it's another opportunity to stand up, rather than give in to fear. What are your 'defining moments'?
How do you want to respond when you reach these moments?

Chapter Twenty-One

THE BEGINNING

Seb sat alone in the college canteen, hands wrapped around a cup of coffee, lost in thought. In the last week, he'd been to Denmark, met Søren, lost the world championships with the orchestra, kissed Gemma in front of almost two thousand people and watched Malone get carted away by the police. Whichever way you sliced it, that was not a normal week.

It was as if something had shifted within him. Although he was still Sebastian Hall, he wasn't the same nervous boy that walked through the college doors back in September. He remembered his first day... walking into his first psychology lecture... his first conversation with Sophie... his audition for the orchestra. A smile crept into the corner of his mouth.

"Seb... Oh, Seb."

He looked around to see Alice hurtling across the canteen, hair flying everywhere, knocking into tables and chairs, her bag swinging wildly from her shoulder. He stood up, beaming at her. She dropped her bag on the floor and flung her arms around him.

"I'm so sorry," she said. "Mark told me everything. And to think... I thought you didn't trust me. But you were... you were trying to protect me."

Seb wrapped his arms around her as she sobbed into his shoulder. "I'm sorry too," he said. "I just didn't know what to do."

"I know… I know," she said between sniffs and sobs. She lifted her head from his shoulder, which was now soaked with tears. "I should never have doubted you," she said sincerely.

He smiled. "Friends?" he asked.

"Best friends," she said with a watery smile. She dabbed her face with her sleeve.

"I'm really happy for you and Gemma, you know," she said a little awkwardly. "She's lovely."

Seb nodded, not quite sure how to respond. "Thanks," he said finally. "I haven't really seen her since we got back from Denmark. After everything that happened, I don't know whether she wants to see me. I'm not sure what to do."

Alice smiled. "You'll figure it out, I'm sure," she said.

The two of them sat and caught up on their adventures. He told her all about the Demon, the orchestra and Malone. Alice simply sat and listened. It seemed that she was just glad to have her friend back too. Occasionally, she would interject with a "Wow" or "How did you do that?". He didn't know whether they'd been there minutes or hours when Alice's phone rang.

"It's my lift," she said as she answered the phone. "Be there in a minute, Mum," she called down the phone, then hung up. She looked Seb in the eye. "It's great to have my best friend back," she said.

"Ditto," replied Seb. He gave her a hug and she picked up her bag.

"Give me a buzz during the holidays," he said. "There's a nice new coffee shop in town. I reckon we should give it a try."

She gave one last smile, turned and headed for the door.

Seb sat for a moment, enjoying the warm glow that radiated somewhere deep inside him. Then he reached into his pocket and pulled out his phone. He found Gemma's number and opened up a text.

Fancy a walk by the river? X

Almost immediately the reply landed.

You bet! XX

He took a final sip of coffee, slung his bag over his shoulder and, with a contented smile, headed for the door.

All was well with the world.

THE END

How to Silence Your Demons

This book has been written to help you with your own demons. What have you learned through Seb's journey that can help you?

The Story Behind the Story

Writing a fictional book is one of the greatest challenges I've ever faced. You'll probably have noticed that Seb encounters a few seemingly impossible challenges during his journey. It's been a similar experience for me writing it!

Although I've written eight non-fiction books, this is completely new territory for me.

It's taken me over five years to write this book. During its life, I've completed twelve full edits. It's also on its third title and its second mythical creature.

Along the way, I've written a couple of diary entries, to capture my thoughts at a few 'defining moments'.

We've made this available as a downloadable PDF on the *Silence Your Demons* website.

I hope it's helpful and provides a little inspiration when you need it most.

Acknowledgements

It's taken many years to get this book from the spark of an idea to a published final copy.

I have so many people to thank for helping me get this far.

Firstly, to my wife Caroline and my daughters, for their unwavering support, their patience and for reading so many draft chapters (particularly the terrible ones in the early days).
My youngest, Francesca, did an amazing job helping to write the 'How to Silence Your Demons' pages at the end of each chapter.

I also owe enormous thanks to…
my friend Nick Warren and my editor Lucy York, for their kind but candid feedback,
book genius Colette Mason, for keeping me on course,
Sammie Covington, for her amazing cover designs,
Darren Swanborough for creating the amazing sculpture that we used to create the cover,
and David Exley at Beamreach, for printing the final book.

I am also incredibly grateful to…
The Blair Project for their permission to use extracts from the Harry Potter stories,
Harper Collins and Middle Earth for allowing me to use extracts from *The Hobbit* and *The Lord of the Rings*,
Irvin Welsh for his permission to adapt the brilliant "Choose Life" lyrics from *Trainspotting*,
and
Hal Leonard Permissions, for obtaining the rights to use the lyrics from *Diamonds* and *Demons*.

And, of course, you… for reading it and sharing it!
Thank you!

The Author

Hi, I'm Simon.

I'm passionate about helping people overcome their mental and emotional challenges … and become masters of their own heads!

My background is sport psychology. I've spent much of my career working with elite athletes and sports teams, helping them to get their mindset right.

After a few years I started to realise that what I called 'sport psychology', is actually human psychology.

It doesn't just work for athletes.

It works for everyone!

Since then, I've been using exactly the same approaches in business, education, healthcare, charities and the military.

Over the years, I've written a few non-fiction books, to share what I've learned about mindset and world class performance.

I also share these lessons through my coaching and speaking work, and through a few digital programmes.

Feel free to check them out.

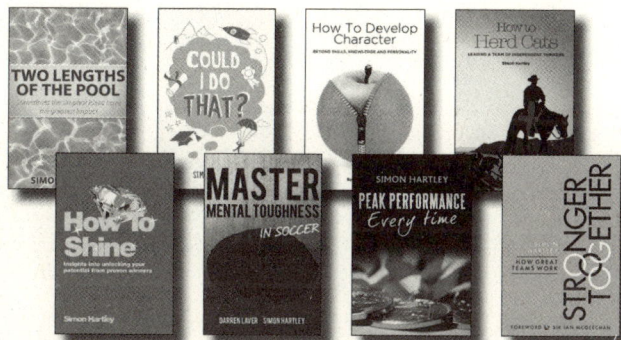

And, if you'd like a little more, hit the Be World Class website

https://be-world-class.com/